Desire's Blessing

Maricca Wood

DESIRE'S BLESSING:
Cover Design: Books and Moods
Editor: The Havoc Archives

ALSO BY MARICCA WOOD

DESIRE SERIES
Desire's Curse
Desire's Blessing

TRIGGER WARNING

Dear Wicked Readers,

Before immersing yourself in this roller coaster of emotions, please be aware that this book is indeed a dark romance. Our female main character finds herself in a bit of a sticky situation as she tries to find a date for her best friend's wedding.

This book contains conversations, actions, or situations that might be triggering and not suitable for some readers. 18+ is advised. Some triggers include manipulation, stalking, domestic abuse (emotional and verbal), car/motorcycle accident (non-fatal), attempted rape, graphic violence, guns, kidnapping, masturbation, explicit sexual scenes, voyeurism, blood (gore), attempted murder, bodies/corpses, and death/dying.

With all that being said, there may be some triggers within the book that I have not listed. Things will not be easy for our female lead so strap in for this crazy and twisted journey.

-Enjoy

To the ones who would burn the world down to get us back.
And to the ones who have someone like that to call your own.

PLAYLIST

Bleed it out – Linkin Park
Hero – Skillet
Voices – Motionless In White
Animals - Nickelback
I'm Just a Kid – Simple Plan
My Happy Ending – Avril Lavigne
Unwell – Matchbox Twenty
Talk Dirty – Jason Derulo
Shake It – Metro Station

CHAPTER 1

FRIDAY – 13 DAYS TILL DEPARTURE

The brutal August heat had let up a little, allowing a nice breeze to cool the Oklahoma night air. With her radio set to a classic rock station at almost maximum volume, Serenity rolled down the front windows of her newer cherry-red Honda Civic and sang along.

Completely lost in the second verse of "Summer of 69" by Bryan Adams, the loud high-pitched sounds of emergency vehicles eluded Serenity. Her only indication that something was wrong was the faint glow of red and blue lights that illuminated her darkened neighborhood. She pinched her black brows together in confusion as she muted the radio, the sounds of sirens replacing her music, growing louder the closer she got.

She prayed no one was severely injured as she reluctantly turned down her street. The sight before her had her heart stopping, her stomach churning, and her face draining of its usual tan color. A few cop cars, an ambulance, and two fire trucks were parked in front of her house, which was completely engulfed in bright yellow and orange flames.

4 HOURS EARLIER

"Do you have a date for the wedding yet?" Addison asked around a mouthful of a tortilla chip that she had dunked completely in her small bowl of white queso.

"Not yet." Serenity sighed heavily as she took a rather large gulp from her frozen strawberry margarita, pinched her brows together, and squeezed her bottle-green eyes shut to try and fight off her oncoming brain freeze.

Every Friday night after work for the last four years, the two best friends had met up at a restaurant for dinner and drinks. This week's choice was Mexican.

Serenity *had* a date for Addi's wedding. She and Noah, her boyfriend of two years, had everything planned out. Plane tickets were bought, and a luxurious room at the resort had been booked for the entire weekend, but that was before she found him in bed with another woman. She valued trust more than anything in a relationship, so the moment Noah broke that trust, there was no going back. She dumped him right then and there.

It had been over three months since that dreadful evening, and she still heard from him. Too often for her liking. Sometimes he would call and leave a voicemail saying how sorry he was. Other times he would text her how much he loved her, that it would never happen again, and ask for her to take him back. Because she never responded, she'd found him waiting for her on her front porch one evening after work. That led her to threaten him with a potential restraining order just to keep him away, but that didn't stop the periodic calls or texts.

"Renny, we leave for Hawaii in thirteen days. If you don't find a replacement date by then, you'll end up having to spend the weekend with my cousin trying to hit on you the whole time," Addi teased with a half-laugh, her dark brown eyes full of amusement.

Addi was getting married to the man of her dreams, who just so happened to be a highly renowned criminal defense attorney and was rather wealthy. Jack wanted her to have the wedding of her dreams, which is why they were getting married on a white-sanded beach in Hawaii at a beautiful five-star resort.

"It might be easier for you to find a new maid of honor before I find a new date," Serenity joked as she dunked a tortilla chip in her queso and popped it into her mouth, the chip crunching loudly under her straight pearl teeth.

"I would cancel my wedding before I found a new maid of honor." Addi spoke in all seriousness, pointing a manicured finger at her friend.

"Well, we can't have that now, can we? So, any ideas? I'm open to suggestions."

Their waitress brought out their steaming fajita platter and the savory smell of fresh tortillas, peppers, rice, and beans filled the air around them.

"Have you tried online dating? A girl at my gym met her boyfriend on one. It's called Desire, I believe." Addi wrapped up her chicken fajita and took a large bite, moaning slightly at the delicious taste.

"There is no way I would be able to find someone in such a short time. Well, someone that doesn't want to murder me and wear my skin, that is."

Though she was joking, she could not stop the chill that rolled down her spine at the image she'd accidentally created in her mind. She'd heard some horror stories of online dating. Not all were happy tales.

"How about you try a type of 'speed dating?'" Addi put up air quotes with her fingers.

Two creases formed between Serenity's brows as she spoke around a mouthful of food. "I'm listening."

"Ok," Addi said, setting her half-eaten fajita back on her plate and wiping her mouth with her napkin. "You scroll through profiles, pick out like seven or eight potential guys. Each day, go on a date with a new one. Get to know them, talk to them, and see if they give off any creepy vibes or not. The ones who pass the test go on a list. The ones who fail… Well, just forget about them." She waved her hand dismissively. "After you've dated them all, go back over the list and make a final selection. Hell, you could even go on a second date with them if you want to be *extra* sure. Then ask them to go with you to my wedding."

Serenity perched a brow high on her forehead. "Even if this goes well, which is highly doubtful, you expect me to take a random stranger on a weekend getaway?"

"No one said you have to sleep with them, Renny. Unless you want to." Addi's thick brown brows wiggled with mischief. "Make that a stipulation up front so they understand your rules and boundaries. Tell them it would just be a fun weekend away on a tropical island, all expenses paid. People put out ads like this on Craigslist for companions for occasions such as these."

"You really are trying to get me murdered, aren't you?" Serenity shook her head, laughing. The action sent her long raven hair dancing across her back.

Addi reached across the table and placed her hand gently over Serenity's. "Come on, sweetie, it's been months. You deserve to have a little fun."

The image of Noah's betrayal flashed through her mind,

causing a jolt of pain to ache deep within her chest cavity. She had tried hard to scrub her brain clean of that horrific scene, but it's as if it had been seared to the organ with a branding iron.

Not wanting to ruin her girl's night out, she shook her head clear, took a deep breath, and willed all things Noah related from her mind. She was hesitant to indulge Addi's bizarre idea, but if she were being honest with herself, she didn't want to attend this wedding alone.

Serenity pointed her fork at her friend. "Ok, ok, fine. But if I get a creeper and end up dead, I'll come back and haunt you for the rest of your miserable life."

"Deal!" Addi threw her head back with laughter, sending her brown and blonde hair spilling over her shoulders.

After finishing their dinner, Serenity and Addi moved to the L-shaped bar in the restaurant so their table was free to seat more hungry customers. A few hours and a few more drinks later, they called it a night, hugging each other and parting ways to head home.

Serenity pulled over and parked next to the curb across the street, got out, and rushed over to a cop who was standing by his squad car.

"Oh my God! What happened?" she asked frantically.

The cop quickly stepped in front of her with a hand held out, blocking her path to the danger ahead. "Ma'am, it's not safe over here. We need everyone to stay back until the fire is out."

"That's my house," she said in a half-daze.

Her voice was barely loud enough to hear over the roaring of the fire. She peeked around the officer, her eyes following the chaotic dance of the enormous flames.

"Does anyone else live in the home that could still be inside?" the cop inquired.

Without removing her eyes from the blazing inferno, she answered. "No... No, I live alone."

Shock and disbelief were starting to take hold of her as she watched thousands of gallons of water being sprayed into what used to be her house. The cop took down her information for the police report and directed her to wait by her car across the street until the fire was completely extinguished.

This can't be happening...

Serenity numbly walked over and leaned against the hood. It was gone. It was all gone. Everything she owned was in that house. She had renters' insurance, thank goodness, and they would cover everything she lost, but that was beside the point. Unfortunately, not everything could be replaced: keepsakes, photo albums from her childhood, and other sentimental objects that were irreplaceable and priceless to her.

She pulled out her cell phone from the back pocket of her blue jeans. Her thumb moved hurriedly over the screen as she dialed her friend.

"Addi..." She trailed off, her voice cracking with emotion.

Addi's tone turned serious. "Renny, what's wrong?"

"My house... It's gone... A fire," she choked out between the soft sobs she was fighting desperately to keep in.

"Oh, fuck... I'm on my way, sweetie. I'll be there in five minutes!" Addi spoke quickly before hanging up.

Serenity tucked her phone back into her jeans and turned her attention toward the collapsing structure that used to be her home. Thankfully, the flames were getting smaller with each passing second.

The sound of an approaching car pulled her from her thoughts as she turned to see Jack's shiny new black Corvette with a single blue racing stripe across the top pull to the curb behind her car. Addi barely waited for him to stop before she threw open her passenger side door, ran over, and threw her arms around her friend.

"Oh, Renny," she said, her voice filled with sympathy. "How are you holding up?"

Addi pulled away and turned to the house that was badly charred and half-standing. Her eyes widened with horror at the sight before her.

"I'm ok," Serenity said with a soft smile as she quickly wiped her cheeks to hide any evidence of the tears that betrayed her by falling.

Serenity turned her head and watched Jack approach. He wore a grey polo shirt that was tucked into a pair of black slacks and a pair of black Italian leather shoes. He brought up a muscular arm wrapped in a gold Rolex and ran his fingers through his wavy brown hair.

He walked straight up to Serenity, wrapped his strong arms around her in a tight hug, and pulled her against his lean frame.

"I'm so sorry, Renny. Are you ok?" He pulled back enough so his deep emeralds could gaze into her mossy greens.

Serenity tried to give him a believable smile. "Yeah, as ok as I can be right now."

Jack broke the hug and leaned against her car as they waited. Another ten minutes passed before the fire was finally lifeless. The ambulance and fire trucks made their way back to their stations while the cop approached Serenity again.

The officer asked, "Do you have a place you can stay at tonight?"

Serenity opened her mouth but then closed it again, unsure of how to respond. The only family she had nearby were her parents who lived an hour away and were out of the state on vacation. So, their place was out of the question. A hotel, maybe?

Addi spoke up, deciding for her. "She'll be staying with us."

The officer spoke with the utmost sincerity as he handed her a copy of the police report for her records. "I'll have a team out here first thing tomorrow to investigate the cause of the fire. I'll give you a call once the investigation is complete. I suggest calling your insurance company right away to start your claim. I'm glad no one was hurt."

Serenity thanked him and watched as the cop got back into his squad car and drove off.

Jack turned toward the girls. "Well, it's late and Renny has been through a lot. Let's go home and get some rest."

Everyone got into their vehicles, Serenity following in her car back to Jack and Addi's place.

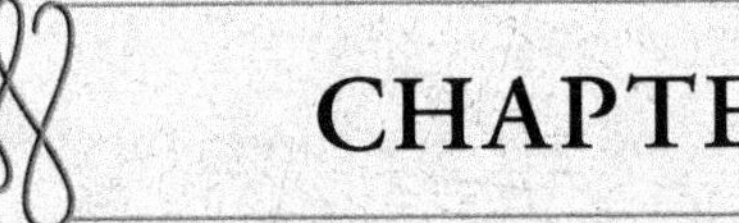

CHAPTER 2

FRIDAY – 13 DAYS TILL DEPARTURE

Serenity pulled into the gated community where Jack and Addi lived. She couldn't help but practically drool at the massive newer homes. Jack had already owned the property when he started dating Addi a few years back and she had been living with him for almost seven months now.

Each of the homes in the neighborhood was a different combination of rock, brick, or both, and each sat on an acre of professionally manicured lawns. A variety of expensive cars, boats, and RVs that probably cost more than she made in a year filled the driveways.

She followed behind Jack's Corvette as he pulled into a long-paved driveway that led to a massive single-story house covered in rock. Large windows framed with black shutters lined the front and it was topped with a black metal roof.

After parking, Serenity followed the couple into the house. She couldn't help but sigh in relief at being in a calm, familiar place. The entire drive over, she was on the phone with her insurance company through her car's Bluetooth, letting them know what happened. She gave them the information from the police report, and they said that once the investigation was completed and they received the paperwork with an itemized list of every possession that burnt in the fire, a check covering the expenses would be mailed to her. She was mentally exhausted at this point.

"Come on, I'll get you some clothes and get the guest room ready for you," Addi said as she walked down the hall toward her and Jack's bedroom.

The home was completely open-concept, updated, and clean. Everything had a place, and everything was in its place. Various photos of the happy couple hung sporadically along the tan walls. Addi walked over to her wooden dresser and withdrew a pair of shorts and a tank top. She turned and handed them to Serenity before she escorted Serenity down the hall to a guest bedroom and bathroom.

"You sure you're ok?" Addi asked as she turned down the ocean blue covers on the bed and turned the ceiling fan on to help circulate the air.

"Really, I'm good. Everything can be replaced. On a happy note, now I have a legit reason to go clothes shopping without getting buyer's remorse." Serenity laughed, though it sounded a bit hollow.

She did love shopping and couldn't wait to rebuild her wardrobe. Good thing she had a plush savings account. She would have to use that until she got the check from the insurance company.

"Ok, well, we're right down the hall if you need anything." Addi smiled, kissed her lightly on the cheek, and left, shutting the bedroom door behind her.

Serenity walked into the attached bathroom and immediately

turned on the shower. While the water warmed up, she got undressed and stepped in, closing the glass door behind her. A soft moan escaped her lips when the hot water fell against her tensed muscles. She closed her eyes and lost herself in the warmth for a while, just letting the water roll down her body, feeling the tension leave her muscles with each passing minute.

After getting washed up, she climbed out, toweled off, and got dressed. Thankfully, her best friend kept this bathroom fully stocked with everything anyone could ever need. She ran a brush through her wet raven strands before braiding it back, turned off the bathroom light, and closed the door behind her. Exhaustion was weighing on her as she yawned and crawled into the queen-sized bed. After snuggling into the fluffy covers, it took no time for sleep to take her.

Addi walked into her bathroom where she undressed and started up the shower. After climbing in, Jack entered and started to shed his own clothes. She couldn't help but watch the man reveal every inch of his six-foot body packed with lean muscles to her. Even though she had seen it a thousand times, each time was like the first all over again.

Jack climbed into the shower behind her, wrapped his arms around her middle, and pulled her back into his front while the hot water fell over them both.

"I can't believe that happened." She spoke as she leaned her head against his strong chest.

"I know, but Renny is a strong woman. She'll bounce back quickly," he reassured her, placing a soft kiss against the top of her wet hair.

"She will. That I have no doubt. Just what are the odds, you know? I wonder what caused it." She closed her eyes, loving the feel of his body against hers. Need quickly flooded her core.

"It could've been a number of things honestly. I'm just glad it happened when she wasn't home." Jack pulled her flatter against himself, sensing the shift in her breathing.

"I wish there was something we could do for her."

He began to place kisses down the column of his fiancée's neck. "Well, she could always stay at my parent's old house until she finds a new place. That way she can take her time with a proper house search."

Addi opened her eyes and craned her head up to meet his gaze. "You mean that? You would do that for her?" Hope and admiration began to fill her voice.

"Of course. She's your best friend," he said, not letting up on the kisses he placed against her creamy skin. "Besides, that house has been empty since they died. It's about time someone used it."

She spun around and wrapped her arms around his neck, her full and heavy breasts pressing into his hard chest. She could feel his fully hardened erection pressing into her stomach and the thought of it had her squeezing her thighs together to relieve the ache between her legs.

"I love you." Her bright smile fully touched her chocolate eyes.

"I had a feeling," he said with a wicked grin as he crushed his lips against hers, their mouths instantly parting, their tongues dancing together in a familiar rhythm.

Jack ran his hands down her back and over her full ass as he gripped the back of her thick thighs and hoisted her up, turned, and pinned her against the tiled wall. She paid the cool mosaic no mind. Her attention was solely on the man about to enter her.

She reached down between them and gripped his thick cock in her hand. Her fingers and thumb lightly touched around his girth as she stroked the entirety of his long shaft slowly a few times, causing pre-cum to bead on the swollen tip before aligning it at her wet entrance. He groaned and with a single thrust, buried himself inside of her, causing her to moan loudly and himself to grunt in approval.

With his head buried in the crook of her neck, he quickly began to thrust into her in a hard, rough manner that they both craved at that moment. Addi brought her hand down, grabbed a handful of soft tissue, and began to massage it and rub her thumb over her hardened nipple. That combination had an orgasm building fast inside her.

"Harder!" She moaned in approval. "Yes, just like that!"

"You like when I fuck you against the wall like this?" Jack growled against her sensitive skin as he pumped harder into her.

"Oh God, yes!" She tipped her head back and closed her eyes, focusing solely on the euphoric feeling.

After a few more violent thrusts, she came undone, her core convulsing around him tightly. Her orgasm rocked through her as she screamed his name and clawed at his back, leaving bright red scratches across his lean muscles.

Not letting up on his pace, he kept moving inside of her, chasing his own finish. With her tight muscles constricting around him in a death grip, he spilled deep inside of her. He groaned as he milked every last drop before pulling out and gently setting her back down on shaky legs. They both breathed heavily as they got cleaned up and climbed out of the shower. After getting dressed, they crawled into bed and held each other closely until they fell asleep.

CHAPTER 3

SATURDAY – 12 DAYS TILL DEPARTURE

The delicious smell of eggs, bacon, and pancakes filled Serenity's room, rousing her from a restless sleep. She slowly worked her heavy eyes open and took in her surroundings. Her brows furrowed as she tried to recall why she woke up in her best friend's guest room. A loud groan escaped her mouth as clarity finally settled over her mind. Her house and all her possessions, minus her car and quite literally the clothes on her back, were no more than charred rubble and mountains of ash.

She reached over and grabbed her phone off the dark wood nightstand. The blinding screen showed 8:30 a.m. After yawning and stretching, she rolled out of bed and fixed the covers and pillows back into place. She padded her way to the updated bathroom, brushed her teeth, and fixed her hair, undoing the braid and brushing out her straight, long black strands, letting them fall freely down her back.

The mouthwatering smell of food only grew stronger the closer Serenity got to the kitchen. Addi was sitting on a wooden barstool at the large island, drooling over the sight before her. Jack, flipping pancakes over the griddle part of the stove, wearing only a pair of black pajama pants, his lean and muscular torso on full display.

"Why do you have to be so damn hot?" Addi asked with a dreamy sigh, her elbow propped on the granite counter and her chin resting in her hand.

"I don't know. Ask God. He built me." Jack chuckled and shook his head, sending his wavy brown hair swaying from side to side.

"Good morning," Serenity greeted them, sleep still heavy in her voice.

Addi beamed. "Good morning, Renny!"

She patted the barstool next to her with a smile. Serenity pulled out the dark stool, sat down, leaned back, and crossed her arms over her chest.

"Morning," Jack called over his shoulder, only sparing her a glance as he worked on filling their plates.

"How did you sleep?" Addi asked.

"I slept alright, given the circumstances," Serenity answered and tried her best to make her small smile believable. "Jack, could you please put on a shirt? Your muscles are very distracting, and I haven't even had coffee yet." She laughed.

"Don't act like you don't like the view," he teased, handing her and Addi each a steamy plate of eggs, bacon, and two pancakes.

Addi took a bite of her crispy bacon, still ogling Jack. "I happen to enjoy this view first thing in the morning. It's a great start to my day."

Smiling and shaking her head, Serenity grabbed her utensils and dug into her food. Jack remained on the other side of the bar, standing while he ate. A comfortable silence fell around them for a while, the only sounds were from forks scraping against plates.

Jack cleared his throat as he set his fork down and wiped his mouth with his napkin. "Addi and I talked last night, and if you want to stay in my parent's old house, you're more than welcome to."

Serenity jerked her head up and looked at him in complete shock. She hadn't even thought about her next move yet. Everything was still fresh; the reality of being homeless hadn't truly sunk in. What *was* her next move though? She couldn't stay here. She would never intrude on them like that. Although they would both argue that it would be no trouble at all.

She would have to find a new place and finding the right one could take some time. She didn't want to apply for the first rental property she saw. She would want to check out the neighborhood, view the property, see businesses close by and what amenities it offered, and most importantly, the distance to her job.

All that took planning and time she did not have, not to mention the application process would take a few days, at least. They were leaving for Hawaii next weekend, so she couldn't truly begin a proper house search until they got back. She could stay in a hotel until she found a place… but that could get expensive. Jack's parent's house was a beautiful two-story family home in a nice and quiet neighborhood.

His parents had died almost two years ago in a car accident. They were killed on impact by a drunk driver. Since Jack was an only child, they left everything to him.

He could never get himself to sell it. Growing up in that house was all he ever knew, but he couldn't get himself to move into it just yet either. He already had this property, and it was too soon for him. Every time he was over there, he was reminded of the wonderful parents he lost. Serenity knew he had hired a cleaning lady to go over there twice a month to keep it up, and a lawn company to visit weekly so it never got neglected or run-down.

"Oh, I could never intrude on y'all like that. I was thinking of just staying in a hotel until I found a place." Love filled her heart from being surrounded by such great friends.

"That would get way too expensive. We wouldn't have offered if it was an intrusion on us." Addi kept her voice light and her big chocolate eyes were filled with kindness.

Jack cleared his plate off, put it in the sink, and walked back to the island. "House searches can take at least a few weeks for the whole process. You can stay in the home and take your time finding the right one. It's clean and ready for someone to live in it again."

They both made valid points, and it was hard to argue with that.

"Ok, but I *will* pay you for the utilities I use. I shouldn't be there for more than a few weeks at the most."

She put her foot down. Well, she tried to. There was no way she was going to live in that place rent-free.

"No can do," Jack said with a genuine smile as he ran a hand through his soft brown hair.

"You're already providing me with a place to stay. Please let me pay."

"Sorry Renny, we won't accept a penny. Put all of that toward furnishing your new house." Addi suddenly clapped her hands together with excitement. "Oh! We have so much shopping to do! We get to furnish a whole new house. Hello, Home Store!" She squirmed atop the barstool, unable to contain her smile and giddiness.

"Leave it to you to find the good in any situation." Jack shook his head as he took both of their empty plates away and placed them in the sink.

Addi shrugged her shoulders and laughed. "It's a gift."

"Thank you, both of you. Honestly, this means the world to me." Serenity shifted her gaze between her two friends and gave them a genuine smile.

"Get dressed and we'll take you over there so you know where it's at and we can show you around," Jack called over his shoulder as he left the kitchen, heading toward his room to get dressed for the day.

Serenity put the jeans she wore yesterday back on, and Addi lent her a fresh shirt. They'd just arrived at Jack's childhood home, Serenity pulling into the driveway behind Jack's car. The beautiful two-story wooden home was painted in a calming blue with pearl white accents. It stood littered with windows and was surrounded by beautiful gardens filled with shrubs, bushes, and an assortment of colorful flowers.

Jack unlocked the front door and led them inside, where they were greeted with a carpeted staircase that led to the second floor. All the rooms were connected on the bottom floor, creating a flowing floor plan around the staircase. To the left of the front door was the large den/family room with a seating area positioned in front of a mounted flatscreen. That led into the combined kitchen and dining room, then around to the formal living room, and then back around to the front door. Three bedrooms and two bathrooms filled the upstairs.

Jack showed Serenity around all the ins and outs of the place. "Here's the key. It unlocks the front door, back door, and the door to the garage." He handed Serenity a brass key and she looped it through the ring alongside her car keys. "Addi has the spare key to the place if you get locked out or need it for any reason."

"Thank you again. This is a huge weight lifted off my shoulders." Serenity smiled.

"It's no problem at all. Now, have fun shopping," he said before he winked at Serenity, kissed Addi on the forehead, and shut the front door behind him.

"Aw, he wasn't up for shopping today?" Serenity teased.

She looked over at Addi, and they both burst out laughing. What man would want to go shopping with two women?

"Hell no! He has to go into the office anyway. He'll be working late until we leave for the wedding to make sure all his case files are as completed as possible, so no one bugs him on our honeymoon." Addi followed her friend out the front door and climbed into Serenity's Honda.

CHAPTER 4

SATURDAY – 12 DAYS TILL DEPARTURE

Serenity pulled her car into the mall parking lot, and the girls could barely contain their excitement as they entered the automated sliding doors, revealing dozens of shops ripe for the picking. Agreeing that necessities should be first—bras and underwear—they started in Victoria's Secret. After stocking up on a drawer full of lace underwear, numerous bras for different occasions, swimsuits she'd need while in Hawaii, and pajama sets, they moved on.

They stepped into a cute little boutique that sold nothing but women's workout clothes. After restocking her supply of sports bras, leggings, and tank tops, work attire was next. For business clothes, they stopped at JCPenney and Kohl's. They made out like bandits with dresses, skirts, blouses, and slacks.

Accessories were next so they stopped at Claire's, buying different kinds of bracelets, necklaces, and earrings. Both women had bags lined up both arms and they quickly realized they needed to make a trip to Serenity's car.

After placing their loot in the trunk of her Civic, Addi looked over to Serenity and practically begged, "Food?"

Serenity closed her trunk and winced at her sore muscles. "Yes, please! I need a break!"

Shopping was fun, but buying a whole new wardrobe? That would take the energy out of the most veteran of shoppers. There was a pizza place in the food court that was calling their names. After getting their slices and sodas, they sat down at a table, both sighing in relief at the pleasure of getting off their feet for a little while.

After resting and refueling, they were ready to go for another round. Shoes were the last stop for mall shopping. After getting a few pairs of tennis shoes, heels, boots, and sandals, they put them all in the trunk of her car and sat in silence as the air conditioning cooled them off and the radio played lightly in the background.

"Walmart?" Addi grimaced.

Serenity nodded. "Walmart. Then home."

She would definitely need to soak in a hot bath after this. She got basic everyday bathroom stuff: a razor, deodorant, toothbrush, and other toiletries. She also picked up a new laptop and some groceries to get her through a few days.

Serenity shifted in the driver's seat and looked at her friend hesitantly. "Addi?"

"Oh, God. What?"

Serenity couldn't contain her smile. "Let's go home."

Addi smacked Serenity's shoulder as a bubble of hysterical laughter escaped her mouth. "Don't do that! I literally almost cried."

On her way to take Addi back home, Serenity kept thinking about the proposition her friend suggested yesterday at dinner. A proposition she'd nearly forgotten about from dealing with the aftermath of her house fire. Could she truly do something that bold, that crazy, dating multiple guys to try and find a date for the wedding? She'd always been a rule follower, never doing anything too adventurous. This would be something far outside her comfort zone. However, she didn't want to attend Addi and Jack's wedding alone.

The roar of a passing motorcycle pulled her from her thoughts as she peered to her right. A man on an all-black Harley Sportster rode past her, putting his blinker on and sticking out his right arm, signaling that he was turning that way. As he slowed to make the turn, the car behind him wasn't paying attention and slammed into the back of his bike.

The loud sound of a crash rang through the air, overpowering the music that was playing on her radio. The biker was thrown back onto the hood of the stranger's car. The driver slammed on their brakes, causing the biker to fall off, land hard against the pavement, and roll a few times before coming to a stop flat on his back.

"Oh my God!" Serenity and Addi both shouted in unison.

She quickly pulled over, threw her car in park, got out, and made her way over to the man who was lying idly on the road. *Please don't be dead! Please don't be dead!* Serenity repeated over and over in her head as she finally reached the biker.

Addi stood off to the side, pulled out her phone, and dialed for help.

A female operator's calm voice came through her phone. "9-1-1, what's your emergency?"

"There's been an accident on Fifth Street, right before the intersection of Fifth and Amber. A car rear-ended a motorcyclist." Addi spoke quickly as she peered around to ensure she gave as accurate a location as possible.

The clicking of a keyboard could be heard through the operator's end of the phone. "Is anyone severely injured?"

"I'm not sure, just send help quickly!"

"I've dispatched a unit to your location. They should be there in a matter of minutes." The operator never once let her calm voice falter.

Serenity knelt beside the man, flipped up the face shield on his black and red full-face helmet, and was met with the most beautiful and unique pair of ice-blue eyes with a golden hazel center staring back at her.

"Sir, can you hear me?" She tried to keep her tone gentle and calm.

God, please tell me he didn't die with his eyes open, she feared. The man stayed silent. Only the blinking of his eyes and the gentle rise and fall of his chest confirmed that he was still alive.

Groaning, the biker tried to get up, only to be halted in place by Serenity's hands pushing against his chest. "No! Don't move. The paramedics will be here soon."

The gentleman who hit the motorcyclist got out of his car and ran over to them. "I'm so sorry! I didn't see him. Is he ok?" the man asked frantically, his face drained of color. The driver had to be mid-thirties, balding, and clearly had never seen the inside of a gym before.

"No, of course you didn't see him. When I passed you, you had your face buried in your fucking phone!" Serenity spat at the balding man. "You could have taken a man's life today. I hope whatever was on your phone was worth it."

"It was an accident, lady. Jeez. I would never touch my phone while driving!" the man lied, trying to save his own ass. "How dare you speak to me like that!"

"Two car lengths away," Serenity gritted through her teeth, turning her mossy gaze back to the biker.

The bald man cocked his head in confusion. "What?"

She whipped her head back toward him, sending her hair flying over her shoulder. "Two car lengths away, AT LEAST! That's how much distance you put between a motorcycle and yourself. If they stop, you stop. If they're turning, you slow down. You never get closer than that. You're protected by a fiberglass body if, God forbid, you ever got hit. They have nothing to protect themselves except the clothes on their body and a helmet. Don't be sorry, be better. Go sit over there and wait for the cops to arrive. You've done enough."

She was seething as she looked away from the complete imbecile. She forced herself to take a deep breath. She needed to remain calm if she wanted the biker to stay calm too. He could be in shock.

As the driver walked away, her bright green eyes met his again, compassion and worry filling them. "You're probably in shock, but know that you'll be ok." Gentleness filled her tone. "What's your name?"

"Hunter," he answered in a deep voice, causing her eyes to slightly widen in surprise.

"He speaks!" Serenity teased, trying to keep the mood light. "That's great. Well, from what I can see, your clothes and helmet protected you. Dress for the slide, not the ride, am I right?" She laughed lightly as her vision slid down his body and back up again, taking in the pair of blue jeans, a solid black riding jacket, and a pair of black riding gloves he wore.

He arched a thick brow as if her words surprised him. "Since you won't let me get up, can I at least take my helmet off?"

She gave him a hesitant but reassuring smile. "No, I'm sorry. I don't know if you have a back injury or not. Moving your head to take off the helmet might further injure your spine. Don't worry though, the paramedics should be here any minute."

Small creases formed beneath the outsides of his stunning eyes. Was he smiling? He was probably thinking the same thing she was. That if he truly wanted to get up, there would be no stopping him. Though it was hard to guess with him laying down, she figured he was well over six-feet and by the way his clothes stretched around him, he was broad and muscular.

"What's your name?" She could hear the amusement in his rich voice and her stomach did a little flip.

"Serenity, but my friends call me Renny."

Sirens began to wail in the distance, and he asked with hesitation, "Is my bike ok?"

Serenity turned her head as she gazed upon the Harley lying over on its side about fifteen feet away. From what she could see, scratches and scuffs marred the black paint of the Sportster.

"Um... it's not that bad." She tried hard to hide her grimace.

He chuckled but it turned into a groan. "You're a terrible liar."

As the ambulance pulled up, a paramedic with a medical bag jumped out of the doors on the back and rushed over to them.

"Help is here now. You're going to be just fine, alright?" She gave him one last smile as she stood and walked over with Addi to the curb so the first responders could do their job.

A moment later, a cop car pulled up. As he began to question Addi and Serenity about what happened, Serenity's vision shifted back to the biker. She sighed in relief when she saw him sitting up, thankful that he wasn't severely injured. Once the officer was through with his questions, the girls climbed back into her little red car and drove off.

After dropping off her very exhausted friend at her house, Serenity made the quick drive to her new temporary house. It took about ten trips to unload everything, just dumping all the sacks on the floor of the family room. She would go through and put everything up later. She quickly made her way into the kitchen, put away her groceries, and then made a beeline up the stairs straight to her new bathroom.

After filling up the tub and pouring lavender bath soap into the hot water, she undressed and sank down, submerging her whole body except her head. She closed her eyes, and let her body completely relax, almost causing herself to fall asleep.

Forcing herself out of the almost orgasmic waters, she cleaned up and headed downstairs to wash and put everything away. After hanging up her clothes and putting everything in the dresser, it was almost 9:00 p.m. Serenity decided to put everything else off till tomorrow as she crawled her completely exhausted body into bed and was out before her head hit the pillow.

CHAPTER 5

Serenity woke up to the sounds of birds chirping and the sun peeking through the sheer drapes as she reached for her phone on the whitewashed nightstand. Upon checking the time, she was surprised to see a text message but then groaned loudly once she saw who it was from.

Noah, her ex-boyfriend. *What the hell does he want now?* She couldn't stop herself from the thought. You would think after three months of no communication, the man would take a hint.

Noah: Hey. I know you probably won't reply to this, but Alex told me your house caught fire. I just wanted to say I hope you're ok. If you need anything, please don't hesitate to reach out.

Alex was one of Noah's friends. He was a firefighter and happened to be part of the crew that responded to her house fire call. She didn't speak to Alex, too in shock to hardly even think, and the man was busy at work trying to put out the wild flames.

Alex must have seen her and put two and two together and then told Noah.

She groaned loudly as she tossed around the idea of replying just this once. It was a crazy situation, and he just wanted to know if she was ok. He wasn't asking her to take him back or anything. Sighing heavily, she started typing.

Serenity: I'm only responding this one time. I'm ok. I don't need anything but thank you for your concern. Goodbye.

She set her phone aside and got ready for the day. She didn't plan on leaving the house, so she threw on a pair of black leggings and a T-shirt. Serenity padded down the carpeted stairs and began sorting through the rest of the bags still sitting on the living room floor.

An hour into her organization, her phone rang loudly, scaring her half to death. She walked over to the coffee table and picked it up. A number she didn't recognize caused her to pinch her brows together in wonder.

"Hello?" she answered hesitantly.

"Hello, is this Ms. Serenity Jinx?" a man asked in a deep tone.

"It is," she responded cautiously. "Who is this?"

"This is Detective Tanner. I was calling to inform you that the Fire Investigation Unit has completed their inspection on the cause of your house fire."

"Oh, that's great." Her tone was lighter now that she knew who was calling. "What did they find?" She held her breath in anticipation.

"Unfortunately, ma'am, it's not good news." Detective Tanner softened his voice. "They found evidence of foul play. The fire was intentional, and they've declared it arson."

"Oh my God!" she gasped. "Wait… you don't think it was me that started it, right?"

If that were the case, her insurance would never cover the loss, and she would be held liable.

"No, ma'am. Well, unless you're a closet arsonist," he joked, trying to keep the mood light. "The materials that were used were high grade, not easy to come by. Whoever did this knew what they were doing and knew how to cover their tracks."

Questions started spilling out of her mouth, one following quickly after another as they popped into her brain. "Do you have any suspects? Do you think someone meant to hurt me? Am I in danger?"

"We have no solid evidence, but the pattern of this fits the profile of numerous unsolved arson cases. We believe the person is a serial arsonist. The places were all abandoned or empty, no one had ever been injured. This person just likes to watch buildings burn. I don't believe you're in any danger. But if you feel like you are, please don't hesitate to reach out. We'll continue the investigation on our end and hope we can catch them soon."

Serenity forced her lunch to not reappear. "Ok, thank you for updating me."

"No problem. Have a good rest of your day," Detective Tanner said before the call went quiet.

She couldn't believe what she'd just heard. On one hand, she was relieved that the person wasn't targeting her specifically, but she was also scared. Why choose her house of all places? There was nothing special about it. You would think an arsonist would choose a bigger target or one that had special meaning to them, not a random person's house in the middle of a quiet neighborhood.

Needing a distraction, she forced her mind to shut off as she went back to her organizing.

Once everything was sorted and put away to Serenity's liking, she grabbed the box that contained her new laptop, poured herself a rather full glass of red wine, and sat down on the couch. She placed her wine on a coaster on the glass side table as she opened her computer and began the setup process. Once it was completed, she went to the Desire dating website.

As she occasionally sipped from her wine, she began to create her profile. She couldn't help but feel silly while inputting her information though. She never had to resort to this method before, and here she was now, using it to hopefully secure a new date for Addi's wedding.

A memory popped into her head of numerous headlines that broke out across all social media and news outlets not even a few weeks ago. A woman, around the same age as her if she remembered correctly, ended up with a stalker after meeting a man on a dating site. *Was it this same one?* She tried to recall its name, but for the life of her, it evaded her memory.

Serenity knew the dating site wasn't to blame. It was just an unfortunate accident. Luckily, the woman, with the help of a close family friend and former Navy SEAL, was able to stop that creep before he could seriously hurt her, or any other woman for that matter.

Please, just don't let me get any psychos. She sent up the silent prayer as she completed her profile and began searching for local men in her area.

After taking a few deep breaths, she began to slowly scroll

through the hundreds of available men. Then she began to wonder just how "available" some of these men truly were. *Stop it. That's why you'll do a test date beforehand, to feel them out.* She would be damned if she ever became the "other woman" in someone's life. She had more respect for herself than that. Plus, after being on the affected side of that situation, she would never willingly put a woman through that type of pain, heartache, and grief.

She filtered down her search to a thirty-mile radius and put the age range between twenty-five and thirty. With herself being twenty-three, she'd always been interested in older men. They were more mature. Well... most of the time. She skimmed through each of the men's bios. If they sounded interesting, then she would look through a few of their pictures.

She examined each picture closely, like a scientist peering through a microscope. Some of them she could clearly tell were photoshopped. Those got deleted from the potential list right away. When she found a few that passed her checklist, she clicked "interested." It was a waiting game now. If the men viewed her profile and were interested as well, then a chat thread was created where they could communicate with each other.

Serenity let out a long breath as she set her computer on the couch cushion next to her and grabbed the remote to the mounted TV, flipping through the channels for anything good to watch. She came upon a channel that had just started showing *The Mummy* and clicked on it, never one to turn down a Brendan Fraser movie.

Thirty minutes later, her computer dinged, pulling her gaze from the large flat-screen. She grabbed her laptop and was pleased to see that she had a few messages from some of the guys that she was interested in. After sending each of them a message, they chatted for a minute before agreeing to meet at a certain day and time this week. She had arranged a date for each day of the next week.

Shaking her head from side to side, she sighed, realizing she felt… dirty, somehow. She wasn't going to sleep with these men or even kiss them, but having a date with a new guy every day was a weird feeling for her. She shook it off, closed her computer, and finished her movie.

After it was over, she got up and placed her empty wine glass in the sink, yawned, and made her way to her bedroom. After brushing her teeth and braiding back her long black hair, she made sure her alarms were set on her phone, plugged it into the charger, and climbed beneath her warm covers.

She knew this next week was going to be hectic, but she hoped that at least one of these men proved to be somewhat worthy of going on her "maybe" list. She forced her brain to shut off as she closed her eyes, snuggled into her pillow, and eventually drifted off to sleep.

With the cover of nightfall giving him a veil of shadows to hide within, The Figure walked down the side of the two-story family home, coming to a stop outside a window that gave him a clear view into the dimly lit family room. A vision of Serenity curled up on the couch sent a wicked smile spreading across his face as he backed himself up into the privacy trees that lined the property, so he was safely out of view.

He stood there casually, with his hands in his pockets, long enough to leave shoe impressions in the grass as he lost track of time. The sight of the unaware woman inside the home sent a rush of excitement through his veins, like an addict chasing their next fix. The feeling of watching someone who was oblivious was freeing and addicting. *You are so fucking beautiful,* he thought as he watched her type away on her computer.

She would occasionally smile, a smile that caused him to groan inwardly and adjust his hardening cock to a more comfortable angle in his pants. He wondered what she was doing. Was she watching something? Was she talking to someone? *I can't wait for you to smile at me like that. Soon.*

As Serenity closed her computer and turned off the TV and lamp, his gaze followed her darkened form as she moved through the room and disappeared up the stairs.

The Figure spoke as a wicked grin curled his face. "And so, it begins."

Though he was missing the sight of her already, he turned and left the property, casually walking off down the street with his hands still in his pockets.

CHAPTER 6

MONDAY – 10 DAYS TILL DEPARTURE

The chiming of Serenity's phone alarm shattered the silence in her bedroom, pulling her from a wonderful dream where Ryan Gosling had bought her a drink at a bar, and they were currently back at her place, promptly removing each other's clothes.

Groaning, and a little sexually frustrated, she grabbed her phone off the whitewashed nightstand and turned off her alarm. She squinted from the blinding light of her screen, the time of 5:30 a.m. taunting her. *Do I really need this job?* She'd asked herself that question almost every morning for the last four years since working at MoneyFirst Bank.

Why couldn't I have been born rich? She kept waiting for the day when her parents would call and tell her that they lied to her and that they were wealthy and just wanted her to learn the value of a dollar. But that phone call had yet to come. So, she did in fact need her job if she planned on living in a house with electricity, running water, and food. *Being an adult is overrated*, she thought as she threw off her covers and climbed out of bed.

She placed her phone back on the nightstand and quickly made the bed, smoothing out the dark purple and black bedcover and neatly propping the matching pillows against the whitewashed wooden headboard. Serenity shuffled, still half asleep, into the attached bathroom, rinsed her face with some cold water, brushed her teeth, put on deodorant, and started on her makeup.

Even as a girl, she was never big into makeup like others her age. She always felt that natural beauty was the best kind of beauty there was. All she wore was some light eye makeup that made her green eyes pop more, and if it was a special occasion, lip gloss or lipstick. Once her makeup was applied, she ran a brush through her black-as-night hair and braided the fine strands back into an elegant French braid.

As she walked into the small walk-in closet, she sifted through all her stylish dresses, blouses, skirts, and slacks ranging in various colors and patterns that were hung neatly on wooden hangers. She always made it a habit to check the weather before picking her outfit and groaned when she saw that it was going to be triple digits today.

Apparently, Oklahoma was trying to push its limits for August weather. She voted for a black short-sleeve dress with tiny flowers covering it that hugged her slim torso tightly and then flowed from her hips down to her knees. She grabbed a pair of black stiletto heels and descended the stairs, setting her heels by the front door, and followed the rich smell of brewing coffee into the kitchen.

She grabbed a white mug from a top cabinet and poured the freshly brewed coffee almost to the rim before sitting at the table and scrolling through social media. She sipped her drink, loving the feel of it waking up her body.

She checked her messages on the Desire app she had

downloaded last night to see if there were any changes to the dates that she'd set up. Seeing no new messages, she sighed half in relief, half in nervousness. She did, however, have plenty of new men who clicked "interested" and were waiting on a response from her. Well, they could continue to wait. She already had her plate full of dates this week.

As she finished off her coffee, she placed the empty mug into the sink, slipped her heels on, grabbed her keys and purse, and walked out the door. Her commute wasn't long, lucking out with this new place being only ten minutes from the bank. The classic rock radio station played low through the speakers as she battled the morning traffic through the city.

Upon arriving at the bank, she parked in the staff parking lot and made her way inside, scanning her badge at the door to get in. She walked into her office, flipped on the light, woke her computer up, and put her stuff away.

The space was small but her own, containing a massive L-shaped desk with plenty of upper cabinets and shelves for storage. Two small wooden armchairs faced her desk, and a row of low cabinets lined the back wall, tucked perfectly beneath the massive window.

After filtering through emails for almost twenty minutes, Serenity pulled up her schedule of appointments so she understood what her day would look like. Once the bank opened and her appointments started filtering in, the morning went by quickly and before she knew it, it was lunchtime.

Right on cue, Addi strode into her office with a Panda Express food bag that she DoorDashed for their lunch. She was a teller and they lucked out with their lunches lining up with each other's, so they ate together just about every day. Addi wore a dark blue cashmere tank top and a pair of grey slacks that hugged her round ass and thick legs tightly. She played sports in high school and had the typical thick, muscular build of an athletic woman.

"So, did you set up a dating profile?" Addi asked her by way of greeting as she handed Serenity her bowl of fried rice and orange chicken.

"I did, actually." Serenity unwrapped her plastic utensils and took a bite of her chicken. "And I have a date scheduled each day this week after work and a few this weekend." She pinched her brows together in thought, trying to recall them all.

"You skank," Addi joked and smiled at her best friend. "So, where are you going today? What's the guy look like?"

Serenity rolled her eyes at her crazy friend as she grabbed her phone and pulled up the Desire app so she could show her the photos of Thomas, whom she would be having dinner with that evening.

"Oh, he's cute! You could get lost in those ocean eyes." Addi swooned over the photos of him. Then she began to read his bio. "Thomas, twenty-eight, works in sales and he loves fishing, sports, and movies. He sounds interesting."

"Let's just hope that when he shows up, he looks just like his photos," Serenity said between bites. "I don't have time to be catfished."

She'd already prepared herself for the possibility and was currently working on an escape plan if need be.

"Send me an SOS if you need an out. I got you." Addi smiled and took a large gulp from her Pepsi.

"I got a call from Detective Tanner yesterday." Serenity took a deep breath to calm her rising anxiety. "He told me some… interesting information about my house fire."

She had forced herself not to think about it. So, talking about it now brought up all those raw feelings again.

Addi straightened her spine in her chair. "What did they find?"

"They declared it arson. Apparently, the pattern fits a serial arsonist they've been trying to catch."

Addi put her hand on her chest in worry. "Holy shit! Do they think the person was trying to hurt you?"

"No, the wacko just likes to watch stuff burn."

Addi sighed. "That's good news. I think… I'm just glad they did it while you weren't home."

Serenity agreed and went back to eating the rest of her lunch. They went over some more wedding details, and she helped Addi make a list of everything they would need to pack and bring with them to the resort. Thankfully, her maid of honor's dress was with the tailor and didn't suffer the same horrible fate as the rest of her belongings. Trying to find a new dress so close to the wedding and have it altered would've been a nightmare.

Serenity's afternoon flew by after lunch, the hours passing like minutes. A part of her was thankful that her workday was quickly approaching its end, but the other part of her was cursing Father Time because each minute that passed by was another minute closer to her dinner date.

Since her break up with Noah over three months ago, she hadn't gotten back into the dating field yet. They had been together for two years, and for it to come to a sudden, fiery end as it did, she was taking her time with the healing process before dating again. Unfortunately, with her best friend's wedding less than two weeks away, she didn't have much time to find a replacement.

She'd wondered, on numerous occasions, if she even wanted to bring a new date. Especially now, having to go through the headache of vetting men out to make sure they weren't serial killers was going to be exhausting mentally, physically, and emotionally. Showing up to a wedding alone wasn't that bad, was it? It was being held on a beach in Hawaii, at a beautiful resort. She was confident that she could find ways to fill her time by herself. Who knows, maybe she would even meet a guy at the resort and could ask him to the wedding.

However, she did miss the companionship she had with Noah. Before his companionship extended to include another woman, that is. Serenity knew that whoever she brought to the wedding, she wasn't going to sleep with. She wasn't ready for that kind of emotional commitment yet so that took some of the pressure off her shoulders. All she needed was to find a man who had a good sense of humor and was open to a new adventure. Someone she could share this experience with as just a friend.

That's it! she thought as she smiled to herself. She was vetting these men, looking for a new friend. That was a good way for her to look at it. The new angle on her unique situation sparked hope and a little excitement inside of her.

As her workday ended, she shut down her computer, turned off the lights in her small office, and was out the door. She turned up her music and sang along with the radio, trying to get her mind in the right headspace for her date, not caring how ridiculous she might look to passing cars.

Upon reaching one of the handfuls of Olive Gardens in the state of Oklahoma, one luckily being in her city, she pulled into the parking lot and made her way inside the beautiful rock building. The inside was updated and elegant, with a soft cream coloring the walls and a combination of grey, brown, and tan slate tiles covering the restaurant floor. Different-sized dark brown wooden tables and booths filled the inside of the restaurant.

The air around her smelled of pasta and freshly baked breadsticks and the sounds of people chatting fluttered past her. Waiting inside the entryway, she opened her Desire app and sent Thomas a quick message.

Serenity: I'm here.

Thomas: Me too. I grabbed us a table in the bar section. I'm wearing a Hawaiian shirt.

She took a deep breath in through her nose and released it in a long exhale through her mouth as she walked further into the restaurant, to the bar area, her gaze scanning the room. She looked down at his photo again and then scanned the space a second time. Her brows pinched together tightly. The only person wearing a Hawaiian shirt looked nothing like Thomas and was about twice as old.

"Serenity, over here!" Thomas called to her, raising a hand so she could easily find him.

Her heart sank to the pit of her stomach as her gaze landed on the older gentleman with salt and pepper hair. *Shit...* she thought, taking a deep breath before she walked over to the man.

"Thomas?" She was trying hard to hide the questionable look she knew was on her face. She would make a terrible poker player.

"That's me." He gave her a large smile as he motioned his hand out to the chair across from him, signaling for her to sit.

She looked down at her phone again, his picture still filling her screen. Well, a photo of what he was supposed to look like anyway. Then slowly her gaze lifted back up to his face. The black hair, blue eyes, and creamy skin of what was supposed to be a twenty-eight-year-old Thomas looked nothing like the man in front of her. This man had to be mid-forties, his once black hair was now heavily peppered with grey, and his blue eyes were framed with laugh lines. He was clean-shaven with a slim build.

Thomas spoke when she didn't move from her spot, as if her feet were rooted deep within the floor. "I know. I look a little different than my photo."

She perched one eyebrow high up on her forehead. "A little?"

He laughed lightly as if there was absolutely nothing wrong with this. "I promise that is me in the photo. It's just a few years old."

"A few?" Serenity asked in disbelief.

She was speechless. She wasn't trying to be rude, but this had thrown her completely off guard. Knowing that getting catfished was a possibility of online dating, she had created an exit strategy in case that happened, but for the life of her, she couldn't recall what that plan was. She started to panic, and her hands became clammy.

"Ok, more than a few. But please, give me a chance. If anything, you'll get a free dinner out of this." He motioned again for her to sit.

Not knowing what else to do, she obliged.

"Good afternoon. My name is Alisha and I'll be taking care of you guys today. What can I get you to drink?" their server asked with a bright smile. The girl was around Serenity's age with blonde hair and big brown eyes.

"I'll take a Coors Light in the bottle," Thomas ordered first then looked to Serenity.

"I'll have a glass of Stella Rosa Black Cherry, please."

"Can do, and might I just say, I love this!" Alisha motioned between Thomas and Serenity.

"Love what?" Serenity inquired, confusion lacing every letter.

"I wish my dad took me out to dinner like this." Alisha's smile was sweet and innocent before she turned on her heel and headed back toward the kitchen.

Serenity was at a loss for words, and she could feel her cheeks starting to heat from embarrassment. There was no way on earth this would ever work. Some people like silver foxes, and she did like her men older, but not this old.

"I'm so sorry. But this," she motioned between them, "just isn't going to work. You seem like a nice guy, truly, but I have to go. Goodbye."

Not giving him a chance to rebuke, she jumped up and practically sprinted from the restaurant. She climbed into her car and let out a loud frustrated groan. *Well, this was a promising start to my little experiment.* She sent up a silent prayer that this would be the only time she got catfished, then started up her car and drove home in complete silence.

As she readied herself for bed, she dreaded work tomorrow because she knew Addi would never let her live this one down. Although, it was her friend's fault that she was even in this mess to begin with. Serenity had a few choice words she planned on saying to Addi.

After brushing her teeth and braiding back her hair, she checked her phone alarms, plugged it into the charger, and crawled beneath her warm covers. Forcing her overthinking mind to turn off for the night, she started counting. She reached sixty-seven before her eyes grew too heavy and she drifted off to sleep.

CHAPTER 7

The house was dark and quiet, signaling that Serenity must have gone to bed already. Slithering through the shadows, The Figure worked the lock to her back door until he heard a soft click. He opened and closed the door quietly, turned around, and scanned the space, taking in the dark dining room and kitchen.

He made sure to keep his steps light as he walked through the kitchen, flipped the switch on her coffee maker off, and continued through to the living room. He spotted her keys hanging on a hook by the front door and carefully grabbed them, shifted them over a few hooks, and rehung them.

These small changes, he knew, would make his presence known to her. Not exposing who he was just yet but letting her know that someone was with her. Watching over her. However, he knew that he would have to break her down before he could finally claim her as his. Turning, he slowly made his way up the stairs, creeping one step at a time, knowing that with each stair he climbed, he got closer to the sleeping beauty that unknowingly waited for him.

The Figure reached the second floor landing, turned, and walked down the carpeted hallway, past the first bedroom. He peered into the open door, finding it empty, peered into the second bedroom's wide doorway, and found that room deserted as well. He approached the primary bedroom's unbarred door and found a small form lying in the middle of the bed. The sight before him caused him to pause in the doorway as he watched her for a moment, excitement and thrill flooding through him. The only sound that could be heard was her shallow breaths.

Finally, he entered the dark room. A few strides from his long legs were all it took before he was standing next to the bed. He gazed down, allowing his eyes to roam over his sleeping beauty's body, the covers stopping just above her chest.

He hooked a finger lightly under the top of the covers, and ever so gently pulled them down a few inches, exposing her round breasts and the perky nipples pebbling beneath her thin tank top. The sight before him had his already hard cock throbbing and his tongue sweeping out, wetting his lips. He groaned inwardly as he pressed the palm of his hand over the bulge straining against his zipper.

He shifted his gaze back up to her angelic face as he gently tucked a few loose strands of her raven hair behind her ear. Slowly, he bent toward the crook of her neck and took a long, slow, deep breath, letting her coconut body lotion fill him. He placed a gentle kiss on her forehead before he whispered one word to her.

"Soon."

With that, he straightened, allowing himself a few more minutes to watch her sleeping form before he turned and left back the way he came.

TUESDAY – 9 DAYS TILL DEPARTURE

Serenity's phone alarm chiming pulled her from a restless sleep. Groaning, she got up, made the bed, and shuffled into the bathroom to start her morning routine. After doing her makeup and pulling her black strands up into a tight bun, she walked to the closet and picked a light pink satin tank top with a cowl neckline and a black pencil skirt that stopped at her knees with a four-inch slit in the back.

She hiked down the stairs and into the kitchen only to freeze when realization hit her. She turned her nose up, took a big breath in, and smelled... nothing. Her brows knitted tightly, and she frowned. The wonderful aroma of freshly brewed coffee should be filling her nose by now. As she stepped over to the coffee maker, she found it cold and empty. *I know I turned it on last night. I even double-checked it.*

Her eyes went to the clock that should have had glowing red numbers on it, but it was dark. Her gaze spotted the cord around the back and followed it to the outlet, confirming it was plugged in. She then shifted her eyes to the power button and frowned even deeper. It was off. *What the hell?*

Serenity gazed at her phone and realized she didn't have time to turn it on and wait for a pot. She would have to stop and get some on her way to work. As she crossed through the main floor to the front door, she reached for her keys, only to find them hanging two hooks down from where she remembered putting them. Groaning out loud, she rolled her eyes and pushed it from her mind. She wasn't nearly awake enough to try and process that one.

After stopping at a coffee shop, she was feeling more herself now that she had some caffeine working its way through her system. Once she arrived at work and started up her computer, she combed through her emails and checked her appointment schedule for the day. She wouldn't be as busy as yesterday and she was thankful, needing some time to start her search for a new rental home.

Lunch came before she knew it and Addi strolled into her office carrying a bag from Santa Fe Cattle Co.

"Hey, girly!" Addi sang as she placed the brown bag atop Serenity's desk. She fished out a blackened sirloin salad and set it in front of her friend, as she pulled out a fiesta salad for herself and sat down in a chair.

"Huh? Oh, hi Addi," Serenity said, a little distracted, not hearing her friend come in. *Was it lunchtime already?*

Addi perched an eyebrow high on her head as she poured a few packets of ranch over her grilled chicken and began to toss her salad. "Is everything ok?"

Serenity opened her salad and dug in. "Yeah, I was searching for rental properties and lost track of time."

"Renny, take your time. We told you that you could stay in the house as long as you needed to. Months if that's what it takes. Anyway," Addi let a suggestive grin slide across her full lips, "how was your date last night?"

"Ugh!" Serenity groaned, avoiding eye contact.

Addi laughed, not able to control herself. "Oh, no. Was it that bad?"

"I got catfished. Those pictures of Thomas were about... Oh, twenty years old or so." Serenity shook her head in embarrassment.

"In fact, he was so much older that our server actually thought he was my dad."

Addi was doubled over in her chair, practically choking on her salad from laughing so hard. Serenity grabbed a packet of salt and threw it at her friend.

"Stop laughing!" she said, half-laughing herself.

Looking back on it now, it was rather funny. Her very first date with online dating went so terribly that she couldn't help but laugh a little.

"I... can't... help it," Addi choked out between laughs. She was gasping for air by the end. "Who's your date with tonight?"

Serenity pulled up his profile on Desire and slid her phone over to Addi. "Elijah. We're going to see a movie."

"A movie?" Addi questioned as she read through his profile.

"Yeah, I thought the same thing. We won't really get much time to get to know each other, just beforehand and maybe while the previews are playing."

Addi slid the phone back to her friend. "Well, I hope this one is at least true to his photos."

Serenity groaned. "No joke!"

As Serenity pulled into the movie theater parking lot, she sent up another silent prayer. *Go easy on me with this one, please.* She pulled down her visor and checked her reflection before grabbing her purse and making her way to the ticket booth where they agreed to meet. Looking through the crowd of people, she tried to find one that looked like Elijah's picture.

"Serenity?"

A man called from behind her. She turned around and was

met with slate grey eyes and a beautiful smile that was framed by a neatly trimmed reddish-brown beard.

"Elijah," she smiled. *Thank you,* she thought. Then she peered up at the board above the ticket window that listed all the movies and showtimes. "So, what movie do you want to see?"

After running a large hand through his shoulder-length dark red hair, he pulled out two tickets from the back pocket of his jeans. "It's called *Watch Out*. It starts in ten minutes."

"Oh, ok. Well, I love a good scary movie."

"After you." He smiled and motioned toward the doors.

She turned and walked inside, disappointed that he didn't open the door for her. She even hesitated to see if he would, but he didn't. It wasn't a deal breaker, but she did want a man with at least some chivalry.

"What can I get for you?" a young kid behind the concession counter asked with a smile.

"A large popcorn and two drinks," Elijah answered. "A Coke and for her..." He turned to Serenity.

"I'll have a Sprite, please."

"Ok, that'll be $22.50," the kid said as he started to fill their drinks.

When Elijah didn't make a move for his wallet, she turned to him with hesitation. Before she could ask the awkward question, he spoke around a mouth full of popcorn.

"Since I got the tickets, could you get this? Money's kind of tight right now."

Are you serious? She didn't mind going Dutch or anything, it just caught her off guard. Why go on a date if money is tight? What struck her as odd was the expensive clothes he wore. Was money tight because he liked to buy expensive things? Luckily, she always kept cash on her for times like this. She paid the kid and grabbed her drink.

She followed Elijah down the hall and into the auditorium where they found their seats and got settled as they made small talk. Well, he did most of the talking actually... About himself. She thought going to the movies would be bad because they wouldn't be able to talk much but she found herself *begging* for the movie to start so he would shut up.

To her dismay, the movie playing didn't stop the man from talking. Instead, he made comments. The. Entire. Time. Not to mention he ate all the popcorn. Popcorn that *she* paid for. Once the ending credits played and the lights came on, she was ready to get the hell out of there.

"That was a good movie," he commented.

I wouldn't know. I missed half of it because you kept talking, she wanted to say, but thought better of it. Without warning, he stood up and started walking out, leaving his trash behind, and expecting her to follow. *What a dick,* she thought as she grabbed both cups and the empty bucket of popcorn, got up, and followed him out, scowling at him the whole way.

"The people who work here are not your personal maids." She didn't bother hiding the annoyance in her tone as she dropped their trash in the bins right outside the auditorium doors.

"They basically are." He shrugged casually. "They get paid to clean up the theaters. I'm just making sure they don't get bored." He laughed as if it were all a big joke.

As they left the theater, he stopped on the sidewalk and handed her his phone, flashing her a suggestive grin that had her recoiling. "Put your number in. We should go out again soon."

The poor excuse for a man was so clueless. She couldn't have been more turned off the entire date. How could he possibly think she had a good time and would want to do it again? That was the problem. Elijah wasn't thinking about Serenity. He only thought of himself and what he wanted.

"No, I'm going to have to pass. Thank you though. Goodbye." She turned and walked off before he could try to argue.

The sun was just beginning to set as she pulled into her driveway. Going straight to the kitchen, she poured herself a large glass of wine and went straight upstairs to run a bath. She grabbed a few candles, lit them, and placed them around the tub. She turned off the lights, causing the flames to cast dancing shadows across the bathroom walls.

Then, she grabbed her phone and turned on some relaxing spa music as she stripped down and climbed into pure heaven. She leaned back and rested her head against a rolled-up towel, closed her eyes, and drank her wine. A sigh of pleasure escaped her lips. That was just what she needed after her second horrible date.

She was beginning to fear that maybe this whole experiment thing wasn't worth it. So far, she hadn't had a good track record with her Desire dates. *Third time's a charm, right?* She made up her mind though. She was going to give herself one more chance. If this next date was another bust, she wouldn't go out anymore. If this next one went well, then she would continue her experiment. Maybe.

CHAPTER 8

TUESDAY – 9 DAYS TILL DEPARTURE

Since the sun was just beginning to set, The Figure wouldn't have the cover of shadows to conceal himself. He would have to be extra careful if he didn't want to get caught. Carefully, he snuck around to the back, peering into every window, trying to locate where Serenity might be. After not seeing her, he figured she had to be upstairs. He came to a stop outside the back door of the two-story home as he worked it like yesterday until the soft click granted him access.

He eased inside and slowly closed the door behind himself as he moved through the house with assassin-like stealth, never once making the floor creak beneath his weight. As he passed through the family room, he grabbed the remote to the flat-screen mounted on the wall and turned it on, making sure to turn the volume low. He flipped through the channels until he found a local news station.

The headline across the bottom of the screen read *Oklahoma woman gained herself a stalker after using popular dating site.* They briefly showed a picture of a beautiful blonde-haired, blue-eyed young woman. The Figure observed the screen before the photo disappeared and the newscasters carried on with their story. *How unfortunate.* He chuckled to himself.

He returned the remote to its spot on a couch cushion before he walked to the front door, removed her car keys from the hook, and gently placed them on the wooden table below. A buzz of excitement filled him as he slowly stalked his way up the stairs. Soft music filled the air around him, getting louder as he got closer, confirming his suspicion that Serenity was indeed upstairs.

Anticipation and heat filled him as he made his way down the long, carpeted hallway, peering into each room as he passed. The instrumental music grew louder the closer he got to the primary bedroom. The Figure stopped just outside of view as he peered around the open doorway, finding the room vacant.

The light to the attached bathroom was off but what looked like the glow of candlelight flickered through the crack in the door. He crept in, thankful that the carpet absorbed his steps as he stopped just outside the bathroom.

The thin crack through the door granted him a sight that sent his heart racing and blood flooding straight to his groin, making him fully hard in a matter of seconds. Serenity leaned back in the tub, eyes closed, her wine glass nearly empty. She hadn't added any bubble soap to the water, which gave him an unobstructed view of her naked body.

His gaze started at her raven hair that she had pulled back into a clip to keep it dry. The tanned skin from her cheeks to her chest bore a slight flush, most likely due to the wine. His gaze shifted lower to her perky tits that were half submerged in the water. Her nipples were hard, begging to be sucked on, which sent his tongue darting out to lick his lips.

Shifting lower, he observed the planes of her flat stomach to the curve of her hips and stopped only when his eyes landed on the smooth skin of her core. What he wouldn't give to be buried in that wet heat of hers. *Soon,* he reminded himself. His eyes continued their journey, following the length of her toned legs which were slightly bent and propped on the foot of the tub.

What happened next took him by surprise and had his cock twitching with need. She set the wine glass aside, closed her eyes again, and allowed her hand to slowly and lightly trail down the length of her torso, stopping at her core.

A small moan escaped Serenity's mouth as she slowly circled her clit with a single finger. The Figure turned abruptly, walked to her dresser, slowly opened a drawer and grabbed a T-shirt from inside before returning to his spot outside the door.

He hastily but cautiously unbuttoned and unzipped his pants as he worked them and his boxers down just enough to free his throbbing erection. He hissed quietly as he took his aching and sensitive shaft in his hand and slowly began to jerk himself off at the sight of Serenity playing with herself, thankful for the music that drowned out any noise from him.

She slipped a finger inside of herself and brought her other hand up to massage one of her full mounds, working her hard nipple between her thumb and finger. A moment later, she added a second finger, her moans growing louder.

That's it. Fuck that pretty pussy of yours with your fingers like a good girl. You like touching yourself, don't you? Fuck, you are doing such a good job. You have my dick aching with the need to fill you. The Figure wished more than anything that he could say those filthy words to her out loud.

The shift in her short, ragged breaths signaled to him that she was getting close to an orgasm. *You better not stop. I want to see you come all over those delicate little fingers.* He worked himself faster as he felt his own orgasm about to hit. After a few more pumps from her fingers, her cries of pleasure drowned out the music. The sound was unlike anything he'd ever heard before. It was pure ecstasy to his ears.

The symphony of her finish rocking through her had his following a second later as he shot hot beads of cum into her T-shirt, imagining it was her chest he was coming on. *Fuck, Serenity!* he screamed inside his head, wishing he could shout it to the moon and the stars for real. As Serenity came down from the high of her finish, he tugged at himself a few more times, making sure he got every last drop out.

He folded up the T-shirt and set it aside as he dressed himself again. He allowed himself to gaze upon the half-sated Serenity one last time before he grabbed the T-shirt and left with a wicked smile on his face.

WEDNESDAY – 8 DAYS TILL DEPARTURE

The familiar chime from her phone at 5:30 a.m. pulled a small whimper from Serenity's lips. To her, it felt as if she'd only closed her eyes not five minutes ago, even though she went to bed early yesterday after her bath. She turned off her alarm, made the bed, did her usual routine in the bathroom, and wandered to the closet while checking her weather app. To her surprise, it would be in the 80s with a nice breeze.

She was thankful for the brief break from the brutal heat as she pulled off a sleeveless, high-neck, solid dark blue, form-fitting dress that stopped at her knees from its wooden hanger. The fabric clung tight to her breasts, curves, and ass nicely, all while maintaining a professional appearance.

She grabbed a pair of black open-toed heels that strapped around her ankle before she padded her way down the carpeted stairs and dropped them by the front door. Her eyes snagged on the keys that were lying on the wooden table. *I thought I hung those up?* Shrugging, she chalked it up to sitting them down in her haste to get upstairs and lose herself in a bath.

The smell of coffee filled her senses as she turned to make her way into the kitchen, only to stop dead in her tracks. The mounted flat-screen was turned on. The volume was so low that she didn't hear it until she turned her full attention toward it. Her heart sank into her stomach and an uneasy feeling consumed her. She knew she didn't turn it on yesterday. When she got home last night, she went straight upstairs, soaked in the bath, and went straight to bed.

So, who turned the TV on? A rush of fear filled her as she ran through the home, checking the locks on all the doors. The uneasy feeling only intensified when she found them all locked with no evidence of being tampered with. Grabbing her phone with shaky hands, she pulled up her messages and shot a text to Jack.

Serenity: Hey, got a weird question for you.

Jack: I like weird. (Tongue out emoji) What's up?

Serenity: Is it possible that your house is… haunted?

Jack: Don't tell me you're one of those who believe in ghosts. lol

Serenity: Hell yeah, I do! I've seen too much in my life to not believe in them. So… is it??

Jack: I've never seen anything. If my parents had, they never said anything to me.

Jack: Wait… What if it's the ghosts of my parents? You know, like a whole Beetlejuice situation.

Serenity: OMG! Why would you joke like that? That's wrong on so many levels!

Jack: Keep that in mind if you ever bring a guy home or feel like playing with yourself. They might be watching… (eyes emoji)

Serenity: Well, now I'm going to have nightmares… Thanks! (Middle finger emoji)

Jack: You're welcome! (Kissy face emoji)

She tried to calm herself down as she poured a cup of coffee and sat at the dinner table, considering the possibilities. Three, to be exact. One, the house truly was haunted, and a ghost, or worse, was messing with her. Two, she was losing her mind and didn't remember turning on the TV, misplacing her keys twice, and turning off the coffee pot. Or three, someone was coming into the house and deliberately doing those things.

The last one almost made her throw up at the thought, but it was highly unlikely. She didn't know anyone around here, and no one knew she had moved except Jack and Addi. Also, there was no sign of forced entry, and the doors were all locked. She doubted that someone who picked a lock to get in would remember to lock it back as they left, which means it would have to be someone with a key. There were only two keys to this house, one of which she had, and the other Addi had.

Was Addi messing with her? No, she wouldn't do that. So,

either she was losing her mind, or this place was haunted. *Great...* She ran a hand through her long hair that she decided to leave down today. Letting out a frustrated sigh, she placed her mug in the sink and left for work.

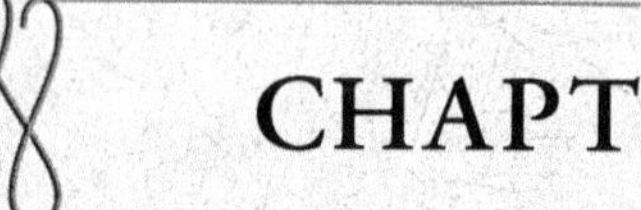

CHAPTER 9

WEDNESDAY – 8 DAYS TILL DEPARTURE

Serenity's morning drug by, the minutes passing like long, excruciating hours. She tried to lose herself in her work, but her mind kept wandering back to her little situation at home. She thought about it so much that she could feel a headache coming on. She opened one of her desk drawers and grabbed some Tylenol while she prayed it would be gone before her date tonight.

"Hey!" Addi entered her office right on time, providing Serenity with a much-needed distraction.

"Hey, Addi." She greeted her friend with a smile, the smell of their lunch instantly filling her office.

"Don't keep me in suspense." Addi began to distribute their lunch from Chili's. "How was your date with Elijah?"

"Dear God, he wouldn't shut up!" Serenity groaned, leaning back in her chair as she drank her Sprite.

Her best friend furrowed her brows in confusion. "Y'all went to a movie, right?"

"Yeah, but let me start at the beginning." Serenity sat up in her chair.

"Oh, I feel like there should be wine for this conversation."

Serenity laughed in agreement. "Ha! Maybe we should have gone out for lunch today so we could have gotten a stiff drink."

Addi got comfortable in her chair before motioning for her friend to start her story. Serenity spilled it all, not wanting to leave out a single horrible detail.

By the end, Addi's mouth was hung open in shock. "Wow… what a dick."

"Right! Ugh, anyway, I just hope tonight is better. If not, I'm done with this experiment."

"No! We had a deal, girl. What happens if date number five or even seven is the man of your dreams? You would never meet him if tonight doesn't go well. That's not fair. Sometimes we have to date an entire city of jerks before we find a good one." Addi tried hard to keep her friend motivated to see this through to the end.

"Fine." Serenity gave in, shaking her head. "Anyway, how's the wedding planning going?" she asked, wanting to change the subject.

Addi beamed. "Great! I'll pick up my dress the day before we leave, and Jack will pick up his tux that day too. Everything else is pretty much done. The resort did the majority of the planning, which has been a blessing."

Serenity couldn't help but smile as well. She loved seeing her friend so happy and in love.

"Has Jack been home much?"

"No, he's been staying late at the firm to get caught up on his work before we leave. Which is fine." She shrugged her shoulders. "We text all the time and I spend my evenings watching trashy reality TV so I'm content."

Serenity laughed lightly at her friend as they finished their lunch and got back to work. She found herself praying the last few hours would go by quicker than the morning had.

As Serenity climbed into her car after work, her phone buzzed. Before pulling out of the parking lot, she checked it and found herself wishing she hadn't.

Noah: Hey, Renny. Been thinking about you a lot. I miss you!

She groaned out loud and rolled her eyes as she ignored him… again! *When will he get the hint that I'm not interested anymore?* She tossed her phone into her purse, turned up her radio, and sang along to the music as she made her way to the meeting spot for date number three, with Owen. Her "maybe" list was still bare, hoping she could add a name to it by the end of the night. *Stay positive,* she told herself.

She lucked out by finding an empty parking space along the street and parallel parked. She quickly checked her reflection, grabbed her purse, and walked down the sidewalk to a small mom-and-pop ice cream shop they agreed to meet at. As she entered, her eyes landed on Owen right away. His pictures did not do him justice. He was standing off to the side by an empty table and she couldn't help but rake her gaze down his front.

His neatly trimmed black hair was cut short and lightly peppered, giving him an older sophisticated look that she enjoyed very much. His eyes were so grey that they appeared silver, which popped against his creamy clean-shaven skin, showing off a stunning jawline. He wore a white polo shirt that stretched over his muscular torso and was tucked into a pair of black slacks that hugged his legs. She forced herself to snap out of the trance he put her in as she smiled and walked over to him.

"Serenity?" Owen gave her a shy smile that made butterflies take flight in her stomach.

She returned a warm smile of her own. "That's me. I'm guessing that makes you Owen?"

"Wow, you look beautiful." He looked down her front and back up again, purposely not letting his gaze linger too long on any particular part.

A gentleman, she thought in amazement.

"Thank you. You look pretty good yourself."

That compliment earned herself another gorgeous smile from him.

"You're too kind. Are you hungry?" He motioned to the counter that contained dozens of ice cream flavors and numerous toppings to add in.

"I'm not one to ever turn down ice cream." She laughed.

"Good to know." He joined in on the laughter as he placed his hand in the middle of her back and walked with her to stand in line. The butterflies were erratic now, thanks to his warm touch that she could feel through the fabric of her dress. "What do you do for work?"

"I'm a loan officer at a bank."

"Oh, nice. Do you like it?" He sounded genuinely interested.

It threw her off but in a good way. It was a breath of fresh air to have someone ask you a question that they truly wanted to hear the answer to.

"It's a good job and pays the bills, so I can't complain," she said lightly. "What about you?"

"I'm a veterinarian and own my own clinic," Owen answered then laughed. "So, if I smell like a dog, that would be why. I promise I showered before coming here."

Serenity fully laughed at that. "No, you smell nice. And that's awesome that you get to be your own boss and play with puppies and kittens all day."

"It has its perks. I like your laugh."

Now she was blushing. As they walked up to the counter, he motioned for her to order first, then he gave his order. As they moved down the line, they picked their toppings and approached the register. He paid without hesitation and handed her the ice cream and a spoon. After grabbing his ice cream, they left and made small talk while walking around the city.

Since the weather was nice that day, they found themselves at a local park. After finishing their ice cream, he took her trash and threw it away along with his. She found herself not wanting this date to end. It was such a drastic change compared to her last two dates.

She might finally have a name to add to her "maybe" list and the thought excited her. From just the short little while they had spent together, she found herself easily picturing bringing him to the wedding. Which equally scared and excited her.

They got along so well. She loved the intellectual conversations they found themselves having. And it helped that he was easy on the eyes too. Although, if she spent a long weekend with this man, she didn't think she could stay true to her "no sex" rule.

As they made their way back to her vehicle, sadness crept in. She didn't want this night to end.

"Well, this is me." She pointed to the Honda she stopped next to.

Owen met her gaze, and her heart did a little flip. "Can I be honest and a little forward with you?"

"Of course." She waited with bated breath and was unable to tear her eyes away.

"This was the most fun I've had on a date in a while." He took a small step toward her. "I would very much like to kiss you."

Her breath hitched and her words swelled in her throat. All she could do was nod her head. Not wasting any time or giving her a chance to possibly change her mind, he closed the distance between them, pulled her against his muscular front, and kissed her pink lips.

She snaked her arms around his creamy neck, and leaned into that kiss, deepening it. His hands found the small of her back as he gently pulled her further into him, trying to eliminate any space between their bodies. His tongue slid across her lips, seeking entrance. She promptly accepted, opening her mouth as their tongues tasted each other's mouths fully.

For a few minutes, they enjoyed the feel of each other's bodies against their own, the heat rising between them, only breaking the kiss when they both needed air. He pulled away enough to look into her bottle-green eyes as he spoke with lust heavy in his voice.

"Please forgive me if I come on too strong or sound presumptuous, but I must ask. Do you want to come back to my place?"

Still trying to catch her breath, Serenity smiled brightly. "I love how forward you are. You know what you want and aren't afraid to ask for it. I respect that. Unfortunately, I have one rule that I always follow, the three date rule."

Two deep creases formed between his dark brows as he cocked his head to the side and asked, "The three date rule?"

"I never go home with a guy until after at least three dates."

"Ah, I understand. It sucks but I respect that." He chuckled softly and slowly released his hold on her. "Does that mean I have future dates to look forward to?" He fully smiled at her as he opened her car door.

"You just might." She smiled sensually, shrugging one shoulder at him as she climbed into her car.

Owen winked at her, shut her door, and walked off with a grin on his handsome face.

The entire drive back to her house, Serenity couldn't stop smiling like an idiot. Her mind kept going back to Owen and the toe-curling make out session they had. At the start of this experiment, she told herself that she wasn't going to do anything with these men while on their dates, but that died when she met Owen.

Then he had the audacity to say he wanted to kiss her, and all her willpower went right out the window. How could she say no to him? She *didn't* want to say no to him. So, she indulged herself and let go. She wouldn't waver on her three date rule though. Never. That was there for her safety—emotional, mental, and physical.

It had been months since she felt that type of spark or connection with another human being and she found herself missing it. Upon arriving home, Serenity showered up, poured herself a glass of wine, and curled up on the couch. She flipped through the TV guide, turned to the Hallmark channel, and fully immersed herself in a sappy rom-com.

CHAPTER 10

Night had fallen, giving The Figure plenty of shadows to obscure him from the sight of any nosy neighbors. Although the fully grown trees and shrubs that lined the two-story property concealed it, giving the plot plenty of privacy, and plenty of spaces to shield himself and watch Serenity through the numerous large windows that lined the home.

The window he was peering into gave him the perfect view of her as she curled up under a blanket on the couch and watched a cheesy love movie. He couldn't help but roll his eyes at that.

Those movies were all the same. Yeah, you can change their names, what their job is, and even the name of their hometown, but the fundamentals were all alike. Someone with a fancy job in the city has to go back to their tiny hometown for whatever reason where they end up running into their first love and get a second chance at happiness. Gross.

But their love story, his and Serenity's, would be rare, unbreakable, wonderful, and filled with so much passion and adventure. He watched as the ending credits rolled across the screen and was surprised when she hadn't moved yet. Upon closer inspection, he noticed that she ended up falling asleep on the couch.

He smiled as he made his way into the home in his usual fashion. As he slowly shut the back door, he walked by the coffee maker that was already prepped and ready for tomorrow morning and unplugged it from the wall. He stalked through the main floor as he entered the family room and came to a stop behind the couch, gazing down at his sleeping beauty.

The Figure gently brushed some black strands out of her face and tucked them behind her ear as he slowly stroked his long fingers through her soft silky locks. He lightly walked around to the coffee table and picked up her phone. A frown creased his face when he saw it was password protected. That frown was short-lived though when he noticed that she had Face ID set up. He turned the screen toward her sleeping face and tried again, this time gaining access.

He snapped a photo of her unbelievable beauty before he walked around to the back of the couch, taking another photo of his fingers laced through her silky hair. *I want you to know someone is watching over you.* A wicked grin tugged his lips up at the thought of the last photo he wanted to take. Slowly he removed the blanket, exposing her torso that was enveloped in a baby blue tank top.

With one hand, he gently cupped the pebbled mound that was closest to him. A small sleepy moan escaped from her lips, and he froze. Had he woken her? Was she that gentle of a sleeper? When her eyes didn't open and she didn't move, he slowly let out the breath he was holding and gave her breast a tender squeeze.

He snapped the photo quickly before focusing all his attention on his hand. A quiet groan of pleasure fell from his lips as he gave her breast another light squeeze, loving the feeling of the soft supple tissue in his large hand. Another small moan left her lips but again she didn't stir awake.

Not able to contain his urge anymore, he closed the camera app and locked the phone. He set it back in its place on the coffee table before he grabbed a dish towel from the kitchen and took up his place again back behind the couch.

The Figure softly unzipped his pants and pulled them down low enough to free his throbbing erection. He laid out the dish towel across the back of the couch and gently cupped her breast in his hand again. He clutched his cock in excitement as he began to tug on himself, making sure to keep his other hand as still as possible so he wouldn't rouse her.

He gave her tit another delicate squeeze and held it for a few seconds. Another sleepy moan escaped from her lips, driving him wild. *You like that, don't you? You respond so fucking well to my touch.* Her nipples pebbled further, and it drove him even more mad with lust. He knew it wouldn't take long for him to come. The possibility of getting caught only added to the thrill of it.

Gently grazing his thumb over her hard perky nipple sent him over the edge. He clamped his mouth shut as he continued to tug on himself until he shot his white seed onto the dish towel.

Reluctantly removing his hand, he folded up the dish towel, cleaned himself off completely, and tucked himself back into his pants. He lightly tucked her back under the blanket as he grabbed the ruined dish towel and left with a pep in his step and a smile wide across his shadowed face.

THURSDAY – 7 DAYS TILL DEPARTURE

Serenity's eyes fluttered open as she awoke the next morning. Two creases formed between her brows as confusion clouded her sleep-filled brain. Her memories from last night came flooding back to her all at once.

She got up, folded the dark grey microfiber blanket that she was covered up with, and draped it over the back of the couch. As she climbed the stairs and wiped sleep from her eyes, she couldn't contain the smile that forced itself wide across her face as she remembered Owen and their wonderful date yesterday.

The tsunami of emotions that flooded her could only be compared to that of a teen's first love. The new feelings of giddiness, the constant butterflies, the unwavering smiles that surfaced anytime you thought about them, wanting to doodle his name in a notebook surrounded with hearts.

Finally, she had a name she could add to her "maybe" list and the excitement and possibilities filled her with newfound hope. As she flowed through her morning routine on autopilot, her mind replayed their date and all the conversations they had, as if trying to memorize everything she learned about the wonderful man.

After adorning a maroon form-fitting dress with a sweetheart neckline that stopped right above her knees, she checked herself over in the bathroom mirror and danced down the stairs as she hummed a chipper tune. Serenity came to a stop in front of her coffee pot with her hand half stretched toward it before she froze. That once happy and magical mood she was in vanished, replaced with dread and fear that sent the hairs on the back of her neck standing up.

The coffee pot was empty, and no red numbers illuminated

where the time should have been. Slowly, her gaze followed the black cord that ran from the back of the machine to the outlet. At least, it was supposed to. It wasn't. The cord was now lying on the white granite countertop.

"There's no way..." she whispered, unable to get her voice any louder from being in utter disbelief.

She could chalk the movement of her keys to her being in a rush, and the TV being on and not turning on the coffee pot to being forgetful, but this... How could she even begin to explain this?

Her haunted house theory was starting to sound less probable. Unless she had a demonic spirit as a roommate, there was no way a simple ghost could unplug a cord from the wall. Which left her with her other theory, that someone had been coming into the house.

She cursed herself for being such a heavy sleeper. She'd slept downstairs last night and heard nothing that should've roused her from slumber. No jiggling of the doorknobs, no tampering of a window, no creaky floorboards caused by heavy footsteps. Serenity quickly dashed across the main floor, checking all three entry doors again, and just like last time, they were all locked with no signs of being tampered with.

If someone was getting into the house, how were they accomplishing it? *Am I truly losing my mind?* She could deal with being crazy, but the thought of a strange person being in a house with her without her knowledge made her skin crawl, and her paranoia kick in.

She threw up her hands in defeat. "That's it... I'm buying a gun today."

If someone was breaking into the house, she would be ready

for them, and she wouldn't hesitate to send them to meet whatever god they believed in. After grabbing her things and sliding into her heels, she locked her door and made her way to work.

CHAPTER 11

THURSDAY – 7 DAYS TILL DEPARTURE

Serenity's morning at work went rather quickly, which she was thankful for, each appointment went smoothly and was over before she knew it. Right on time, Addi walked through her office door, carrying the lunch they DoorDashed that day.

"How was your date yesterday?" Addi skipped the small talk, wanting to get right down to the juicy details.

Another smile spread across Serenity's face as she was reminded once again of Owen.

"Shut the fuck up!" Addi beamed after observing the pure delight brightening her friend's angular features. "Spill!" She distributed their food before sitting in a chair next to the large desk.

"It was wonderful! Now, I know it was only the first date, and I shouldn't get my hopes up too quickly, but it's hard not to. From what I observed, Owen is smart, kind, funny, and breathtakingly handsome!" Serenity swooned as she filled Addi in about the entirety of her date.

"So, you finally added a name to your list?" Addi questioned around a mouthful of her deli sandwich.

"Top of the list, in bold, underlined with a few exclamation points at the end." Serenity laughed. "Jeez, I sound like a teenager who just went out on a date with their crush."

Addi laughed. "I fucking love it! It's so good to see you smile again, Renny."

It was nice for Serenity to feel herself smile again too. Her breakup with Noah was sudden and rough and the healing process was extensive and ugly. Despite the odds, she mended the broken pieces of her heart back together, allowing herself to be open and ready for love again, no matter how much the thought of new love scared her.

Serenity took a deep breath and sighed heavily. "I hate to ruin this moment, but something's happened, and I need to talk to you about it."

Addi straightened in her chair, her food momentarily forgotten. "What's wrong? Is everything ok?"

"I could be overthinking this but… either the house is haunted, I'm losing my mind, or someone has been breaking in." A cautious and unsure look marred Serenity's face.

"I'm sorry, someone *has been* breaking in? As in more than once?" Addi asked, emphasizing the words as she scooted to the edge of her chair in anticipation. She looked both angry and hurt that this was the first time she was hearing anything about it. "Renny, what's going on?"

Serenity filled her in on all the weird occurrences that had happened since moving into Jack's parents' house. It felt good to be able to talk to someone about this, but it was also scary because speaking about it made it all that more real.

Addi sat there, her mouth gaping in shock. "Maybe this dating thing is stressing you out so much that you're becoming forgetful?"

"That is a possibility, but I need to consider my worst options. Someone could be getting into the house. I haven't the slightest clue who it would be or why, but if that's the case, I need to arm myself and be more cautious."

Serenity reached for her Sprite, letting the carbonation burn her throat as she drank and pondered over who the mystery person could be and their motive, since they never took anything.

Noah? It was possible. He does know her house burnt down and that she relocated somewhere new. Plus, he still messaged her saying he missed her. Maybe this was him trying to get close to her again. The arsonist who burnt her house down? Possibly, although she couldn't think of a motive for the person.

The detective mentioned the arsonist wasn't ever violent toward people, just liked to watch buildings burn. Maybe it was a neighbor who didn't like that someone was now living in that house and was trying to scare her into moving away. That was highly possible. The home had been vacant for years. Maybe the neighbor was afraid she would be a nuisance to the street since she was so young.

"I'll speak with Jack. Maybe he can set up some security cameras around the house?" Addi offered.

"That would be wonderful, thank you. It would give me some peace of mind." Serenity sighed with relief, thankful that her friend believed her and was willing to help.

The second half of her day flew by as quickly as her morning had. Serenity was thankful as she pulled out of the bank's parking lot and drove to her local Academy. She would feel safer once she got a weapon that she could defend herself with.

She entered through the automated sliding glass doors of the store and made her way to the back, where the outdoor and shooting department was located. Her heels echoed loudly with each step against the white tiled floor. She stopped in front of a glass counter that housed pistols, weapon attachments, and an assortment of knives. Various rifles and shotguns hung along the back wall behind the counter.

An older bald man who looked to be in his mid-fifties walked up to her from behind the counter wearing the typical tan khaki pants and blue collared uniform. "Good afternoon, ma'am. Can I help you find anything specific you're looking for?" A welcoming smile spread across his heavily bearded face, putting some of Serenity's nerves to ease.

She greeted the gentleman with a small smile of her own. "Yes, I was looking for something that would be great for home defense?"

"Alright," he gave her a small nod. "You have a few options with that. A pistol would work great. It's compact, lightweight, and easy to use." He motioned his hand down toward the glass display case in between them. "A shotgun would work too. They're bulkier, but you don't have to aim as hard to hit your target with these. The further the target, the more spread out the pellets will become. Those work great in homes with a lot of open space. If your home is more compact, a shotgun would be hard to maneuver around corners and such." He motioned to the shotguns hanging on the wall behind him.

"Maybe one of each? A shotgun for my downstairs which is rather open and a pistol to keep upstairs?" Serenity suggested as she looked over her options.

"A woman after my own heart," the man joked, causing her to blush slightly.

"Alright, let's start with pistols. For home defense, you won't really need anything more powerful than a 9mm, unless you want something with more kick." He laughed.

He opened the door to the display case and pulled out a Glock G17 for her to hold. He cleared the weapon, making sure it was safe before he handed it to her. She liked the weight of it and her hands fit around the grip comfortably.

"I like it." She placed it back on the counter gently.

He handed her a few more options and told her a little about each one. After some consideration, she ended up picking the Glock.

"Now for the big boys," he joked as he grabbed a shotgun from the wall and cleared it before he handed it to her. "With these, I would suggest a 12-gauge. It will do the job, and it won't have as much recoil as some of the more powerful ones do."

He handed her a few options as she aimed at an invisible target with each one, studying the weight of them and how they fit her reach and against her shoulder. She decided on a Remington 870 Tactical. The weight and the shorter barrel felt more comfortable in her hold than the others she tried.

"I will get those guns for you as well as a box of ammo for each while you fill out the paperwork for the background check."

He handed some papers to her and disappeared through a door off the back wall. As he pushed his way through the door, he placed the boxes on the counter and rang everything up on the register. She handed him her completed paperwork and swiped her bank card. The total was rather large, but it was money well spent for her peace of mind.

After waiting a while for the initial background check to clear, he bagged up her purchases and said goodbye as Serenity turned and left the store. She placed her items in the front passenger seat and checked the clock, sending up a silent thank you that she had enough time to get them before her date with Hunter.

She turned up her radio and sang along to the classic rock station as she drove to a local bar and grill. With her mind more at ease now, she found herself relaxing and looking forward to this date. She wondered if her good luck would continue, allowing her to add another name to her list.

CHAPTER 12

THURSDAY – 7 DAYS TILL DEPARTURE

Serenity parked her Honda in the half-empty parking lot. It was a Thursday, just past the main dinner rush, so most customers would have cleared out. She flipped down her visor and checked her makeup in the attached mirror. After applying some clear lip gloss, she closed the visor and sent a quick message to Hunter.

Serenity: Hey, I'm here.
Hunter: Me too. I got us a table in the bar section.

She took a deep breath and willed the nervous butterflies in her stomach to settle down as she entered the restaurant. She didn't understand why she was so nervous. She had been on dates all week, she should be used to them by now, but she wasn't. As she rounded the corner into the bar area, she slowed her steps and peered around, trying to locate her date.

A few tables around the room were sporadically filled with people conversing, eating, and drinking, causing laughter to fill the air around her. After a quick scan around the room, a man snagged her attention as he stood from his table. His gaze alone rooted her to the floor as his eyes locked onto hers and time ceased to exist. All she could do was stare as a rather large man slowly stalked toward her, never once averting his gaze from her and sporting a devilish grin that pulled at one side of his full lips.

Though he was tall and packed with large muscles, it was his presence that dominated the room, drawing other customers' eyes in his direction. His walk was lethal, every muscle, every move so precise as if he were in complete control of every inch of his body. His long legs ate up the distance between them. Even though he was dressed casually in a black T-shirt that stretched across his broad shoulders and hugged his bulging biceps tightly, and a pair of blue jeans that were snug around his thick legs and pulled over a pair of boots, he was hands down the sexiest man she ever laid eyes on. He had his long brown hair pulled high into a knot behind his head and the brown beard that lined his cheeks and jawline was trimmed neatly to his face.

Holy… fucking… hell… she thought as she watched this god of a man approach. She wasn't even sure if she was breathing.

"Hello, Angel." His deep voice washed over her and nearly brought her to her knees.

Her body responded instantly to the sound, heat sparking deep in her core. Serenity forced her emotions back in check and she finally found her voice as she tilted her head up to meet his gaze.

"Hunter?" She inwardly cursed herself for allowing that to come out a bit breathlessly.

"The one and only." He captured her delicate hand in his large grasp.

She looked down in shock at where their hands were connected and took in the tattoos that painted both of his arms. Sporadic scars varying from small to large disturbed some of the artwork. Curiosity struck her as she found herself wanting to hear the story behind each one. Without saying another word, he turned and led her to their table, pulling out her chair for her before returning to his seat.

"It's nice to meet you."

Serenity reached for the glass of water in front of her with a slightly shaky hand. *Get it together! This is not the first hot guy you've seen,* she scolded herself.

He chuckled lightly, the sound so deep that it caused her toes to curl and wings to explode in her stomach. "This isn't the first time we've met."

Her brows furrowed as she cocked her head to the side. "It isn't?"

She studied his face more intently, trying to figure out where they could have previously met. She took in an old scar that ran vertically through his left eyebrow, bisecting it, the full brown scruff that covered his jaw, and the fullness of his kissable lips. Then she saw it. His eyes. They were a beautiful shade of ice-blue with a bright hazel center. Recognition flashed in her brain at their uniqueness, but she couldn't place where she'd seen them before.

She couldn't stop the nervous laughter that bubbled up. "I'm sorry, I think you might have me confused with someone else. I would definitely remember meeting you."

"Oh, it was you all right," he drawled. "Those green eyes of yours have plagued my dreams every night since meeting you."

Before she could question him further, their waitress came to the table, introducing herself.

"Hi, my name is Cassie and I'll be taking care of y'all this evening. What can I get you to drink?" She turned her full attention to Hunter and gave him a bright smile.

Serenity groaned inwardly. The girl was trying so hard that even she could see it, the way she pushed her chest out a bit more so her breasts were more prominent in the low-cut tank top she was wearing.

Hunter shifted his gaze toward Serenity, not even sparing their waitress a second glance. "What would you like to drink, Angel?"

Shock flashed across Cassie's face. Clearly, she wasn't one used to rejection. Then a flash of anger sparked within her vision, but she quickly schooled it and plastered on a fake customer service smile as she turned and looked at Serenity.

"I'll take a sex on the beach, please," she answered.

"And for you?" Cassie clipped out at Hunter as she tried to hide the defeat in her voice.

"I'll have a Coors Light, draft."

Cassie scribbled across her notepad. "Twelve or twenty-four ounces?"

"Twelve is fine, thank you." Hunter went back to skimming over his menu.

Cassie didn't speak again before she turned and strode toward the kitchen.

"Are you trying to get our server to spit in my food?" Serenity shook her head but laughed.

"What?" He peered over his menu at her with a smirk. "She needs to learn her place. Clearly, we're on a date." He shot her a quick wink.

Ugh! How does this man have so much control over my body? Something as simple as a wink caused wetness to dampen her underwear.

"You're not going to tell me where I know you from, are you?" she inquired, narrowing her vision at him.

He shrugged. "Maybe later."

"Jerk," she muttered, but he must've heard because a deep chuckle floated across the table, causing her heart to skip a beat.

Cassie dropped off their drinks and took their food orders. After she left, Hunter leaned back in his chair, casually drinking his beer as he asked, "Want to play a question game?"

"Sure." She sipped from her glass. "You go first."

Unable to take his gaze off the raven-haired beauty sitting across from him, he questioned, "What do you do for work?"

"I'm a loan officer at a bank. What about you?"

"I own a private security company."

Cassie delivered their food before leaving again, clearly still stewing over the rejection that wounded her ego.

Serenity muttered, "Seems fitting," and laughed.

She had guessed either military, police, SWAT, or something along those lines based on his looks, his demeanor, how he moved, and the way he carried himself.

Hunter perched a thick brow high in pure amusement. "Meaning?"

"I just can't picture you behind a desk working eight to five every day."He laughed at that. "Do a lot of people in Oklahoma need private security or do you take clients worldwide?"

"I'll send my men anywhere the client needs protection. We get a lot of celebrities, political officials, or wealthy people who need short-term security for work, vacations, or business trips." He dunked his French fries in his ketchup.

"Sounds fun. Dangerous, but fun. Do you like it?" she

questioned further before taking a bite of her burger.

"I love it. I report to no one, I make my own hours, and the pay is great. Plus, I get to meet a variety of people on a daily basis. What about you? Do you like working at a bank?"

"It's not bad. It pays the bills but it's not my passion."

"What is your passion then?" He gazed deep into her green eyes, waiting patiently for her answer.

A small blush stung her cheeks. "To be a mom and have a family of my own."

She'd secretly hated that question. A part of her always felt bad that she didn't have a big desire for things like saving people, serving her country, wanting to teach young minds, or careers like those. She loved that for others and respected the hell out of them for following their dreams, but her dream was simple. She didn't need a lot to make her happy. All she wanted was a man who came home to her every day more in love than the day before and kids of her own to raise and love unconditionally.

"That's an exceptional passion to have. You'll make a great mother." There was no judgment in his unique eyes. Only honesty.

"You barely know me." She blushed slightly, glancing down to hide the coloring in her cheeks. "How are you so confident that I would be?"

"Because the day I met you, you showed me your willingness to help those in need, your will to protect people you don't know, and that you aren't afraid to hold people accountable for their actions. You also showed me how caring and loving you could be to a total stranger, so I can only imagine how you will be with your own children," he confessed.

Serenity pinched her brows together and cocked her head. What he said was wonderful and it made her heart swell with pride, but she couldn't figure out what he was talking about. Then it hit her. A memory of him lying on the pavement and her staring down into those beautiful eyes of his.

"The biker from the accident? That was you?" she questioned.

The biker had given her his name. How had she not remembered that or put the pieces together when she saw that a Hunter was one of her dates this week? He smiled at her in confirmation, a smile that fully reached his eyes. She indeed was in trouble if she had a man who smiled at her like that.

CHAPTER 13

THURSDAY – 7 DAYS TILL DEPARTURE

Serenity and Hunter ordered another round of drinks after their meal, loving their conversations and each other's company. The night wasn't over yet, but she already knew that she would be adding his name to her list. She glanced at the clock on the wall of the restaurant and winced. *Why did this night have to end so quickly?*

"It's getting late and unfortunately, I have work tomorrow." Sadness filled her voice. Hunter agreed as they got up and left the restaurant.

"Speaking of tomorrow, I would like to see you again," he stated as he escorted her to her car in the dimly lit parking lot. The sun had long set and there were only a handful of cars left.

She kept her voice light and tried not to get too hopeful as she fidgeted with her keys. "Is it safe to say you had a good night if you want to do it again so soon?"

"There wasn't a single moment of this evening that I didn't like."

She stopped beside her car and turned to face him, her breath hitching slightly. Hunter was an intimidating man in the light, but cover this man with shadows and he looked downright sinister, as if he belonged there, waiting to reap the souls of the dead. She wasn't scared though. It was weird and she couldn't explain it, but she felt safe with him.

"I would love to go on another date with you, but I already have one set for tomorrow."

The moment the words left her mouth, her mossy eyes widened in fear. *Why did I just say that?* She cursed herself for not thinking before she spoke. She opened her mouth to try and save herself, but his movements froze the words in her throat.

Slowly, he dipped his head, and his gaze darkened. He took a step closer to her, his shoulders rigid, causing her to take a half step back.

"You have *what* already set for tomorrow?" His voice was low and though he looked frightening, the sound sent the butterflies within her into overdrive.

He took another step toward her, causing her to take another one back, only to be halted by her car. The cold metal pressed into her back, but she paid no mind. She tried to speak again but the words clogged her throat. "Come on, Angel, use your words. Tell me why you can't go out with me tomorrow."

Hunter took one last step, eliminating the gap between them. His large frame hid her body fully from sight. Serenity finally pulled herself together as she took a deep breath and forced the words out.

"I already have a date tomorrow," she choked out, barely above a whisper.

He cocked his head to the side and spoke slowly. "You went out with me tonight knowing you have another date tomorrow with someone else?"

"Y-yes," she stuttered.

Though it was dark, she watched his gaze drop down her front and back up before he spoke again. "Why?"

She tried to keep her voice light. "Um… I'd rather not say. My situation is… well, it's unique, and I don't expect you to understand."

"Count me intrigued." His tone was still low but a hint of amusement crept in.

"Well, my best friend is getting married next weekend at a resort in Hawaii. We had reserved rooms and plane tickets months before my untimely breakup with my long-term boyfriend who would have been my plus one." Once she started, the words wouldn't stop. Even if she wanted them to. "I didn't want to go alone so my friend talked me into using Desire to try a type of speed dating to find a guy to go with me for the weekend."

He crossed his arms over his chest and furrowed his brows. "You planned on asking a random stranger to go out of town with you for the weekend?"

She cleared her throat and angled her chin up. "When you put it like that it sounds bad, but that's what these dates are for. To weed out the crazies."

"I can think of at least fifteen reasons why that is a bad idea," he stated flatly.

"People put ads out for stuff like this all the time. I'm not going to sleep with the person, and they would get their own hotel room at the resort. I just didn't want to go alone."

Serenity saw how crazy it sounded, not to mention how dangerous it could be. She was skeptical from the beginning, but after some consideration, the idea warmed up to her. Of course, she did plan on taking every precaution possible to keep herself safe.

With arms still crossed, he raised a single brow. "So, our date was to see if I was a contender?"

"Y-yes," she stammered again.

He inquired further. "Are there others?"

"Just one, so far." She instantly regretted the words the moment they left her mouth.

A darkness hooded his gaze, one that had nothing to do with the darkness of the night. Was it possession, jealousy, anger, or hurt? She couldn't place it but as soon as it appeared, it was gone, his expression schooled to a calm demeanor once again.

"And even after tonight, you'll continue your dates until you make a decision?" He was fully amused now. Did he think this was a game?

She straightened her shoulders and held her chin up slightly, holding his gaze. "I will." She would hold her ground and not let him deter her.

"Ok."

He agreed so simply that it left her shocked. *That's it?* She expected more back and forth.

"You're… You're not mad?" Serenity was unable to hide the shock from her voice.

Hurting him was not intentional and if she had upset him, she would apologize. If the situation had been reversed, she would have been hurt to discover his intent behind their date.

"No, Angel, I'm not mad. I understand your situation. I don't approve by any means, but I get it. Plus, I'm very confident that no others will compare, and I'll be going with you next weekend." He uncrossed his arms as full amusement, and confidence filled his tone.

"Oh?" She arched her brow and crossed her arms over her chest. "What makes you so confident I'll choose you?"

Without another word, he placed a large hand on the small of her back. The other cupped the back of her neck as he pulled her against his hard frame. He bent his head down and claimed her lips with his. At first, she was shocked. Her arms instinctively went up to push him away but the moment his lips met hers, she found herself wrapping her arms around his neck instead and leaning further into him.

The warmth of his body consumed her, and she smelt the woodsy scent of his cologne. The feeling of his hands on her and her body pressed against his muscular front sent need straight to her center. He took a small step forward, pressing her back against her car. The action surprised her but the moment his tongue slid across her lips seeking entrance, a small moan escaped, and she opened, allowing their tongues to explore.

They only parted when they both came up for air, breathing heavily. He rested his forehead against hers as he spoke. "Any future dates you go on, I want you to remember that. Remember how I made you feel just now and that no other man would be able to surpass it."

"It was just a kiss," she said between pants, still trying to catch her breath.

"Was it? I bet if I reached under that dress of yours, the evidence of how great that kiss truly was would soak my fingers. Am I wrong?" Lust laced every word.

"No," she whispered.

She almost whimpered as he pulled away but refrained. He reached for the handle on her door, opened it for her, and made a questionable face as he took in the items in her front seat.

"Preparing for battle?"

Confused at his question, she followed his gaze to the Academy bag filled with weapons and ammo still occupying her passenger seat.

"Oh, that." She laughed nervously. "Just some things for home defense. You know, a single woman living alone and all. You can never be too careful."

"Right." He drew the word out and nodded skeptically.

Serenity slid into the driver's seat and started her car. "Good night, Hunter."

"Good night, Angel." He gave her a wink, and closed her door before making his way to his motorcycle parked near the front.

As Serenity showered up for the night, she couldn't control her wandering mind from reliving her kiss with Hunter. She could feel her body agreeing with her as wetness started to drip down her thighs, mixing with the hot water. She now had two names on her "maybe" list: Hunter and Owen. Owen… She paused. Not once had he crossed her mind since meeting Hunter.

There was a lot she liked about Owen. He was smart, kind, a gentleman, handsome, and seemed to be interested in her thoughts and opinions on various topics. He had a good, stable career and she enjoyed his company. He made butterflies flutter in her stomach on their date and the kiss with him was wonderful. There were definite sparks, but what she felt with Hunter was different.

Hunter almost brought her to her knees with just his voice alone. He was caring, intelligent, and dangerous in the most delicious way possible. His looks alone had her body screaming for his touch, not to mention that kiss. If his kiss was enough to make her almost forget how to breathe, sex with him would be catastrophic.

Her brain started to wander down a much dirtier path. Sighing in frustration, she removed the shower head and turned it to a higher pressure setting. She angled the water to hit the bundle of nerves at her center. As she closed her eyes, she thought back to Hunter kissing her and what would happen next if they were at her house.

She pictured him ripping her dress clean off her body and lifting her up on the kitchen counter, taking one of her full breasts into his mouth. As he switched to the other one, licking and sucking on her perky nipple, she would work on undoing his pants. He'd pull away and slide his jeans down just far enough to free his hard cock.

She imagined him gripping her waist as he pulled her to the edge of the counter, pulled her panties to the side, and entered her, burying himself to the hilt. There would be no lovemaking, no soft or gentle movements. It would be pure primal need, hot and rough as he stretched and filled her.

He wouldn't give her time to adjust to his size before he would be moving inside of her, hard. Impaling her over and over. She'd wrap her legs around his waist and try to pull him further into her. Her loud moans and his grunts of pleasure would be the only sounds that filled the kitchen.

And it wouldn't take long before he'd come, filling her up with his seed. The thought of Hunter coming inside of her had the shower head sending her into her own orgasm. The ones she gave herself were never as powerful as the ones brought on from sex, but they were enough to hold her over and release some of the pent-up need she felt.

After rinsing off and stepping out of the shower, she toweled off and got dressed in a pastel pink short and tank top pajama set. She brushed out her hair and braided it back, brushed her teeth, and crawled into bed. After checking to make sure her alarms were set for the morning, she plugged in her phone and snuggled into her pillow, sleep taking her quickly.

Addi sat on her couch, curled under a multicolored quilt that her grandmother handcrafted for her as a child. She had been binging one of her favorite reality dating shows all afternoon, a guilty pleasure she had. She would agree with people that those shows could be ridiculous and fake, but for some reason, she couldn't stop watching them.

A noise at the front door caught her attention, drawing her eyes away from the TV. The security system dinged three short and quick chimes, signaling that a door to the home had been opened. Glancing at the time on her phone, it was a little past seven that night.

"Jack, is that you?" she called from the couch.

"Yeah, it's me, babe," Jack answered as he left the foyer and entered the living room where he walked around the couch, leaned down, and pressed his lips to hers.

"You got home early today," she joked.

"I know, I feel like we should celebrate." He smiled and straightened. "I'm going to take a quick shower and then you can catch me up on what I've missed." He pointed to the TV, a guilty pleasure of his too.

She beamed. "Deal!"

About ten minutes later, he came out of their room shirtless with only a pair of blue plaid pajama pants hung low around his waist, allowing his muscular torso to be on full display. Addi opened the covers as he laid down on top of her, his head resting on her ample breasts as he wrapped his arms around her middle. She adjusted the covers back over them before filling him in on what he missed while she ran her fingers through his brown wavy strands.

"So, at lunch today, Renny told me about some weird things that have been going on at the house."

"What kind of weird things?" he questioned, craning his head to meet her gaze, worry filling the emeralds of his eyes.

She filled him in on the things Serenity had mentioned to her. "I told her maybe it was just stress that might be causing her to forget things."

"It could be. What would she be that stressed about though?" Concern filled his tone.

"Trying to find a date for the wedding by next Thursday."

He turned his head and laid it back down against her chest. "I didn't think she would go through with the weird speed dating thing."

"Yeah, she's gone out on a new date each day this week. She has one guy so far that's a possibility."

It could be stress-related. She knew that if she had to go on a new date every day, she would be worn out too.

"Back to the house thing, does she have any weapons in case someone is getting inside?"

She noticed a hint of strain in his voice, but she didn't know why. Was he upset that someone was possibly breaking into his house? Or was it something else?

"She planned on getting something today after work. I also told her I would talk to you about maybe putting up cameras around the outside of the home?"

"Yeah, that's a good idea," Jack agreed. "I know a guy who can come out tomorrow and install some."

They stayed like that for another hour, just loving the warmth and closeness of each other before they called it a night and went to bed.

CHAPTER 14

FRIDAY – 6 DAYS TILL DEPARTURE

Upon waking the next morning, Serenity found nothing amiss with her house. Everything was the way it should be. She unboxed her weapons and loaded them the way the gentleman at the store showed her. She placed the pistol in the nightstand next to her bed and the shotgun inside a hall closet downstairs.

With two weapons in the house, one on each level, she felt some of the worry and fear leaving her. Although her paranoia made her feel like she was being watched anytime she was at the house, she hated it. She hated the person more for making her feel on edge in her own safe space. Her phone chimed from the kitchen, and she made her way back to it to check the notification.

Hunter: Good morning, Angel. I hope you have a wonderful day and remember me while on your date tonight.

Serenity: Good morning to you too! I'm making it a point not to think about you.

Hunter: Good luck with that. (Winky face emoji)

She snorted, knowing she wouldn't be able to stop herself from thinking about him. She woke up with Hunter on her mind and found herself smiling like an idiot. It had been too long since a man sent her a good morning text, let alone doing it without her sending one first. Hope ignited in her chest despite countless tries to squash it. They only had one date, but she had a good feeling about him.

Serenity's morning at work was daunting. Although she had a packed schedule, she found her thoughts filled with Hunter far too often. Addi strode through her office door and placed their lunch on Serenity's desk.

"Please, tell me last night's date was as good as the one with Owen?" Addi smiled, getting right to the point.

"Good morning, Renny. How are you doing today? Oh, I'm great. Thank you for asking. How are you today, Addi?" Serenity mocked. Addi rolled her eyes and stuck her tongue out as she distributed their food. "You remember the guy from the motorcycle accident last weekend?"

"Yeah?" Addi answered in confusion, not sure where she was going with this.

"Well, he was my date yesterday."

"No shit? Huh, small world."

"The date went… fantastic!" She finished the last word with a dreamy sigh.

Two deep creases formed between Addi's brows, although she couldn't contain the smile that worked its way across her lips. "Better than your date with Owen?"

"Way better! You know when you're a teen and your crush finally asks you out, and on the date there are butterflies and it's nice and sweet and innocent?" Serenity asked and Addi nodded her head in understanding. "Well, that's what my date with Owen was like. But with Hunter, the moment I saw him I knew I was in trouble. His voice literally made me weak in the knees. I know that makes me sound like a whore but it's nothing like that."

Serenity described him and their date in more detail. The more she said, the more Addi's face grew with a mixture of shock and excitement.

"Where can I find one of those?" she joked. "I'm so happy for you. Two successful dates in a row and two names added to your list."

It did feel good to have something on that list, and even better to have multiple names on it.

"Did you speak with Jack about putting up cameras?" Serenity asked while the thought was fresh in her mind.

"Yes, he said he knows a guy who can come out today and install some," Addi confirmed around a bite of food.

"Oh, good. With those and the weapons I bought, I feel safer already."

"Renny, please stay with us until you find a new place. I don't like the idea of a stranger possibly getting into a house that you are living in." Worry was heavy in her voice.

"I have a few properties saved that I'll tour when we get back from Hawaii, plus weapons and now cameras. I'll be fine. I will not let a stranger drive me out of my own house."

Well, a house I'm borrowing from a friend, but you get the idea.

Addi tried to protest again but Serenity was adamant about staying.

The rest of the afternoon went quickly, and Serenity was able to add a few more properties to her possible rental search to tour after the wedding. As she pulled into the blue two-story family home, she spotted a white van parked in the driveway along with Jack's black Corvette.

Her face scrunched in worry as she wondered who was currently at the house without her knowledge. She parked her car, got out, and walked hesitantly along the side of the van. A sigh of relief left her lips upon reading the name painted across the side, advertising a security camera company.

"Hey, Renny!" Jack called as he popped out from the far side of the home.

He wore a light blue button-up shirt that was tucked into a pair of suit pants. *He must have come here straight from his office,* she thought.

"Hey, Jack." She walked lightly across the lawn to him, careful not to sink her black heels into the ground.

"I hope this is ok." He motioned to the guy who was high up a ladder attaching a camera to the side of the home. "Addi caught me up on what's been going on and I thought the sooner the better with something like that."

She smiled at him. "Thank you, this really means a lot."

He truly was a good friend, and she was so glad her best friend was marrying a guy like him.

"Of course, Renny. I only wished I'd taken you more seriously when you texted the other day. I apologize for that." He gave her a sincere smile as he ran his hand through his wavy hair.

"Don't feel sorry. There was no way for you to know what was going on."

"Well, he's almost done, and we'll get out of your hair. You could always take up Addi's offer to stay with us," He suggested as he slid his hands into his pockets and walked beside Serenity toward the backyard where the technician was.

She placed a hand on his shoulder and gave him a small smile. "No, I could never impose on y'all like that. I know you'll say it's no problem, but I just can't. I appreciate the offer though."

The technician climbing down the ladder caught their attention as they continued their walk toward him. He walked them both through the ins and outs of the camera system and instructed both Serenity and Jack to download the app to be able to monitor each camera. Once he made sure they were all working properly, he gathered up his tools and left.

Jack walked with Serenity back toward his car. "I hope this helps you feel safer. I am so sorry this is happening to you, especially in my home. I pray it's just stress getting to you."

"Honestly, it probably is. I could be overthinking the whole thing." She laughed because it was true. She'd always struggled with the nuisance and headache of overthinking.

He pulled her into a tight, warm hug as he spoke in a stern voice. "If anything happens, and I mean anything, Renny, call me. I don't care what time it is."

"I will, I promise." She hugged him back, thankful that she had someone reliable to count on if things went south. "Thank you, again."

She prayed it wouldn't come to that though. Jack pulled away and said goodbye as he got into his car.

Serenity climbed the carpeted stairs, having a little bit of time to get ready before her date with Weston. They agreed to meet at a local dive bar in town for a few rounds of pool and maybe some dancing. After touching up her makeup, she brushed out her hair and ran her straightener through it, smoothing out any waves from the braids she wore to work.

She chose a cute yellow spaghetti-strapped sundress that hugged her small waist and stopped mid-thigh, the V-neckline showing off an ample amount of cleavage. A notification sounded from her phone, letting her know that her Uber was outside the house. She always took one on nights like these when she would most likely have more than two drinks. She slipped on her solid brown boots, grabbed her black clutch and her keys, and left the house.

CHAPTER 15

FRIDAY – 6 DAYS TILL DEPARTURE

Serenity's Uber driver was a middle-aged woman that chatted with her the whole way about anything and everything under the sun. She was thankful for the conversation though. It helped distract her from her nerves. She gave up hoping they would go away, but no matter how many first dates she went on, nerves were inevitable. The woman dropped her off in front of the bar and gave her a card with her number on it.

"If you need a ride later, don't hesitate to call. I'll make sure to get you home safely," the woman said to her in a motherly way.

"Thank you." She slipped the card into her clutch and closed the car door.

The exterior of the bar was painted sky blue with spray paint art decorating the length of the building. There were no windows on this side of the building but there was a patio section that had twinkling lights strung overhead, illuminating the area.

As she made her way to the solid blue front door, she passed a line of various motorcycles parked up front. Her mind instantly went to Hunter, wondering what he was up to tonight. *No*, she stopped herself. She wouldn't think about him. She wouldn't let him win that easily. She shook her mind clear as she pushed open the door and walked inside.

The dimly lit interior of the bar was small. A horseshoe bar took up the whole left side with numerous stools lining it. A few rows of pool tables filled a space off to the right, dart boards lined the walls and a small empty space for dancing lay up front next to a neon jukebox.

She preferred these kinds of places versus a large club any day. The people here were more laid back, and the environment was more relaxed. Regulars usually frequented places like this so you never had to worry about being packed shoulder to shoulder like more mainstream bars. She grabbed a wooden stool at the bar as she sent Weston a message.

Serenity: Hey, I'm here. I'm sitting at the bar in a yellow sundress and brown boots.

"What can I get you to drink, hun?" A young woman around her age asked from behind the bar. Her curly blonde hair was pulled up into a messy bun, and bright red painted her lips, popping against her creamy skin.

Serenity spoke a little louder than usual so the bartender could hear her over the music. "I'll take a Michelob Ultra in a bottle, please." The woman turned, grabbed a bottle, popped the top, and handed it to her. "Keep the change." She smiled and passed the woman a five dollar bill.

The bartender smiled and thanked her. A tap on her shoulder caused her to turn around, seeing a tall man with mocha skin and short black hair standing behind her. His straight white smile greeted her as his gaze dropped to her cleavage and snapped back up quickly, but not quick enough. She caught that and groaned inwardly, thankful that he corrected himself before she had to.

"Hey, I'm Weston. It's nice to meet you."

She grabbed her beer and stood. "Serenity. It's nice to meet you too."

He flagged the bartender down and ordered a double whisky and Coke. "Do you want to shoot some pool?"

The bartender handed him his drink and walked off. *He must already have a tab going,* she thought when he didn't pay, and the bartender hadn't asked for a card to keep on file.

"Sure." She smiled at him and walked over to an empty pool table.

Serenity sat her beer down on a small circular table by them and grabbed a pool stick from a rack hanging on the wall. Weston started racking the balls in the middle of the table and grabbed a stick of his own.

"You break first." He shot her a grin as he took a large swig of his drink.

She bent over at the waist, lined up the tip of her stick behind the white cue ball, and shot it forward, sending the ball into the rest waiting across the table, scattering them in various directions. She watched as one with stripes went into a pocket.

"I'm stripes." She straightened and peered over at Weston who was zoned out on her ass.

He snapped his attention back up to her face. "Nice shot!"

Great, she thought. If men were going to look, that was fine. She only wished they would try to be more inconspicuous about it. She walked around, found a clear shot, and took it, pocketing another one.

"What do you do for work?" she asked as she went for a third one but missed.

"I'm a delivery driver for UPS. What about you?" He took a shot and missed, muttering something under his breath that was too low to hear over the music.

"I work at a bank," Serenity answered. "Do you have any siblings?"

"Three brothers. One older, the rest younger."

She laughed as she took her turn. "Wow, that's a big family."

"Yeah." He laughed in agreement. "What's your longest relationship?"

"Two years." She fought off the urge to cringe. She didn't like thinking about Noah. Every time she did, the picture of his betrayal flashed through her mind. "What about yours?"

"Three months." He shrugged casually. "She wanted commitment, but I'm not ready for that."

That struck her as odd. His profile said he was thirty. "If you don't want commitment, why do online dating?" She sipped from her beer.

"To hook up with hot chicks," he admitted, shooting her a wink, taking her by surprise.

I won't be one of those hookups, but I give him points for honesty.

They continued to chat, asking each other random questions as the game went on and they took turns shooting. Weston downed two more double whiskey and Cokes before the game was even over. Serenity didn't have a problem with people drinking but the rate he was going at was excessive, especially for someone on a first date.

She racked the balls in the middle of the table for another

game. "What do you like to do for fun?"

"This," he said, motioning to the bar. "Although I usually win when I play," he grumbled.

Was he upset? She'd won the first game. He, on the other hand, didn't even come close, only pocketing three balls. *Please, don't be the sore loser type,* she prayed silently.

"Well, maybe you just needed to warm up first."

"Maybe," he clipped out. He broke this time, not pocketing a single ball. "Fuck," he muttered under his breath as he wobbled a little, but caught himself and recovered quickly.

You've got to be kidding me. She sighed as she scanned the table and found a clear shot. She bent down and took it, pocketing a solid red ball.

Weston dropped the wooden stick atop the table as he tried and failed to hide the frustration in his voice. "I'm going to get another drink."

Serenity released a heavy breath and placed her stick back on the rack with the others, not wanting to play anymore. She sat at the table and finished off her one and only beer as she waited for him to come back.

She was ready to call it a night. She wasn't having any fun, and at this rate, her date would be blacked out within the next hour, and she didn't plan on sticking around to see that happening.

He weaved his way back to her through the crowd of people with a fresh drink in his hand and a drunken smile on his face. As he placed his glass on the table, she went to tell him she was leaving but his hand cupped the back of her neck, and his lips fell on hers.

Complete shock rocked through her as she stared at him, his eyes closed and his lips moving against hers. She placed her hands on his arms and pushed him away. He straightened with a grin and somehow, during the horrible kiss, managed to step between her legs.

"Let's get out of here." He winked as he rested his other hand on her bare thigh.

"I'm going to go but you won't be coming with me."

She tried to remove his hand from her thigh. When that failed, she tried to get up from the chair, but he pushed against her chest, forcing her further back. His lips went for hers again, but she managed to turn her head away, sending his lips to her neck instead. He didn't protest as he began placing kisses along the column of bare olive skin.

"Weston, stop!" she told him sternly.

"Don't act like you don't want this. You dressed like that to get a man's attention. Well, now you have it," he said in between kisses as he placed his other hand back on her thigh and started sliding it beneath her dress.

"Get the hell off of me!" she shouted as she dug her thumbs into his eyes.

"Ah! You stupid bitch!" he cursed as he straightened and held his palms against his aching vision.

Weston dropped his hands a moment later and the look of pure rage across his face scared her. She saw him raise his right hand to hit her, and instinctively, she threw her hand up, blocking her face for the hit that didn't come.

"Didn't your mother ever teach you not to hit a woman?" A deep voice washed over Serenity, and her breath hitched.

She didn't have to look to see who that voice belonged to. She knew and so did her body, betraying her and awakening at the sound of him.

She dropped her hands and turned her head, the sight before her had her heart skipping a beat. Hunter was standing there with a calm collected expression with Weston's wrist in his large grasp. A group of menacing men stood behind Hunter that she didn't recognize. *They must be with him,* she thought.

"Mind your own business, asshole," Weston spat at him as he tried to yank his arm from Hunter's white-knuckled grasp.

It didn't budge. Clearly, he was wasted because any sober man would think twice about saying something like that to a man as dangerous-looking as Hunter, let alone the four equally frightening men behind him.

"She *is* my business." He spoke calmly, his blue and hazel eyes meeting her bottle-greens. "It's best if you leave."

"Whatever. This teasing slut isn't worth it. You can have her." Weston yanked his arm again, and this time Hunter untightened his grip, allowing Weston to storm off while cursing more colorful insults under his breath.

CHAPTER 16

FRIDAY – 6 DAYS TILL DEPARTURE

All Serenity could do was stare in shock. How was he here? Had he followed her on her date? Was it just a coincidence? She didn't care, she was just thankful he stopped Weston before things got bad.

"Th—thank you." She fumbled with her words.

That seemed to be a recurring thing when she was around him. One day she would be able to talk to him without sounding like a stuttering idiot.

"You're welcome, Angel," Hunter took a step toward her, his long legs eating up the short distance between them too quickly. "Are you ok?" His rough hand cupped her chin gently, completely at odds with each other.

She nodded her head. "Yes."

She averted her eyes from his, feeling embarrassed for letting herself get into this situation, and cursing herself for not stopping it and leaving earlier.

"Did you drive here?"

She shook her head. "No."

"Grab your things. I'll take you home." He never once lost his calm demeanor. In his line of work, this was probably another Tuesday for him.

"Ok." She grabbed her clutch and stood up. He placed a strong hand on the small of her back as he walked her to the door, the group of men with him following closely behind. "Who are they?" She motioned to the men behind them as they left the bar. Her ears rang from the sudden sound difference, needing a moment to adjust to the quiet parking lot.

"These are my friends Fuse, Sweeney, Doc, and Einstein."

Hunter introduced each man to her. As she took them in, each one was scary in their own way, whether it be from their sheer size, noticeable scars both old and fresh, or tattoo choices and placements. They either nodded or said hello after being introduced.

"Hey," she said nervously. "Those are some... interesting names."

They all chuckled, including Hunter. "They work for me. Each one is given a nickname or a call sign specific to them. We use them even when we are off the clock so when shit hits the fan, no one is fumbling over what names to call each other."

"Well, if I ever need a bodyguard, I'm calling y'all. No one would come within fifty yards with men like that by me." She rambled on again due to her stupid nerves. "No offense. I'm sure you guys are lovely people."

They all burst out laughing and color filled her cheeks.

"I like this one, Boss." Fuse laughed and the rest agreed.

He reminded her of a Viking straight from Norway. He was about six feet and packed with bulky muscles. His blond hair was shaven on the sides with the top pulled into a tight braid that hung to his shoulders. His eyes were as blue as ice and his pointed features were covered in a brownish-reddish beard that he kept at a light stubble.

Hunter shot them a glare and shook his head. "Come on, Angel. Hop on."

He patted the back seat of one of the bikes. It looked exactly like the one he was hit on, a matte black Harley Sportster, but there wasn't a single scratch in sight.

"I'm not getting on that." She half-laughed in protest, motioning to the short dress she was wearing. "I'll just call an Uber. Thank you for what you did back there."

She turned to walk back to the door where she would wait for her ride, but a hand wrapped around her wrist, halting her. The grip was gentle but firm. She peered down at her wrist and followed it up Hunter's muscular tattooed arm until she met his piercing gaze.

"I wasn't asking." His tone was low and serious. "Get on the bike."

She gently removed her arm from his grasp and crossed her arms over her chest. "Or what?" she shot back.

What are you doing? Don't make the scary biker mad. Just get on the damn bike, she scolded herself. She didn't know where she got the nerve, but she was going to hold her ground and not let him order her around.

"Oh yeah, we definitely like this one!" Sweeney spoke this time, laughing as Serenity tried to stand up to their boss.

Sweeney was just as tall and broad as Hunter, but his brown hair was cut short on top and faded on the sides. His golden eyes popped against his tanned skin, and he kept himself clean-shaven, making his square jawline more prominent. He only had one arm sleeved out in a bright colorful tattoo that peered out beneath his T-shirt.

Hunter turned and glared at his men again. They all put up their hands in defense and shook their heads laughing. "If you don't get on this bike, I will bend you over this seat and spank you while my men watch."

Serenity's mouth dropped open in utter shock. She could not believe the words that had just left his mouth. "You wouldn't dare." She glared at him. Who did he think he was to threaten her with something like that?

He peered at her through hooded eyes as a wicked grin slid across his handsome face. He gently pulled her toward his bike and bent her over his seat. She tried to fight him, but she was like a child in his grasp, easily movable to him. Once bent over the cushioned seat, she glanced back and saw him raise his large hand, ready to land the first spank across her round ass that was now half exposed to everyone from where her short dress rode up.

"Ok! Ok! Jeez! I'll get on the stupid bike!" she pleaded with him.

Hunter dropped his hand instantly and helped her stand upright again, a satisfied smile pulled at one side of his lips. She didn't need a mirror to know her face was bright red from embarrassment.

She tugged the hem of her dress down, pinched her brows together, and pointed a finger at him sternly, even though he had a good six or seven inches on her. "That was completely inappropriate and wipe that stupid smirk off your face."

Hunter chuckled and handed her his black riding jacket. She yanked it from him and put it on, muttering a colorful string of curses beneath her breath. The jacket swallowed her, like a child trying to wear their father's shirt, but it was surprisingly warm and smelt like him. She fought hard to resist the urge to pull it against her nose and inhale deeply.

He held out his hand and she took it reluctantly as she swung her leg over the back of the bike and sat down, using her other hand to keep her dress pulled down so she didn't flash anyone. She didn't need any more embarrassment tonight. Hunter grabbed the helmet resting on a handlebar and slid it down over her head. Gently, he lifted her chin so he could attach the straps and tighten them.

The helmet smelt like him too, but this one she could take a deep breath of without being obvious. He swung his large muscular leg over the bike and sat down as his men climbed onto their own rides.

"I'll see y'all later. Ride safe." Hunter nodded his head toward the others.

They nodded back and said their goodbyes. One by one they started up their bikes, a loud rumbling filling the quiet night air. They backed out and left, leaving Hunter and Serenity alone, the parking lot falling quiet again.

He handed her his phone with his map app pulled up. "Put in your address, Angel."

She did and gave him the phone back so he could attach it to the phone mount he had for his bike.

He turned his head and glanced back at her. "Have you ever been on a bike before?"

"No." Nerves laced the word.

"Wrap your arms around me and lean into the turns, ok?"

"Um… ok," she agreed hesitantly.

Her nerves were getting the better of her, but her curiosity was starting to override them. Slowly, she leaned against his back and wrapped her arms around his stomach, resting her head against his broad shoulders. Hunter started up the bike and the vibration shook her whole body.

Kicking back the stand, he backed out of the space and pulled out of the parking lot. He started slowly at first, giving her a chance to get used to the bike. She quickly learned what he meant by leaning into the turns with him.

As they rode down the street, she found herself slowly starting to relax and enjoying the ride. She also enjoyed the closeness of him. Every time he moved or turned, she could feel his muscles move underneath his shirt and it took every ounce of restraint to not run her fingers down the rivets of his abs. The closeness to him and the vibrations from the bike had heat rising to her core. She groaned in frustration when she realized she couldn't squeeze her thighs together.

Halfway through the ride, Hunter brought his hand back and rested it atop her left knee, gently tracing circles into her bare skin. Goosebumps rose and she could feel more wetness pooling between her legs. *Don't let there be a wet spot when I get up,* she prayed.

She lost herself in him and the ride and before she knew it, he was pulling into her driveway. He quickly kicked out the stand as he tilted the bike over until it rested on it and turned it off. When he rose from the bike, she instantly missed the warmth of his body, feeling cold even though it was a warm August night.

He turned and helped her unbuckle and pull off the helmet. She quickly smoothed her hair back down and took his hand as he helped her climb off the bike. Hunter let out a deep growl, startling her as she turned to look at him. His gaze was locked on the seat then flicked to her, hunger and lust filling his unique eyes.

Her brows furrowed in confusion as she looked down at her

seat. Flames scorched her cheeks as she took in the small damp spot that she left.

"Oh God, I'm so sorry. That's not what it looks like." She ignored the deep burning in her cheeks as she tried to save herself from any more embarrassment.

"It looks to me like you *really* enjoyed that ride, Angel." Hunter spoke in a dangerously low tone that sent her toes curling in her boots.

As he hung his helmet on a handlebar, he pulled Serenity completely against his front. She didn't fight it, instead, she wrapped her arms around his neck and welcomed the kiss that he didn't hesitate in planting on her full lips. Instantly, his tongue slid across her lips, seeking entrance. She quickly accepted and their tongues explored each other's mouths.

He brought his hand down and trailed his fingers up the outside of her leg, slipped it under her dress, and grabbed a handful of her round ass. He gave it a hard squeeze and she moaned against his mouth, earning her another growl of approval from him. They only pulled away when they both were gasping for air. He made sure she was stable before releasing his hold on her.

He gave her a sly grin as he grabbed his phone off its mount and handed it to her. "Since I now know where you live, it seems only fitting that I get your number."

Serenity stood there considering the idea for a moment before ultimately inputting her number. "I sent myself a text, so I have yours as well." She handed him back his phone.

He shot her a quick wink and smiled. "Good night, Angel."

"Good night, Hunter." She smiled back before she turned and walked inside the house.

She was on cloud nine as she closed the door behind her and

leaned against it, still trying to catch her breath. The sound of his bike starting up and trailing off down the road made her miss him instantly. A part of her was thankful that he didn't expect more from her, but the other part was sad he didn't. Had he asked to come inside, she would have gladly accepted, throwing her three date rule out the window.

CHAPTER 17

FRIDAY – 6 DAYS TILL DEPARTURE

As The Figure walked up the dimly lit street to the blue wooden two-story family home, excitement filled him when he noticed Serenity's Honda Civic parked in the driveway. The house was dark except for a small lamp in the living room and the porch light. *Is she asleep already?* He found himself wondering as he took in the quiet house from the sidewalk.

Something caught his eye that made him smile. *How cute,* he thought as he took in the cameras mounted on the house. He walked up the driveway and down the side of the home in clear view of the cameras as he rounded the back. He let himself in and quietly shut the door behind him as he slowly made his way through the darkened main floor.

He stealthily climbed the stairs and peered into each room, progressively growing more irritated as he found the house to be vacant. *Where the hell is she? Is she out with someone else?* Wandering around her empty bedroom, he trailed his fingers lightly over the cold covers of her bed before stopping in front of her dresser.

A wicked grin spread across his face as he opened the top drawer, revealing laced thongs in various colors as well as a few laced bras. He gripped a bright red little number and held it up, examining it as he pictured Serenity wearing nothing but that for him. The thought had his cock straining against his zipper.

The sound of a motorcycle pulling into the driveway drew his attention back to reality. He put the thong back in its place and shut the drawer before he walked toward the window and peeked out from behind the curtains. A large man he did not recognize turned to help his passenger take off their helmet. *Who the fuck is that?*

When Serenity's face became visible to him, pure rage filled his vision. He quickly but quietly made his way back downstairs to a window in the formal living room by the front door where he would have a better view and be able to hear their conversation.

When he pulled the curtains aside, the sight before him had his blood boiling. Whoever this man was now had his hands and lips all over her. Hurt filled him but he pushed it away and forced himself to take a few deep breaths before he did something stupid. *This is not our time. Soon,* he reminded himself.

He would just have to get rid of this one like he did the last one. That thought sent a spiteful grin across his face as he continued to watch the scene unfold in the driveway. The Figure sank back into the shadows, concealed by the curtains as Serenity entered the home. After she locked the doors and set her coffee pot for the morning, she padded her way upstairs.

Once he heard the shower turn on, he counted to twenty before he slowly crept up the stairs after her. He inched his way to the doorway of her bathroom and lurked just out of her view as he watched her shower. He stood there and admired her beauty as hot soapy water ran down her naked frame before he turned his head and noticed her phone lying on the bed. A sly grin pulled at his lips when he saw it was unlocked.

He grabbed it and pulled up the camera. After swiping it over to video, he pressed record, and stood there silently, filming her shower. When he was happy with the video, he closed out of the app and placed her phone back in its previous spot. As she turned the water off, he slithered from the room and hid in the closet of a spare bedroom.

When The Figure was confident that she was asleep, he emerged and crept back into her room. The sound of her light steady breathing filled the space as he stood beside her. He reached over and unplugged her phone from the charger, taking it with him downstairs.

He sat her phone down on the dining room table and made sure to grab a pencil and a piece of paper, scribbling a note on it before he left the house. He folded the paper and placed it in the bricked-in mailbox by the road before casually walking off down the sidewalk with his hands in his pockets.

SATURDAY – 5 DAYS TILL DEPARTURE

Serenity woke to the peaceful and beautiful melody of birds chirping their morning hymns outside her bedroom window. With her eyes still closed, she couldn't fight off the smile that worked its way across her sleepy features. The dream she thoroughly enjoyed last night that contained a certain sexy biker was fresh in her waking mind.

It had been far too long since she woke up feeling that good.

With all honesty, she hadn't smiled that genuinely since before her abrupt breakup with Noah and she was equally glad and thankful to experience the joys of it again. Slowly with each passing day, her heart became whole again. However, it would never be fully healed, as if a glass plate had been broken and glued back together. It was whole, but it would never be the same again.

Thinking of Hunter had her reaching for her phone. Would there be another good morning text waiting for her? Her heart picked up its pace at the thought and butterflies lightly fluttered in her stomach. Her hand padded across the top of the nightstand in search of it but only a small lamp occupied the surface. She pulled her black brows together and finally opened her eyes as she slightly lifted her head from the pillow and gazed toward the nightstand, no phone in sight.

A spark of panic suddenly replaced the happiness she felt just seconds ago. *Where's my phone?* she asked herself, trying to remember if she plugged it in last night. She could have sworn she did. It was a nightly routine and had become more of muscle memory now to charge it before going to sleep. *Did someone break in again last night?* The thought of a stranger being in her room while she was asleep and unaware had her wanting to vomit.

Calm down, she coached herself through a few deep breaths through her nose as her vision shifted around her room, praying she would find it lying somewhere close by. She had been distracted last night when her mind kept replaying the heated make out session she shared with Hunter in the driveway. That could have easily distracted her enough to leave it somewhere.

She rose from the bed and shuffled across the room, still not fully awake yet, her eyes skimming every surface as she searched. After checking every room on the top floor, she slowly descended the stairs and began scouring the living room before making her way into the kitchen. The smell of freshly brewed coffee filled her senses, and she sent up a silent thank you that it was working properly this morning.

With each passing minute, she grew more nervous and paranoid. She checked each entry door as she passed by them, but she found them like she always had, locked. As she was about to move onto the last room of the house, she caught sight of her phone lying on the dining room table in the same spot she drank her morning coffee.

She quickly grabbed it, punched in her passcode, and pulled up the security camera app, completely ignoring a text message notification, having more pressing things on her mind. She clicked on the live feed and rewound the time until she saw herself and Hunter in the driveway last night. Hitting the fast-forward button, she watched intently for any sign of movement at the front and back doors. Minutes ticked by as she watched with bated breath. A part of her hoped she wouldn't see anything, but the other part of her wished she would so she had an explanation for all the weird occurrences that had been happening lately.

After a while, the feed stopped and began to show live images again. Nothing... No one had entered or exited her home last night. She let out a sigh of relief as she ran a hand through her long black strands flowing loosely down her back. She closed out of the security app and was reminded again of the unread text message she had waiting for her. She clicked on it and instantly smiled when she saw who it was from.

Hunter: Good morning, Angel. I hope you dreamt of me last night.

Serenity: Nope. But I did dream about one of my other dates.
Hunter: For your sake, I hope not.
Serenity: Why? Are you going to threaten to spank me again?

The memory of her bent over his bike last night popped into her mind. She was completely embarrassed in that moment, especially since he did it in front of his men, but she would be in denial if she said she didn't want him to go through with it. Excitement sparked within her and the thought of being spanked by him had her cheeks coloring and desire beginning to ignite within her core.

She'd never been that adventurous with sex before. Especially not with Noah. Their love life wasn't vanilla by any means but something about Hunter had her open to exploration, wanting to push the boundaries of her comfortability. A delicious thrill swirled around in her stomach at all the things he could possibly show her.

The loud ringing of her doorbell sounded through the quiet home, scaring her, causing her to yelp and drop her phone on the table. She cursed at herself as she picked her phone up and walked to the front door. She closed one eye as she peered out through the peephole. The sight before her sent her heart racing, her belly flipping, and her breath hitching.

CHAPTER 18

SATURDAY – 5 DAYS TILL DEPARTURE

Serenity quickly unlocked the door and held it half open, the morning sun causing her to squint as her eyes tried to adjust to the sudden brightness.

"What are you doing here?" she inquired as she took in the sexy biker standing on the front porch.

She couldn't help but wonder what Hunter looked like in a tux if he looked like a god in casual clothes. Who knew a simple dark blue T-shirt and jeans could look so good on a man, but the way they formed around his body, his muscles, tattoos, and scars had her mouth watering. He wore half of his brown hair tied up in a ponytail with the rest flowing down to his broad shoulders.

"It's not a threat, Angel. I *will* spank you if I must." His tone was low as he held up his phone, indicating that he was referring to her last message.

She watched as he tore his eyes from hers and slowly took her in. Her raven hair was down, allowing the strands to hang freely around her shoulders and down her back. She was still in her pajamas, a pastel pink tank top and shorts set. Her perky nipples poked against the thin material, and the shorts allowed the spot where her ass met the back of her thighs to peek out.

His gaze continued down her long legs to the bare feet that had bright red polish painted on the nail of each toe. Slowly his vision met hers and color heated her cheeks when she observed pure hunger filling them.

She was forced to clear her throat before she trusted her voice enough to speak. "What are you doing here, Hunter?" she questioned again, cursing inwardly as that came out softer than she wanted.

"Are you hungry?" His composure was schooled again. Any sign that her body influenced him was gone.

The simple question threw her off. Her face scrunched up. "What?"

Hunter tried hard to keep his eyes on hers. "I thought we could grab some breakfast."

"Hunter, you can't just show up at my house like this. I gave you my address last night so you could take me home, but that wasn't an open invitation to drop by when you feel like it." Serenity tried to scold him but only felt like a child trying to reprimand their parents.

"You're right. I should have texted first," he agreed.

For the second time, this man caught her off guard. She had expected more of an argument, not an agreement.

"Thank you." She tried hard not to sound shocked.

"So, are you hungry?" he inquired again with a hint of amusement in his eyes.

Did he find her attempt to be firm with him amusing or was it the fact that he shocked her when he agreed he was wrong? She couldn't tell which.

"This is why you should've texted first. I already have prior arrangements." She tried hard to avoid the fact that her plans involved another date with a man who was not him.

Any amusement in his eyes was gone as his voice dropped an octave. "Another date?"

She forced her chin up and answered confidently, holding his gaze. "Yes."

"Am I going to have to save you from this one too?" he deadpanned as he arched his scarred brow.

"No!" she said in complete shock. *The audacity of this man!* "And for your information, I didn't need you to save me last night. I could have gotten myself out of that… somehow." She crossed her arms under her breasts, the action making them more prominent.

Hunter flicked his gaze to them, hunger and lust flashing through his irises again before he brought them back up and schooled his features once more. Serenity noticed as she started to shift from one foot to the other nervously. He didn't dignify that with a response. Instead, he just stood there, waiting patiently.

"Ugh!" she groaned as she opened the door wider and turned toward the stairs. "Wait in the family room. I'll go get dressed." She called over her shoulder as she climbed the stairs. Her cheeks colored again as she felt his weighted gaze on her the entire way until she turned down the hall to her room.

She threw on her favorite *Star Wars* T-shirt that had two red lightsabers crisscrossing with the words, *come to the dark side, it's more fun,* written underneath and a pair of Wrangler jeans that hugged her legs and ass like a second skin. She brushed her hair out, deciding to let the strands flow freely down her back today before quickly applying a little eye makeup and calling it good. She grabbed a pair of boots and made her way back downstairs.

As Hunter shut the front door behind him, he couldn't tear his eyes from the view before him. He watched hungrily as Serenity climbed each stair, the movement causing her ass to bounce slightly and her hips to sway from side to side. He felt blood rushing to his cock, and he groaned inwardly as she disappeared down the hallway.

He entered the family room as his mind went back to the day they'd met. Unfortunately, that wasn't his first wreck, and probably wouldn't be his last. Part of the dangers that came with riding. He was jarred a little at first but once he worked through the realization of what happened, he knew nothing was broken.

He knew he was ok to get up, but when the angel next to him forced him to stay still, he laughed on the inside. There was no physical way a small woman like herself could keep a six-foot-three man down, but he let her believe she had full control over the situation.

He was too intrigued by her. Watching her go off on the idiot who had hit him, putting him in his place, he found himself infatuated and a little turned on if he were being honest. She was so beautiful but had a fiery side to her that he would love to discover more of.

Every time that olive-skinned beauty had opened her mouth, he fell even further under her spell. After she had left, he had kicked himself for allowing her to walk out of his life before he got her number. He wanted to take her on a date and thank her properly. Now, life was giving him that second chance and he wasn't about to screw it up.

He took his time observing the house as he walked quietly around the space. His brows pinched together as he took in the photos sporadically displaced around the room. She was in none of them. Only a boy at different stages in life with what must be his parents. *That's odd,* he thought to himself. The sound of her coming down the stairs a few minutes later pulled him from his thoughts.

He turned to meet her, and the view had his words caught in his throat. *Fuck.* He took in the angel standing before him. No matter what she wore, she was breathtaking, even if she wore nothing at all. He quickly shook his head clear of that dangerously wicked thought or else he would have to explain the reason for the hard bulge in his pants.

"You look beautiful." He smiled. "I like the shirt."

That smile turned into a devilish grin as he read it. *So, she prefers the villains,* he observed. *Be careful what you wish for, Angel.*

She looked down at herself and began picking at the hem of her shirt. "Thank you." She smiled sheepishly at him as she tucked a loose strand of hair behind her ear.

"You have a nice home." He gestured toward the open room.

"Oh, it's not mine," Serenity corrected as she bent down to put her boots on, pulling her pant legs down over the top of them. "It's Jack's, my best friend Addi's fiancé. He grew up here and inherited it after his parents died. My house burnt down so they're letting me stay here until I find a new rental."

Despite his years of training, Hunter was unable to hide the shock, disbelief, and concern that filled his voice. "Your house burnt down?"

"Yeah, thankfully I wasn't home when it happened. Apparently, some serial arsonist wanted to watch it burn." She shrugged. "Would you be upset if I asked you to return me home after breakfast, so I didn't miss my date?" She straightened and gazed toward him.

His eyes darkened as he lowered his head to glare at her.

"I'm kidding!" She laughed fully. The sound filled his heart with pure joy, the feeling alien to him, but he welcomed it. "Jeez, you need to relax more. I canceled my date for today since you intended on being so stubbornly insistent."

That feeling of pure joy only blossomed further inside of him at hearing that. *Fuck... I'm in trouble,* he cursed at himself.

CHAPTER 19

The ride to the diner was amazing and Serenity found herself growing fonder and more comfortable on a motorcycle as well as with Hunter. He had brought a spare helmet this time, apparently confident enough that she would take him up on his offer of breakfast, gaining a glare from her when she noticed. She loved the freedom a bike offered—the excitement, the danger, and the closeness to your passenger, which created a certain type of intimacy.

Striding through the doors of the small restaurant was like stepping back into the 50s. Red and white vinyl booths lined the walls, checker-pattern linoleum covered the floor, and a neon jukebox lightly played classic tunes from the era. The young fiery-haired hostess, dressed in a pink short-sleeve, knee-length dress walked them to a booth in the back as Hunter took the side with his back to the wall, giving him a full view of the place.

A middle-aged woman dressed in the same 50s-inspired uniform took their orders and brought their coffees, leaving the pot on the table so they could refill them as needed.

"Tell me about yourself." Serenity spoke as she accepted a steaming cup of coffee that he had poured for her before pouring some into his own mug.

He took a careful sip of the hot liquid. "What do you want to know?"

"Everything?" She laughed. "I feel like I know nothing about you except what you do for work."

"I don't think we could cover everything in the time it will take us to eat." He laughed and shook his head.

"True, I guess it's a good thing I have your number now so we can talk more when we're not together." She paused, taking a sip. "Start with your childhood. What was it like? Do you have any siblings?"

"I was a military brat. My dad was in the Air Force, cyber intelligence, so we moved around a lot. My mom was a stay-at-home mom. I have two younger brothers and our childhood was amazing. My mom is the kind that never stops smiling, always happy and easygoing. My dad was stricter, but he was always there for us. No matter how hard of a day he had, he always put forth an effort to be present and invested in our lives. My parents are still grossly in love and moved back here to their home state after my dad retired."

Hunter kept his face neutral, but she didn't miss the glint of love for his family in his eyes.

"They sound wonderful." She couldn't help but smile. She wanted love and a family like that one day. "What about your brothers?"

"We were all close growing up. Still are to this day. We all followed in our father's footsteps. I joined the Navy and became a SEAL, Adam joined the Army, and Neil, the youngest, joined the Marine Corps. It drove our dad crazy that we didn't choose his branch but secretly he was proud of us. Adam and Neil are still in, making a career out of it, but I got out."

"How come, if you don't mind me asking?" She caught herself, hoping she wasn't overstepping or prodding too much.

"I loved it, but after being surrounded by death for so long, I needed a change. I wanted to protect rather than destroy, so I founded Red Sky Security so I could do just that and still get the freedom to travel the world."

"Wow, that's awesome. Not many people can say they are following their dreams and fully loving what they do." She spoke in awe.

Every time this man opened his mouth, he revealed another layer of himself, exposing more and more of his true nature. She couldn't wait to peel all the layers back and know this man completely, the good as well as the bad.

Without knowing specifics of what he had done, she knew this man was dangerous and probably had a few skeletons in his shadowy closet, but she saw deeper than that. Just from this conversation, she saw a spark of light in the pit of his soul that he didn't like to let shine. She wasn't sure why he kept it hidden but she found herself wanting to discover the reason.

Serenity's phone buzzed in her pocket, drawing her attention from her meal and Hunter, thinking it was Addi. She apologized to him as she quickly removed her phone and froze.

Noah: Hey, Renny. Can we meet up for coffee? Please, I miss you so fucking much that it hurts.

She couldn't contain the groan that slipped out as she read the text, the words almost making her breakfast reappear.

Hunter's tone grew serious. "What's wrong?"

She slid her phone across the table for him to read. He was quiet for a moment, the only indication that what he read bothered him was a slight flair of his nostrils, but he was otherwise composed.

"Is Noah the long-term boyfriend you were supposed to go to Addi's wedding with?" he asked in a calm voice, remembering back to the conversations they had on their first date.

Surprise and shock briefly flashed through her. *He remembered that?* Then she was reminded of what he did for a living. Of course, he would pick up little details like that.

"Yeah. He still texts from time to time with something along the lines of that." She pointed to her phone.

He handed the phone back to her. "Why not just block him?"

"Honestly, I've thought about it, but he was such a huge part of my life for years. Despite what he did, I guess it's just hard for me to close that door indefinitely." Sadness filled her. Sadness at the reminder of how great they were, but also of the unforgivable betrayal his actions caused.

Hunter was quiet for a moment before he spoke. "That's understandable. Will you tell me what happened?" he asked softly, surprising her yet again. Another layer revealed itself. This time, a gentle and compassionate one.

She had to take a deep breath before she could dive into that. The only people she had ever talked to about what happened was her mother and Addi, but she felt whole enough to be able to talk about it openly.

"We met a little bit after I started working at the bank. I was a teller at the time, and he came in to make a deposit. He asked me out and we had been together ever since. It was great and honestly, I thought he was the man I would marry." She paused, needing a minute before continuing to the hard part.

Hunter sat there quietly, looking at her with not a single hint of judgment in his eyes, patiently waiting for her to continue.

"He tended to let his eyes wander occasionally but I never thought anything of it. Those rose-colored glasses were glued to me, I guess, but I never had the feeling he was sneaking around or cheating on me, so I let it go and learned to live with it. I was going to surprise him with dinner at his home when he got off work, but I was the one surprised. When I walked inside, I found him screwing a girl he had bent over the side of his bed. I ended things right then and there and haven't spoken to him since, besides one text I replied to when he found out my house burnt down."

He stayed silent for another minute, processing everything she told him. His face was still neutral but, on the inside, he was a raging mess. He wanted nothing more than to find that piece of shit and make him hurt for hurting her. He couldn't wrap his brain around the fact that the idiot never stopped looking at other women, even when he had the most beautiful creature all to himself. *Well, his loss,* he thought. She wasn't even officially his yet and he was already willing to sacrifice the world for her happiness.

"I'm sorry you had to go through that." Hunter's large hand swallowed up hers, giving it a gentle squeeze. "He didn't deserve you."

She couldn't stop the hysterical laugh and eye roll that his statement drew out of her. He froze and his gaze seared into hers, forcing her to instantly regret her actions.

"Don't ever think negatively about yourself, especially around me. He. Didn't. Deserve. You." He punctuated each word, making his point. "Know your worth and don't ever expect anything less."

All Serenity could do was nod her head in agreement, another layer of his revealing itself.

CHAPTER 20

After breakfast, Hunter took her on a long ride through some of his favorite scenic routes. A ride that was filled with lots of winding backroads, hills, and beautiful landscapes that had her constantly turning her head from side to side so she wouldn't miss anything. They had been riding for hours before he pulled off into the gravel parking lot of a small biker bar on the outskirts of town. Serenity hissed as she climbed off the bike, her legs sore from sitting atop it for so long.

"You'll get used to it." He laughed as he took the helmet from her and placed it on the seat next to his.

In places like these, everyone belonged to the same community and treated you as family, even if you had never met before. So, he was confident no one would try and take the helmets.

"I've noticed you use future tense a lot. How are you so certain this will work out?" She motioned her finger between them.

He struck like a viper, fast but gentle as he grabbed her finger and pulled her into him, catching her off guard as he wrapped a muscular arm around her, resting his calloused hand on the small of her back. He skimmed over her face before locking eyes with her as he brushed a few raven strands behind her ear.

"Because, Angel, now that I've found you, I don't intend on letting you go." His voice was low as a grin pulled at his full lips.

"What if I don't want this?" Serenity's words were no louder than a whisper as she found herself unable to tear her gaze away from his blue and hazel grasp.

"You don't have a choice." The grin turned wicked as he dipped his head toward hers and captured her lips with his.

Those words should have scared her off, but they had the opposite effect on her. It had her wanting to push her limits with him, to explore a side of danger she had only experienced in books, to fulfill a curiosity she had never spoken aloud before.

The kiss was hot, quick, and unfortunately over before she got the chance to fully lean into and enjoy it. The taste of him lingered on her lips as he pulled away and she couldn't help but run her tongue along them. The action earned a low growl of approval from her biker. He captured her hand in his and led her through the door.

"So, you know why I'm using Desire, but you don't strike me as the kind to use online dating," Serenity inquired as she accepted a fresh chilled bottle of beer from Hunter and thanked him.

He followed her to a small round wooden high-top table, took a seat across from her, and took a swig of his beer before he casually shrugged his shoulders and answered. "I lost a bet."

She waited, only growing more curious by the second. "Well, don't keep me in suspense." She laughed, prompting him to continue.

"Sweeney and I were on an assignment guarding a female

celebrity filming some scenes for a new movie. It was obvious that she had a thing for me, but I wasn't interested. I don't fraternize with the clients. Ever. Sweeney bet that she would throw herself at me before the assignment was over. I bet him she wouldn't. A few nights later, a knock sounded on my hotel room door. When I answered it, there she was in nothing but a revealing bathrobe, holding a bottle of wine." He met her gaze and studied her.

She didn't look away as she took another sip of her beer. "What happened next?"

"I held up a hand, stopping her before she could utter a word, and told her that I don't mix business with pleasure. Then I shut the door on her."

Serenity threw her head back in laughter. "Ouch! That was harsh."

"That doesn't bother you?" he inquired.

Her reaction had clearly caught him off guard. Did he fear she would be upset with him for that?

"Why would it?" she questioned back, furrowing her brows and taking another drink.

"All the women I've tried talking to in the past seemed to have the same problem. They were so insecure with themselves that they would demand I only take on male clients."

"You said it yourself that you always keep things professional. Trust is a very big thing for me. If that's what you say, then I'll believe you until you give me a reason not to."

She tried to hide the sting she felt when talking about trust. Noah had completely obliterated her trust beyond any chance of mending. However, with Hunter, it was whole until he proved otherwise. Hesitant, but whole.

"Communication and trust are the biggest values in a

relationship. I can't tell you what a breath of fresh air it is to find a woman who understands and values it just as much." He gave her an appreciative smile before continuing. "Anyway, Sweeney surprised me with a profile on Desire and told me I had to go out with the first woman to ask me on a date." A wicked grin pulled at his lips that sent her heart flipping. "Imagine my surprise when I saw a message from my angel sitting in my inbox."

She wasn't trained in concealing her emotions like he was. The shock was evident across her face. *Maybe this was fate,* she thought but then inwardly groaned at how cheesy that thought was. He simply winked one of his blue and hazel eyes at her and continued to drink his beer.

Hunter pulled into Serenity's driveway and shut the bike off before climbing off and helping her up. She knew her legs would be screaming tomorrow after their day of riding, but she wouldn't trade it for anything.

"Thank you for today. It's been far too long since I've had this much fun." She spoke around a smile.

He sat her helmet down and pulled her into his strong embrace. "Anything to make you smile, Angel."

"Why do you call me that?" she inquired as she instinctively wrapped her arms around his neck and began twirling her fingers lightly through the base of his long brown hair.

"Because," he started as he placed a soft kiss against her forehead, "when I was lying on that pavement, the moment I first saw you leaning over me I thought I had died and went to Heaven. But then I thought there had to be some kind of mistake because if God knew half the things I've done, he would never let me in."

Those words melted her heart into a puddle of emotions. This man was an enigma. When she first met him, he was guarded, rough around the edges, and intimidating, but the more she got to know him, she slowly saw the good inside of him. She saw the love he carried for the people he cared about and the amount of kindness and gentleness he was capable of.

"I disagree. I think you would be the perfect warrior God would be looking for to protect his kingdom."

"I don't deserve you either, but I claimed you the moment I saw you."

"Let me be the judge of who deserves me," Serenity whispered softly as she closed her eyes and kissed him.

His hand came up and grabbed a handful of her hair as he kissed her back with such hunger and need that she felt her core ache.

He groaned loudly as he pulled away. "Before I take this to a place you aren't ready for yet, I think it's time we say good night." He lightly cupped her chin and ran his thumb over her plump lips.

As much as her hormones and heart were screaming that they wanted this, her brain was telling her that he was right. They had one more date to get through before they passed her three date rule. Groaning inwardly, she stepped out of his embrace and watched from her porch as he rode off down the road.

Serenity walked down the driveway toward the bricked-in mailbox and pulled open the metal lid. She grabbed the handful of mail inside, closed the lid, and flipped through each envelope as she walked back toward the front door. A single piece of paper caught her attention and had her brows knitting tightly together. As she unfolded the handwritten letter and read it, she was halted in place as immense fear and panic washed through her like a tsunami.

Do you think a few cameras are enough to keep me away from you?

Her stranger theory was right; someone was breaking into the house and this piece of paper just confirmed that. She sprinted inside and locked the door behind her as she set the mail down on the small wooden table beside the door and pulled out her phone. She pulled up the security camera app, rewound it, and watched it play through as she tried to catch any sign of movement. Unfortunately, the mailbox was out of range for the camera, but she didn't see anything out of place. Not even a shadow moving, indicating someone trying to hide out of the camera's view.

"This can't be happening," she whispered.

Was the person inside the house now? She shook off that thought. The cameras would have picked them up. The stranger must have come by, saw the cameras, and left her the note, trying to scare her. The sound of her phone ringing through the silent home pulled a scream from her throat as she fumbled with it, trying to answer the call.

"Hello?" She tried to catch her breath and slow her speeding heart rate down.

A male voice asked through the phone, "Ms. Serenity Jinx?"

"Yes, who is this?" Fear crept into her mind as she wondered if this was her intruder.

"My apologies, this is Detective Tanner." He kept his tone professional. "I was calling to update you on the case pertaining to your house fire. The arsonist has been apprehended."

Serenity let out a sigh of relief upon hearing it was Detective

Tanner and a weight she didn't realize was there in the first place had lifted from her shoulders on hearing the criminal was now behind bars.

"What time was he arrested? If you don't mind me asking?" That person was one of her own suspects as to who may have been breaking into the house.

"This evening, ma'am. I would say maybe an hour ago," he answered without hesitation.

Her suspects in this theory so far were Noah, the arsonist, or a neighbor. The cameras picked up no one entering her home since the installation yesterday, and with this note found in her mailbox, the arsonist could still be a good contender. They could have planted the note and gotten arrested sometime after.

She would have to wait and see over the next day or two to confirm that. If things were tampered with again, she would be able to eliminate them as a suspect. She didn't want to wait to test her theory but what other choice did she have?

"Ma'am, is everything ok?" Detective Tanner asked.

She hadn't realized the long stretch of silence. She'd been too lost in her mind to respond.

"Yes, I'm sorry. Thank you for letting me know. I appreciate it," she said, not wanting to alert the detective.

There was no point. She had no physical evidence that someone was breaking in. A note just confirmed that someone saw she had cameras up around her house.

"You're welcome. Have a good night." He hung up.

Now, she waited.

CHAPTER 21

SATURDAY – 5 DAYS TILL DEPARTURE

The Figure stood behind the veil of shadows and privacy trees as he peered through the family room window at his goddess curled up under a blanket on the couch. He stood there, losing track of time as he gazed upon Serenity and imagined what their life would be like after he finally claimed her. Eventually, she fell asleep there and he allowed himself an extra twenty minutes before leaving his spot and rounding the back of the home.

He worked the back door of the blue two-story family home, gaining entrance to what should be Serenity's sanctuary, but with him around, there was no place she would be safe until she was finally his. He walked toward the dining room table and grabbed another piece of paper and a pen so he could scribble down his next note.

Thrill flooded him as he wrote the words that he knew would break her just a little bit more. His only regret was that he wouldn't be able to watch her reaction firsthand. Instead of leaving the note in her mailbox like last time, he would leave it right there, on her table. That would get his point across that even though she had cameras, they wouldn't be able to save her from him.

He would never stop getting to her, no matter what obstacle she may place in front of him. After writing his note, he left the paper on the table, crept through the dark rooms of the main floor, and came to a stop behind the couch in the living room. The rush of possibly being caught at any moment had his skin tingling with excitement and anticipation.

The Figure brushed a few stray raven hairs back behind her ear before he ran his fingers through the silky ends, loving the feel of it against his skin and in his grasp. The blanket had fallen down during her sleep, now pooling around her stomach, leaving her breasts exposed for him to fondle over the fabric of her tank top again. *Look at that, even while asleep, your body is begging for my touch.*

He grabbed her phone, unlocked it, and started recording. His heart rate began to pick up as he ran a finger ever so gently down the column of her bare neck, over her exposed collarbone, over her tank top, and down over the side of her round breast. *I want you to see how gentle I can be with you, how good I can make you feel. See, your body is reacting to me on instinct.* Her nipples began to harden and poke against the thin material.

He slowly grabbed a handful of her soft tissue and swiped his thumb back and forth over the hardened mound. A sleepy moan escaped her lips, and he smiled in pure satisfaction. He ended the video and placed her phone in its original spot. He bent down, placed a soft kiss on her forehead, and left.

SUNDAY – 4 DAYS TILL DEPARTURE

Serenity woke to the beam of sunlight shining on her through the large windows of the family room. She had fallen asleep on the couch while watching a movie and apparently stayed there all night, not waking up once. She reached for her phone and smiled as she saw a text waiting for her from Hunter.

Hunter: Good morning, Angel.

Serenity: Good morning. I feel like I need a nickname for you.

Hunter: I prefer my name on those pretty lips of yours. Are you free this afternoon? The guys are wanting to get together and grab a few drinks.

Serenity: I don't know. I'll have to check my schedule. I think I have another date today.

She knew she was playing with fire, but she didn't care. A part of her loved teasing him with this because she loved the possessive reaction that she got from him when she did. It made her body come alive in ways she never knew possible. In ways she'd never experienced with Noah or any previous boyfriends.

Hunter: Not happening. I've already told you that you're mine and I don't share.

Serenity: I never agreed to be yours though.

Hunter: And I remember telling you that you didn't have a choice.

Serenity: Can I invite Addi? I would love for her to meet you.

Hunter: Of course, Angel. I'll pick you up at five.

Serenity: No need, I'll get a ride with Addi and meet y'all there.

She knew that would aggravate him to no end. From what she picked up so far, the man liked being in control and was used to getting what he wanted. Well, he was in for an adjustment if he wanted to be with her. Serenity was strong-willed and stubborn herself. Still lying there on the couch, she dialed her friend.

"Hey, girl!" Addi greeted after a few rings.

"Hey, I know Jack's been working a lot here lately, but do you have plans today?"

"Not a single fucking one!" Addi groaned. "I'm about to go insane with how much alone time I've had this last week."

"I'm sorry, hun. Just a few more days and you will have Jack all to yourself for so long that I'm sure you will be glad to send him back to work," Serenity joked and Addi laughed in agreement. "Hunter and some of his friends are getting together for drinks later, do you want to come?"

"God, yes!" Addi shouted as soon as Serenity asked the question. She didn't even have to think about it.

Serenity laughed as she spoke. "Awesome! Pick me up around 5 p.m."

"You got it! Bye, girl," Addi said all giddy and hung up.

Serenity laughed and rolled her eyes. She hated that her friend was so lonely. She would be too if she were in her shoes.

She threw off the covers, folded the blanket, and made her way into the kitchen to the delicious coffee she knew was waiting for her. She poured herself a cup and walked over to the dining table. As she sat down and placed her coffee cup aside, a piece of paper caught her attention. She pulled her brows together in confusion, wondering what it was.

No! It can't be... She read the note that had her heart stopping and fear flooding her veins.

I told you those cameras wouldn't be able to keep me away from you. Nothing will. You belong to me, and I can't wait to claim you. Soon!

She dropped the note, ran to the half-bathroom on the main floor, and threw up. It was mostly dry heaving since she didn't have anything on her stomach yet. *Calm down, deep breaths,* she tried to coach herself as she sat back against the wall. The thought of the stranger being in the house with her had her wanting to hurl again, but she forced it to stay down.

Being a heavy sleeper was amazing until moments like these. Moments when someone was breaking in and fucking with you. *The cameras!* That thought had her up and moving back to the dining room in search of her phone. With shaky hands, she pulled up the feed from last night and fast-forwarded, looking for her intruder. *That can't be right…*

She rewound and played it again, and then a third time, hoping she just happened to miss him but there was nothing. No person, no shadow, no movement. Two of the cameras were even pointed right at the front and back door and not once did they open.

Serenity's mind raced a million miles a minute as question after question played through her mind. How was he getting into the house? How was he avoiding the cameras? How does he not make a single noise when he's inside? Who was he and why did he want her?

She closed her eyes and took a deep breath, forcing her mind to slow down. She was not going to let this person win. Whoever the sick fuck was. She would be ready for him if she had to strap the gun to her side. She would put up a fight and end that sicko.

The whole day, Serenity kept looking over her shoulder, jumping at every shadow she saw and sound she heard, wondering if it was her intruder coming for her. She indeed had her pistol within arm's reach all day. As she got herself ready, she was thankful for the break she would get from being out of the house for a while. She left her black hair flowing freely down her back and did her eye makeup lightly like always.

She chose a Led Zeppelin cropped tank top that showed off a little of her slim midsection and a pair of Wrangler blue jeans that fit snugly around her. She checked her phone; it was almost five and Addi would be there any minute. She grabbed her boots and made her way downstairs to wait.

Addi rang the doorbell a few minutes later, almost causing Serenity to jump out of her own skin. She slipped her boots on, grabbed her phone and keys, and left.

"You look hot!" Addi said as they walked to her car.

"So do you!" Serenity took in the light blue spaghetti-strapped sundress her friend was wearing. It cut low around her chest, showing off an appropriate amount of cleavage, and stopped mid-thigh, revealing a good amount of her thick legs. "Jack would have a heart attack if he saw you in that."

"He would have hauled me straight to our room." Addi laughed. "We would have never left the house."

They turned up the radio and sang along as they drove to the bar where they were meeting everyone. By the time they pulled into the parking lot, Serenity had forgotten all about her problems at home.

CHAPTER 22

SUNDAY – 4 DAYS TILL DEPARTURE

The gravel crunched beneath their shoes as they walked to the front door of the bar. Serenity saw a line of bikes parked out front and her heart kicked into overdrive with anticipation of seeing Hunter again. They walked through the door and the environment consumed them. Music played over the speakers, glass clinked as drinks were being poured, people were chatting and laughing, and the sound of pool balls being hit across tables filled the air around them.

"Let's grab a drink before we search for the men," Addi suggested as she looped her arm through Serenity's.

"You read my mind. See, this is why we're friends." Serenity smiled as they approached the bar.

"What can I get you ladies?" a gentleman behind the bar asked with a smile.

Addi spoke over the music. "Two Miller Lite's please."

The bartender turned, grabbed their beers, popped the tops, and handed them to the girls.

"Thank you. Keep the change." Addi handed him a five dollar bill and passed a beer to Serenity.

They turned to observe the room, looking for Hunter and his friends, but a stranger stopped in front of them.

"Hey, ladies! Wow, you two look amazing. Do y'all want to hang out with us?" a guy asked as he motioned to a group of men across the bar sitting at a table. Serenity opened her mouth to decline but another voice spoke first.

"Sorry man, they're with us," Sweeney's amused voice sounded from behind the stranger, causing him to turn around and almost stumble backward at the sight before him.

Hunter, Fuse, Sweeney, Doc, and Einstein stood there looking as menacing as always. The man didn't even respond. He simply turned and walked off toward his friends.

The moment Serenity's eyes met Hunter's, her body awakened with need, begging for his touch. They were all dressed casually in jeans and T-shirts, but good God were they a frightening bunch.

"Addi, this is Hunter, Fuse, Sweeney, Doc, and Einstein. Guys, this is my best friend, Addi." She introduced everyone, hoping she had gotten all their names right.

She'd only met them once before and only for a few minutes. Then the memory of her meeting them, where she was bent over Hunter's bike, flashed into her mind and she felt heat starting to color her cheeks.

"It's nice to meet you. You are... holy fuck, the most beautiful woman I've ever seen," Sweeney greeted with a dazzling smile as he stepped forward and extended a large hand to Addi who was blushing like a schoolgirl. She took it and he placed a soft kiss on the back of her hand.

"Yes, and she's getting married this week, so play nice," Hunter warned his friend.

Both women didn't miss the disappointment that flashed through Sweeney's whisky eyes, but it was gone just as quickly, schooling his features back into his normal, charismatic self.

"I always play nice," Sweeney dropped Addi's hand and took a step back before shooting her a quick wink. "Unless I'm asked not to."

Addi leaned in and whispered quietly to her friend. "Exactly what type of men do you keep company with? They seem… scary."

"Private security, ex-military type," she whispered back.

"Ah, gotcha." Addi nodded as if that explained everything, straightened, and took a sip from her beer.

Hunter placed a large hand on the small of Serenity's back and led them to their table. The group talked and laughed and got to know one another over beers that kept coming. The boys excused themselves to shoot a round of pool while the girls stayed at the table, chatting and watching them.

"So, that's Hunter, huh? I like him." Addi smiled.

"I like him too." Serenity laughed. "Like, a scary amount of like."

"Like you want him to take you to bed kind of like?" Addi wiggled her brows suggestively.

"God, yes! Just the sight of this man has my body coming alive in ways I never thought existed outside of books," Serenity confessed.

Her vision shifted toward Hunter, who was casually leaning against the side of a pool table, arms crossed over his chest and one ankle crossed over the other. As if he felt her gaze on him, his eyes shifted up and locked on to hers. A grin slid across his bearded face, and he gave her a quick wink before looking back toward his friends.

"Well, then I say go for it. This is technically y'all's third date, right?" Addi questioned, knowing about Serenity's three date rule.

Serenity blushed so hard she felt like her face was on fire. "I'm considering the possibility." She nudged her shoulder into her friends and smiled. "I've noticed Sweeney can't keep his eyes off you."

Addi blushed and took a sip from her beer. "I've noticed too."

The men finished up their game of pool and walked back to the girls. "May I have this dance?" Hunter extended his hand toward Serenity.

"You know how to dance?" she questioned with a raised brow.

"A little." Hunter grinned wickedly at her.

She set her beer down and took his hand. He escorted her onto the small dance floor up front, pulled her into his arms, and began moving her across the small space with fluid ease. She was stunned. This man was moving like he was born to dance, hitting each step with precision, and spinning her around with ease.

"Just a little, huh?" she asked with a smile.

To her, dancing was such an amazing and intimate experience, and she always wanted a man who knew his way around the floor.

"My mom made sure all of us boys knew how to properly dance with a lady." He spoke as he spun her around and pulled her back to him again.

"Thank her for me, would you?" She laughed, looking into those unique eyes of his.

He winked at her. "You can thank her when y'all meet."

"Wow, meeting the family. That's a big step. We haven't even slept together," she joked and she noticed a shift in his gaze. His eyes instantly became hungry at the thought.

"Yet," he stated simply, but there was a hidden promise behind it.

A promise that sent desire flooding through her veins. As they slowed their movements down, Serenity took the time to glance around and noticed Addi and Sweeney talking and laughing back at their table.

"He'd never overstep," Hunter said. "Although he's dying inside, he'll be nothing short of a gentleman to her."

He must have noticed too. The confirmation made her worry a little less. She knew her friend would never cheat but she didn't want to have to hurt a man who crossed a line with her friend.

"Good, because I'd have to kill him if he wasn't." Serenity laughed, turning back to him, and meeting his gaze again.

"I would pay good money to see that." He fully laughed and the sound was deep and beautiful. It filled her heart with pure happiness. A feeling she hadn't felt in a long time. "Have I told you how beautiful you look?"

"Not today," she teased.

She rose on her tippy toes and placed a kiss right on his lips. He instantly stopped their dance and placed both hands on the small of her back, deepening their connection.

"Get a room!" one of the guys, Einstein maybe, shouted to them.

She pulled back and laughed, and Hunter showed them his middle finger. He took her hand as he led her back to their table.

"Alright, I have to ask. What's with the names?" Addi questioned as she took a sip from her beer.

"Do you know what a call sign is?" Sweeney asked from beside her and Addi nodded in acknowledgment. "Well, each one is unique to us in some way. Whether it be a physical attribute, personality trait, or something that happened that was so memorable, good, or bad, that the nickname just stuck."

"So, Sweeney, how did you get your name?" Addi asked, meeting his golden eyes.

"You know the story of Sweeney Todd?" Both Addi and Serenity shook their heads from side to side. "Well, he was a fictional serial killer from the mid-1800s. He was a barber who killed people with his straight razor."

"So, you, um… kill people with straight razors?" Serenity inquired hesitantly and all the men burst out laughing. She could feel heat stinging her cheeks.

"No, but I do love knives." Sweeney winked at the girls.

"Well, that's a lovely image," Addi said nervously as she took a rather large gulp from her drink.

"What about you? Einstein, is it?" Serenity asked the young man standing across the table from her.

He stood about six feet and was the youngest of the group. The ends of his shaggy black hair stuck out in wings beneath a well-loved grey beanie. His deep blue eyes popped against his pale skin which was free from tattoos and piercings. He was a slender man, his body packed tightly with lean muscles and black polish covered his fingernails.

Addi arched a brow. "I'm guessing you're a genius of some sort?"

"Yes, ma'am. Tech wizard, hacker, gamer. I have many attributes." Einstein flashed a pearl smile at her.

"Fuse, was it? What's your story? Short temper?" Addi joked as she peered into his ice-blue eyes.

Doc laughed. "No, although he did blow up a convenience store because their slushy machine was broken."

"Hey! That was one time! It was our mission objective anyway. Sorry for trying to get a frozen treat before it went up in flames," Fuse shot back at Doc next to him. Everyone at the table burst out laughing. "Explosives expert, pyro enthusiast, pretty much anything that goes boom, I'm your guy."

"That leaves you, Doc." Serenity pointed the tip of her beer bottle toward the man with rich mocha skin.

He was slimmer than the rest, minus Einstein, with lean muscles packed tightly against his frame. His black hair was cut short on the top and faded on the sides. One arm was covered in dark ink and the other sported an old scar that ran in a thin line down the outside length of his forearm, from elbow to wrist. A small silver cross earring hung from his left ear.

"Let me guess, you're a medic of some kind?" Addi asked with a raised eyebrow.

"No." Sweeney chuckled. "That would be too on the nose. Call signs are more elusive than that, more intricate and creative."

"You ever heard of the famous gunslinger, Doc Holliday?" Hunter asked the girls and smiled when they both nodded their heads in confirmation. "Well, if you need a gunslinger at your side or a sniper watching your back from a distance, he's your man. He's one of the handful of snipers that can hit their targets over a mile and a half away."

"Stop it, you're going to make me blush," Doc teased as he shot back the rest of his beer, causing the tiny cross earring to swing erratically from the movement.

"What about you?" Serenity turned her head and looked toward Hunter who was standing next to her with his arm draped around her waist. "What do they call you?"

"Boss," Fuse called out.

"Bossman," Einstein added.

"Big Daddy," Sweeney threw in with a grin as he wiggled his thick brown eyebrows. Everyone laughed again at that one.

"I know, it's not as grand as everyone else's but it's fitting, and I like it." Hunter spoke as he placed a kiss on Serenity's forehead and finished off his drink.

"You've always been a simple, straightforward kind of man, Boss," Fuse said endearingly as he slapped Hunter on the back in a sign of respect.

"Well, it's getting late." Addi checked the time on her phone and dug into her purse for her keys.

"Oh, wow, it is," Serenity agreed with shock in her voice.

Hours had passed by like minutes. Everyone closed out their tabs and filed out into the dimly lit parking lot.

"Thank you so much for inviting me. I had a blast!" Addi hugged Serenity. "Gentleman, it was nice to meet you all." She waved bye as she turned to walk toward her car.

"I'll walk you to your vehicle." Sweeney matched Addi's steps as he walked beside her through the parking lot, purposefully keeping his hands tucked in the front pockets of his jeans.

Everyone got on their bikes and left as Hunter helped Serenity into her helmet and took her home.

CHAPTER 23

SUNDAY – 4 DAYS TILL DEPARTURE

Hunter parked his bike in Serenity's driveway and helped her remove her helmet. He took her hand in his and helped her off the bike as he sat their helmets on the seat.

She stretched her legs and smoothed her hair back down. "I think you're ruining me with this bike."

"How so?" His tone was full of amusement as he turned to look at her.

"It's addicting, freeing, and the rush of thrill is unlike any other. I can see why you have one." Her eyes were bright with excitement.

"Well, anytime you ever want a ride, all you have to do is ask." He grinned at her and pulled her into his strong arms. Her front was pressed into his and it started awakening the need for his touch.

Serenity placed her hands flat against his broad chest. "Do you want to come in?"

A low growl vibrated her hands, and her eyes shot up to meet his. His usual ice-blue and hazel eyes were darkened with barely contained lust.

"Are you sure?" His restraint to tame the beast wanting to tear free was evident in the tightness of his jaw.

"Yes," she whispered, that look of his had her weak in the knees. No man had ever looked at her with such intensity before. As if everything in the world paled in comparison to her beauty.

She clutched his hand and led him to her front door as she unlocked it and stepped inside. She hung up her keys and by the time she turned around, Hunter had the door shut and locked before he cupped her face with his large hands and crushed his lips to hers.

The kiss was hot and passionate as his tongue ran across her lips, asking a silent question. She immediately obliged as she opened, and their tongues fell into a familiar dance. Her hands found the hem of his shirt and she started to tug it up his torso. He raised his arms as she pulled it off, exposing his chiseled body.

"Good Lord," she whispered, her breath hitching as she took in the sight before her.

His naked torso was packed with well-defined muscles, artwork that snaked fully up his arms, a light dusting of chest hair, and a raised line of an old scar was slashed across a few ribs. She couldn't stop herself as she ran her hands up his arms, over his broad shoulders, down his chest, and over the valleys of his abs.

"Your turn," he said hungrily as he pulled her shirt up over her head and tossed it aimlessly to the side. "Fuck," he cursed.

His eyes drank in the sight of her naked slim torso and the black laced bra that cupped her breasts perfectly. He hauled her back into his arms to resume their kissing as his hands roamed her body and cupped her tits through her bra, earning him a moan of pleasure from her.

Before she knew it, he had her bra unclasped and discarded to the side. It had been too long since someone had touched her like that. If she was being honest with herself, she had never had anyone touch her with such passion, such hunger as the man standing in front of her was doing.

She brought her hands down and fumbled with the button and zipper of his pants. He broke the kiss, only long enough to strip off his pants and boxers, exposing his hard cock as it sprang free. She took the time to strip off her own jeans and thong, leaving herself naked as the day she was born.

"Shit..." Serenity choked out when she couldn't take her eyes off his thick erection.

She took a timid step toward him, and he froze, not sure what she was doing until he watched her kneel before him. The sight alone had him ready to come.

She reached up and ran the palm of her hand along his length. The action caused a groan of pleasure from him, so she continued. She wrapped her hand around his veiny member, her fingers and thumb almost able to touch. Slowly, she began to stroke him, the action causing pre-cum to bead at the swollen tip. Her tongue quickly darted out and licked it up.

"Fuck, Angel." Hunter gripped a handful of her raven hair.

She brought him into her mouth as her tongue explored and tasted him. Then she sank further down his length, testing to see how far she could take him. His size caused her eyes to water, but she didn't stop until he hit the back of her throat.

"Do you like the taste of my cock in that pretty mouth of yours?" She moaned in agreement as she bobbed her head up and down his length. The action had him gripping her hair even tighter. "Shit, that feels so fucking good." He groaned.

He would love for this to continue but he needed inside of her before he came. He gently pulled up on her hair, signaling he wanted her to stand. Serenity obeyed and Hunter hoisted her up as if her weight was nothing to him and sat her down on the back edge of the couch. He stood between her parted legs as he reached down with one hand and palmed the outside of her center.

"You're fucking drenched." His tone dripped with need.

He slipped a thick finger deep inside of her, pumping it in and out before adding a second digit, stretching her out further. She gasped at the sudden intrusion but moaned in pleasure as she held on to his broad shoulders for support. He continued that motion as he dipped his head down and pulled one of her breasts into his mouth, licking, sucking, and biting on her hardened nipple.

It had been too long since she had a man touching her like that and she felt her orgasm quickly approaching in the pit of her stomach.

"Oh, God. Don't stop!" she moaned.

As if reading her body, he hooked those fingers into the soft spot inside her and it sent her over the edge as her orgasm rocked through her.

"Hunter!" she screamed as the tsunami crashed through her.

"That's it, soak my fucking hand, Angel," he demanded.

As she came down from the rush, panting for breath, he withdrew his fingers and sucked them clean.

"Fuck me," she whispered at the sight.

"Oh, trust me, I'm about to." He grinned wickedly, sending more wetness between her legs that now began to soak the back of the couch.

"Just so you know, I'm on birth control," she panted, still

trying to catch her breath.

"Is that a challenge?"

The sinful threat in his eyes had a wave of arousal crashing through her. She found herself wondering why that threat turned her on even more. But before she could give it much thought, he aligned the swollen tip of his cock at her slick entrance and thrust in, burying the entirety of his dick deep within her.

"Oh, God!" Serenity moaned as she gripped his shoulders, digging her nails deep into his skin, leaving red crescent marks.

"Shit, Angel! Your pussy is so fucking tight." He paused for a minute, allowing her to stretch around the size of him.

He filled her completely. It had been a while since she'd had sex, and she had never been with anyone close to his size, but damn if it didn't feel amazing.

"I'm good," she whispered.

He pulled out to the tip and buried himself in her again, over and over, before he picked up more speed. She became a moaning mess as he pounded into her as she sat on the edge of the couch; each thrust sent the furniture scooting further back across the floor. Already, she could feel another orgasm starting to build.

"Hold on tight," he warned her.

She quickly wrapped her legs around his waist and wrapped her arms around his neck before he lifted her off the couch and started up the stairs, all while never pulling out of her heat. He only made it halfway up the stairs before he laid her down and started thrusting into her again.

"Hunter!" Serenity moaned. "Fuck, this feels so good."

She panted as he took her right there on the stairs, thankful that they were carpeted. They still bit into her back, but she didn't mind one bit.

"We're moving again," he warned her with a grin, and she held on tightly as he lifted her and continued up the stairs. "Which one is your room?" He pulled away only long enough to ask before assaulting her neck with kisses.

"End of the hall," was all she could get out as she pulled out the half ponytail he had, allowing his long brown hair to flow freely down to his shoulders.

His long strides had them in her room before she knew it as he pulled out long enough to stand her up. She whimpered in protest, but he quickly spun her around and bent her over the bed before he entered her again.

His large hand grabbed a handful of her raven hair as he pulled back on it, causing her to arch her back as he took her from behind. The coil in her stomach grew with each thrust he drove into her.

"I've felt you come around my fingers. Now I want to feel you come around my cock." he growled as he reached around with his free hand and started rubbing circles against her already sensitive clit.

It didn't take long before she was screaming his name again as another orgasm hit her like a freight train. The sound of his name on her lips and the feel of her clenching around him had his own finish following close behind. With a few more hard thrusts, he spilled inside of her.

"Serenity! Oh, fuck..." Hunter groaned, filling her up and marking her as his in the most primal way.

They stayed like that for a moment as they tried to catch their breath. Finally, he withdrew and collapsed on the bed with her lying next to him. He pulled her against his hard chest as he wrapped a large arm around her.

"That was... wow," Serenity said in a fully sated daze.

Hunter laughed and placed a gentle kiss on the top of her head. "I agree."

She craned her head up and kissed his full lips. A fresh wave of heat instantly flooded her again as he cupped her cheek and deepened it.

"Let's get you cleaned up." He rose from the bed and walked into the bathroom.

CHAPTER 24

SUNDAY – 4 DAYS TILL DEPARTURE

Serenity followed Hunter's retreating form with her gaze. His backside was just as sexy as his front, as if he was sculpted by the gods. The sound of the shower turning on had her up and moving toward the bathroom. Halfway there, she felt his finish begin to run down the inside of her thigh, and she almost cried with pleasure. She wanted nothing more than for that man to use her body and fill her repeatedly.

He held open the shower door for her as she climbed in with him. He took the bar of soap and began to run his hands along her whole body, taking the time to memorize every freckle, every curve, every muscle of her figure. He crouched behind her and slowly ran his hands up and down her legs, and over her round ass. He stood and continued across the plains of her stomach, and over her breasts, giving each of them a gentle massage. She tipped her head back and rested it against his strong chest as he touched her.

The feeling of his hands all over her had her body humming with an intense tingle that she was quickly becoming dangerously addicted to. A moan slipped free as he started placing gentle kisses against the sensitive column of her neck. After she rinsed off, she took the soap and began to wash him, taking her time and loving the feeling of her hands all over his chiseled body.

"What happened here?" Her fingers lightly traced the scar that slashed across a few ribs.

"Hazards of my job," he said gently as he watched her place a soft kiss against it.

"What about these?" she asked as she came across a few more, one a couple of inches long across a bicep and another horizontally across one of his forearms, both disturbing the dark ink around them in a dangerously delicious way. "Are they from work as well?"

"Yes." He watched her place a kiss on each one. When she looked up at him, there was so much emotion in his ice-blue and hazel eyes, emotions she couldn't quite decipher.

She pointed to the scar that bisected his left eyebrow. "And that one?"

"Hazards of growing up with brothers." He chuckled.

Serenity cupped his cheeks and gently lowered his head toward her so she could place a kiss against it as well.

"I don't deserve you either." His thick tone was barely above a whisper.

"Like I said before, that's for me to decide."

She removed the shower head and started rinsing him off. He stood still for her, letting her work. He towered over her, and her shower wasn't that large, so he was careful with his movements. She replaced it when she was satisfied that she had removed all the suds. Before she knew it, he guided her a few steps back against the wall of the shower as he dropped down to his knees.

"What are you doing?" she asked breathlessly.

"Worshiping you." He threw one of her legs over his shoulder and ran his tongue along her entrance, gaining another moan from her.

Her hand gripped his long wet hair as he feasted on her, devouring her as if she were the salvation to a starving man only minutes from death.

"God help me," she choked out with pleasure and her eyes fluttered closed.

He growled against her center, the vibrations causing her back to arch off the wall. "God can't save this, Angel. You're at *my* mercy now."

His tongue went to work on her swollen clit, licking, biting, and sucking as he entered two fingers straight into her. She was pleased to find a man who knew what he was doing. The way his tongue worked her core with such precision would be her undoing.

"It should be illegal for a man to be this good with his tongue," she panted as she felt her stomach tightening again.

Hunter chuckled and the vibrations sent her into a frenzy. She moaned out in pleasure as she ground her hips against his face. He hooked his fingers and sent her over the edge as her body convulsed, her screams of pleasure echoing off the tiled walls.

"I knew you would taste like heaven." He withdrew his fingers and licked slowly up and down her folds, cleaning her up. When he raised, she could barely stand, and he laughed. "Do I make you weak in the knees?" Serenity nodded, her energy spent from her multiple orgasms. "Here, let me help you."

He held her against the wall with his torso and lifted one of her slender legs up behind her knee. "Stay with me, Angel. I'm not quite done with you yet." His voice was deep and promising.

"Don't ever stop fucking me! If I die, I'll die happy," she said in a haze of ecstasy and pleasure.

He reached between them and angled his cock at her entrance. With a single shift of his hips, he was buried inside her warmth again. She cried at the pleasure overload as he stretched her, and he didn't spare a minute before he began moving inside of her.

"I fucking love the way your tits bounce when I pound into you," he growled as he watched them move with each thrust.

His mouth covered one of them as he took her hardened nipple between his teeth, biting down just enough to blend pain with pleasure, using his tongue to ease the sting. This time they came in unison. Her screams of pleasure and his grunts filled the shower as she clenched around him, and he spilled deep into her. Hunter withdrew and didn't release his hold on her shoulders until her legs were stable beneath her. They quickly finished their shower, got out, and dried off.

They made their way into her bedroom where she put on a pair of blue lace cheeky underwear as he went downstairs to retrieve his boxers. Upon returning, one sight of her in nothing but her panties had his blood rushing.

"You're going to be the death of me, Angel. You're so fucking gorgeous." Hunter drew the covers back and climbed into bed, pulling Serenity against him as he wrapped his arms around her.

"I guess I can officially ask you, even though we both already know the answer." She laughed lightly and then asked around a yawn, "Do you want to go to Addi's wedding with me?"

"I've already cleared my schedule."

"What if I didn't choose you?" she inquired.

"It's cute that you thought you had a choice. The night of our first date when I learned about your little… experiment, I cleared my calendar so I could go with you. You're stuck with me, forever."

His arms tightened around her in a comfortable hold.

"Mmm," she hummed sleepily as she snuggled into the warmth of his bare chest. "We'll see."

"I do have to go out of town tomorrow for a few days on an assignment, but I'll be back Wednesday night," he informed her.

"I'll miss you. Be safe, ok?"

"I always am." He placed a soft kiss atop her head. "Good night, Angel."

"Good night," Serenity mumbled as sleep took her quickly.

Hunter lay there for a while, holding her and listening to the sounds of her steady breathing before sleep eventually overtook him too.

The Figure strolled down the sidewalk with his hands casually in his pockets as he came to the all too familiar blue two-story family home. Excitement filled him and he couldn't contain the smile working its way across his face at the thought of seeing Serenity again. That excitement was short-lived though. Confusion stopped him in his tracks and then anger filled him as he noticed the motorcycle parked in the driveway.

It was late at night, and the house was dark, which could only mean one thing. She had a guest staying over. Rage tried to consume him as he made his way around to the back door. He worked it and let himself in, quietly closing it behind him. The scene before him had that restraint on his rage breaking completely loose. Discarded clothes were tossed aimlessly around the family room and the couch was turned at a weird angle.

He tried to take deep breaths through his nose but the thought of another man's hands on her, another man's cock filling what was his had him wanting to murder the man. He turned and climbed the stairs quicker tonight, his long legs only requiring a few strides before he stopped at the entryway to her bedroom. His face contorted into a snarl when he saw a large man lying next to her in bed, his arms wrapped around her naked torso, both sound asleep.

His hands twitched for something to smash the biker's head in, but he stopped himself. There was no way he would be able to kill him without waking Serenity up and exposing his identity. It wasn't quite their time. He needed to be patient if he was to have her in the end. *I'll get rid of this one like I did with the last one.* That thought had a wicked grin creeping across his features. He took one last look at her before he turned and made his way downstairs. He had another note to leave.

Hunter's eyes shot open, and he sat up abruptly, looking around the darkened room. The feeling of being watched woke him from a deep sleep, but no one was there. He slowly got up, making sure not to wake Serenity as he began to clear the house one room at a time. After walking through the whole house and checking all the doors, he shook off the feeling, chalking it up to a new place, and made his way back upstairs. He slowly eased back into the bed and pulled Serenity's back against his front, wrapping his arms around her, and drifted back to sleep.

CHAPTER 25

MONDAY – 3 DAYS TILL DEPARTURE

Serenity stirred the next morning, feeling better than she had in a long time. She woke with a smile on her face as she sent herself into a satisfied stretch, only to bump into something solid. Her sleepy face scrunched in confusion. There shouldn't be anything in her bed except herself. Then she froze and fear sent her skin prickling. Was it her intruder? Her eyes flew open as she jolted upright, glancing at the solid form next to her.

"What is it? What's wrong?" Hunter was now wide awake, his eyes expertly scanning the room for any possible threat.

She released a heavy breath as clarity dawned on her. "I'm sorry, you just scared me. It's been a while since I've woken up next to someone."

She placed a hand on her bare chest and forced herself to take deep breaths through her nose. He sat up and began to rub small delicate circles across her back. The touch was gentle given his hand was rough and calloused.

He placed a soft kiss atop her bare shoulder. "You have no

need to apologize, Angel."

His grip on her shoulder was soft as he pulled her down on top of his chest. He wrapped an arm around her and twirled the ends of her long raven hair through his fingers. She snuggled into his comforting warmth and inhaled deeply, loving the manly scent of his faded cologne. With each deep breath, she felt her body growing more relaxed. It was hard for her to explain, but there was something about being in his arms that made her feel like she was invincible, like there was nothing in the world that could hurt her.

"How did you sleep?"

"Like a baby." Serenity couldn't contain the smile that slipped across her sleepy features. "How did you sleep?"

"Pretty good, other than being woken up from your snoring."

She shot up, using her elbow as support, and slapped his chest playfully. "I do not snore!"

He grabbed her wrist and flipped her over on her back, nestling himself between her legs. She blinked in shock at the sudden angle change. He had her on her back in seconds and by God if that wasn't a turn on for her.

"I'm only joking." He laughed as he lowered his head and placed a few soft kisses along her collarbone. "How are you feeling this morning? I hope I wasn't too rough with you last night."

She was quiet for a moment as she recalled their adventures. She couldn't stop the smile that fully touched her eyes at the memory.

"A little sore but I wouldn't change a thing. I don't want you to feel like you have to hold back either. I don't think that it's possible, but I promise you, I will tell you if you ever get too rough with me."

"Oh, believe me, I can get animalistic if I don't exercise

restraint." The promise in his eyes should've scared her but it only sent a wave of arousal coursing through her body at the thought.

"I'd like to see that," she purred sensually as she sucked her bottom lip between her teeth.

His eyes darted toward her full lips as they filled with lust and hunger. A low rumble ripped deep in his chest.

"If I didn't have a plane to catch, I'd show you now. Then again after lunch and twice tonight."

Hunter lowered his head and sucked her bottom lip into his mouth, biting down a little before releasing it. A moan escaped her lips at the action, but she groaned inwardly knowing he wouldn't be able to take care of her needs before he left.

Serenity looked toward the clock on her dresser and pouted. She had to get up and get ready for work or she would be late. Reluctantly, they untangled themselves and got out of bed. He made his way downstairs to retrieve his clothes as she made the bed and got herself ready.

"Do you want some coffee before you leave?" she offered as she padded down the last few steps and rounded the corner to the living room.

He was fully dressed and in the process of scooting the couch back to its original place. She couldn't stop a grin as the memory of what happened on the back of that couch last night flashed through her mind.

"I'd love some, thank you." He followed her into the kitchen.

Her chipper mood was short-lived when she stopped in the doorway, causing Hunter to suddenly halt to avoid bumping into her. Her mossy eyes landed on the piece of paper that was lying atop the dining room table, causing her shoulders to go ridged and her face to drain of color.

Her body started to tremble, and her breathing became ragged as if an elephant was sitting on her chest and she couldn't take a full breath. He noticed the sudden shift in her body, and he went into fight mode, his honed skills of fighting and protecting kicking in. He grabbed her biceps and moved her aside, putting his body between her and whatever threat was in her house.

His eyes scanned the room like a hawk but found no threat. He turned to her, and his heart nearly broke at the sight of her terrified expression.

"Serenity, what's wrong?" he questioned in a serious tone he only used at work. She didn't answer, her body was locked with fear. "Angel, look at me," he said a bit softer as he cupped her cheeks and forced her eyes to meet his. "What's wrong?"

Serenity finally shifted her eyes toward him and forced her words past the fear clogging her throat. If the intruder was in here, Hunter would stop them. That thought had some of the terror leaving her body long enough for her to move and form sentences again.

She pointed with a shaky hand. "The note... there, on the table."

He turned and followed the direction of her finger. He saw the paper she was talking about and started moving toward it without hesitation. He picked it up and read it. His training allowed him to stay calm in this situation, the only emotion he expressed was the tick of his jaw and the pure rage that filled his eyes.

"What does it say?" Her tone was barely above a whisper as she stood rooted to the floor.

He read the note in a strained voice. "How dare you bring another man home and let him touch what's mine! Let him fuck what's mine! Do you think some big strong man will keep me from you? I told you before, you belong to me. See you soon!" He tore his gaze from the paper and strode back over to her, his long legs putting him in front of her in a few strides. "Care to fill me in?" he clipped out.

She closed her eyes and took a deep breath before she told him about what's been going on. How sometimes things would be moved or turned on or off and the previous notes.

"That's why you bought those guns."

Though Hunter's words were more of a statement than a question, Serenity still answered. "Yes."

"Why didn't you say something sooner? Do you know how much danger you put yourself in by keeping this a secret? Why haven't you reached out to the police and why the hell are you still in this house?"

He forced his tone to stay even. She could tell he was furious with her, but that he was trying hard not to shout. She knew he simply wanted his questions answered.

She exhaled heavily. "Because I'll be damned if I let someone run me out of my own house and I have no physical evidence to go to the cops with besides those notes. I have security cameras, but the person is never spotted in them. It's like they're a ghost or something."

"Show me the other notes and the camera footage," he insisted.

She pulled the previous two notes from a drawer in the kitchen and pulled up the security camera app on her phone. He read both notes before moving on to the camera feed. Maybe his trained eyes would be able to catch something she missed, but he found nothing as well.

"Are you the only one with access to the cameras?"

"No." She shook her head and chewed nervously on the inside

of her cheek. "Jack does on his phone since this is his house."

Hunter looked at her but kept his thoughts to himself. "Who has keys to the house?"

"Just me and Addi."

He let out a frustrated sigh as he ran his hand through his long brown hair that flowed loosely across his shoulders. "I want you to stay at my place while I'm out of town. I don't like knowing someone is getting into your house, let alone when I'm thousands of miles away."

"I appreciate the offer, but no. Like I said, I'm not about to let this person run me out." She knew he wouldn't like that, but it wasn't his decision.

"It wasn't an offer," he growled in a dangerous tone, but Serenity steeled her spine and held her ground.

"I'm not leaving, Hunter. Look, clearly whoever this is has had multiple chances to hurt me, but they haven't. They want me, so I'll be fine. I have two weapons in the house and will barricade myself in my room at night so if they try to get in, I'll hear it and wake up."

She tried hard to make him see reason. She appreciated his offer, and it warmed her heart to know he cared enough about her to want to keep her safe, but it wasn't his decision, it was hers.

"Damnit, Serenity! If anything were to happen to you…" He didn't finish that thought. He *couldn't.*

"Hey." She gently cupped his bearded cheek. He closed his eyes and turned his face into her delicate touch. "Nothing's going to happen to me."

Hunter opened his eyes and met her gaze. The promise of what he would do burned brightly in his colorful irises, and it caused a warm smile to appear on her face. That look spoke louder than words ever could, expressing that he'd burn the world with his rage and grief if he ever lost her.

"I'm going to take these." He folded the notes and tucked them into his pocket. "I want to see if Einstein can make anything of them."

Serenity nodded as she stood on her tiptoes and placed a kiss on his lips. He instantly wrapped his arms around her waist and pulled her front completely against his, as if some phantom was about to crawl out of the shadows and take off with her.

He rested his forehead against hers. "I'll be back Wednesday evening. If anything happens, and I mean anything, call me. I'll send some of my men over right away."

"I will, 1 promise. I want you to be safe, ok?"

She pushed away the spike of fear that tried to consume her. He was good at his job. She needed to be confident that his skills would bring him home to her in one piece.

"I should be saying that to you." He half-laughed in irony. "I'll miss you, Angel." Hunter claimed her lips one last time before reluctantly pulling away and leaving.

CHAPTER 26

MONDAY – 3 DAYS TILL DEPARTURE

Hunter rode back to his place where he changed, packed a duffle bag for his trip, and headed to Red Sky Security in his gunmetal grey Jeep Wrangler. He didn't feel like trying to strap a duffle bag to the back of his Harley. He pulled into the parking lot and stopped in front of the standalone brick building with bulletproof windows lining the front. He threw the duffle bag over his shoulder and headed inside.

"Good morning, Boss," a young woman with rounded features, light blonde hair highlighted with baby blue, and colorful glasses called from behind a dark mahogany receptionist's desk.

"Good morning, Blue," Hunter greeted Phoebe with a smile.

She'd worked for him for almost two years now. Within her very first week, the men had already accepted her as part of the family. A little sister they would protect with their lives. They gifted her with her very own nickname. It came rather naturally, due to the blue highlights in her hair.

The lobby was bright and open. A neutral grey color covered

the walls, and a few black armchairs lined the back wall. Dark hardwood floors were laid horizontally, making the space appear bigger.

He turned right and walked down the hall of offices that lined both walls, the same hardwood floors connecting the spaces. He turned into the last office on the left where a silver nameplate was tacked to the wooden door. It stated the space was his. He dropped his duffle bag on top of his mahogany desk before he left back down the hallway and through the large wooden double doors that led into an open briefing room. He kept walking back, through another door that led into their fully stocked armory and into a large single office off to the side.

A large wooden L-shaped desk filled the left side of the space. Numerous monitors ranging in size were mounted on the wall above. A large flat-screen TV was mounted on the opposite wall with a sofa positioned in front of it. Hunter tapped his knuckles on the thick wooden door, announcing his presence.

"Hey, Einstein. You got a minute?" He entered the office and stood in front of the large desk.

Einstein paused his game and removed his headset. "Yeah, Bossman. What's up?"

"What have I said about gaming in here?" Hunter sighed and shook his head, a grin trying to tug at one side of his lips.

Einstein pressed a few buttons on his keyboard and all the monitors changed, hiding his video game. "What game?" He sucked his lips between his teeth, trying not to smile.

"I need you to investigate some things for me. A stranger has been getting into Serenity's house somehow. She has cameras up but never catches any movement. I want you to look and see if your eyes can find anything we might be missing. Also, they've been leaving these notes. Is there any way you can try and identify the handwriting?" He unfolded the notes and placed them on Einstein's desk.

The tech genius grabbed them and read through each one. "Jesus, this dude's a creep." He grimaced and turned his chair around, so he was facing his numerous monitors. "I have a program where I can upload this and run it against all public and some... not-so-public documents. What security system does she have and what's the address?"

Hunter gave him the info and watched in silence as his friend's pale fingers now topped with dark purple polish moved like lightning across his keyboard. For the years he's known the little genius, Einstein's always kept his fingers painted. Curiosity almost had Hunter asking a few times why he paints them, but he stopped himself every time. The men there, though they were as close as brothers, liked their privacy on certain matters. So, if Einstein has never voiced the reason why he does it, if there even is a reason, he wasn't about to pry by asking.

"I'm not sure how often the person visits the home, but she had them installed on Friday," Hunter said.

Einstein turned back toward his boss, the movement sending the ends of his shaggy black hair sticking out beneath his grey beanie swaying. "Ok, I'll pull all the footage and filter through it, see what I can find."

"I appreciate it." Hunter ran his hands through his long hair, gathered it up, and tied it into a knot on the back of his head.

"Anything to help, you know that. Is she still staying at the house, or did you move her to a safe location?"

"She refused to leave," Hunter gritted through his teeth, his jaw ticking in annoyance.

Einstein couldn't contain the laugh that escaped his throat. "I'm sorry, Bossman. You've got your hands full with that one."

"Tell me something I don't know." He released a long breath and groaned. "I won't be back until Wednesday evening, so the moment you find anything, call me."

"Will do. Are you going to station men outside her house while you're gone?" Einstein questioned, although he already knew the answer to that.

"Obviously."

"Does she know?"

"Nope." Hunter turned and left the office.

Einstein's laughter followed as he made his way back to his office. It might be crossing some invisible boundary with his angel, but he didn't care. Now that they were together, he'd do everything in his power to protect the woman he was quickly falling for. Even if they weren't together, it's his nature to protect as if it were engraved in his DNA.

From standing up to bullies in school, his time as a Navy SEAL, and now with his security company. If he knew one thing for certain, it was that he was put on this earth to help and protect those who couldn't. So yeah, he would station his men outside of Serenity's place until he got back, and he won't apologize for it because all that matters in the end is her safety.

The Figure strolled down the sidewalk with his hands casually in his pockets, ready to see his love again. He hoped that biker wouldn't be there again tonight, but if he was, he would contain his rage better.

He won't be around for long. I already have a plan to get rid of him. That thought had an evil grin pulling across his face. The blue two-story home came into view and his heart rate picked up a bit in excitement. He cherished the moments when he got to see her.

As he crossed the property line of privacy trees and turned to walk up the driveway, he stopped dead in his tracks. A bike was parked out front. It was a red and black BMW sports bike instead of the full black Harley that was there yesterday. *What the fuck! Does she have a different man over?* Anger tried to work its way through him, but a shadow moving near the far side of the house distracted him.

A tall man came into view, veiled in the darkness of nightfall. *Who the hell is that? Does she have someone watching her house at night?* The thought made him laugh inwardly. As if that would be able to keep him away from her. Both men stood there, staring each other down before The Figure turned on his heels and took off running down the street.

"Hey, get the fuck back here, you piece of shit!" Doc called after The Figure as he began to chase him down the street. "What? You're fine stalking an innocent woman, but you're too chicken shit to face a man?" he taunted him.

The Figure kept running until he came across an alley and quickly turned down it. He didn't feel like testing his luck in a fight or risk exposing his identity. He could feel the stranger closing the distance, but The Figure had the advantage. He knew this neighborhood well from his frequent trips to see Serenity. He cut through a few more properties and zig-zagged down into another alley until the tree line of nearby woods came into view.

He didn't dare slow his pace, even if his lungs were screaming at him and he didn't risk looking back to see if the stranger was still pursuing him. He would risk tripping and getting caught. He didn't slow as he broke the tree line and darted further into the woods.

Doc stopped pursuing the intruder who wandered onto Serenity's property when he disappeared into the shadows of the woods. He withdrew his phone and dialed his boss, who answered after the first ring.

"Is Angel ok?" Hunter asked by way of greeting.

"Yeah, Boss, she's ok. Her intruder showed up." Doc made his way back through the neighborhood, not even winded in the slightest. "He took off when he saw me. I chased him, but he disappeared into the nearby woods. I'm on my way back to her house now."

"Did you get a good look at the fucker?" Hunter forced his words out through gritted teeth.

"It was dark." Doc released a heavy breath that wasn't due to exhaustion from running. "All I could make out was that he was tall, at least six feet, and had a slim build. He had a black hoodie on with the hood pulled up so I couldn't make out any defining features."

"Motherfucker," Hunter muttered under his breath. "Alright, just get back to her house and keep your eyes open. Call me if anything changes."

"Will do, Boss." Doc hung up and made his way back to Serenity's house to stand guard for the night.

CHAPTER 27

WEDNESDAY – 1 DAY TILL DEPARTURE

Serenity lost herself in thought on her drive home from work Wednesday afternoon. It had been two days since she found that last note from her intruder and each night since, she'd locked her bedroom door and angled a chair underneath the knob. Each morning, she checked the entire house, looking for anything that had been moved or messed with, or even worse, another note.

However, each morning, she found nothing amiss and no fresh notes. She was guessing that had something to do with the men who walked around her house all night. That first night she almost had a heart attack as she lay in bed and viewed the live footage of her cameras. When she saw a man walking around, she almost screamed until she got a better look at him and realized it was Doc.

She put two and two together and figured Hunter asked some of his men to guard the property while he was away. That notion sent a flood of emotions for the man straight to her heart. She had missed him like crazy while he was gone. They had texted often but that wasn't the same as seeing him in person. Every night she prayed that he would come home safely to her and tonight he would be. She could barely contain her excitement.

A little bit of that excitement had dimmed as she pulled into the driveway. Her once safe haven had become a beacon of dread. A place where she once was happy and able to relax on the couch now only brought her fear and paranoia at every sound she heard, every shadow that caught her eye.

She smiled a little when she saw a bike parked in the driveway. Not Hunter's bike, but one that belonged to one of his men. As she got out of her car and turned, she saw Doc round the corner of the house and stride toward her.

"Hey, Doc. Hunter will be back today. You don't have to stay here," she said as he escorted her to her front door.

"I know, I'll leave once he gets here. I'm sure you're probably ready to get rid of me," he joked, flashing her a bright white smile that popped against his bronzed skin.

She gave him a shy smile. "Not at all. Honestly, your presence is what has helped me sleep these last few nights."

"Glad I could be of service." He tipped an invisible hat to her. She unlocked her front door but was halted from entering. "Let me clear the house real quick. I've been out here for a while, but just in case that freak snuck in somehow. Take this and wait here." He reached into his pocket and pulled out a scary-looking pocketknife. He opened it, revealing the three-inch razor-sharp blade. "Scream if you need me. Oh, and don't close it."

Serenity hesitantly took the knife from him and furrowed her brows together. "Why not?"

"It's bad luck to close a knife you didn't open yourself."

Doc grinned at her as he pulled a pistol from a holster that was concealed behind his shirt. Serenity waited there on the porch nervously as she watched the man move with practiced movements through the home, clearing each corner and room as he went until he disappeared up the stairs.

She scanned her surroundings as she waited for him to come back. Paranoia tried to take over, making her feel like eyes were watching her from within the trees.

"House is all clear." Doc descended the last stair and walked out the front door.

"Thank you. Are you hungry or thirsty?" she offered before she entered the house.

"No, I'm alright. Thanks though." He smiled as he walked down the porch steps and turned to continue his rounds around the property.

Serenity shut and locked the door behind her before she climbed the stairs and showered, putting on a cute black spaghetti-strapped nightgown that stopped mid-thigh.

Once Hunter made it back to his place, he got showered up and repacked his duffle bag with everything he would need for their trip to Hawaii. He planned on staying the night at Serenity's house and going straight to the airport with her in the morning. He was almost at her house when a call sounded through the Bluetooth of his Jeep Wrangler.

He pushed the phone button on his steering wheel. "Any news, Einstein?"

"No match on the handwriting yet. That could take a few more days though. There are a lot of documents worldwide for the software to filter through. But I do have news about the camera footage. I noticed there were splices cut into the feed once every night, starting on the first day they were installed."

"What do you mean by splices?" Hunter asked. There was a reason Einstein was the tech genius and not him.

"It's like someone cut out a section of the footage and replaced it with a clean roll of video. The cameras did capture someone coming and going from the house, but they scrubbed the footage, erasing themselves."

"Are you able to… un-scrub it?" he questioned as he pulled into Serenity's driveway, hoping that was the right terminology for what he meant.

"Usually I could, but whoever did this is a pro. They covered their tracks and left almost no evidence. I nearly missed the glitches myself."

Hunter began muttering a very colorful string of curses that would make a nun blush. There was a moment of silence before he asked, "How long were the sections that were scrubbed?"

It was Einstein's turn to mutter as he released a breath. "I was hoping you wouldn't ask that."

"Tell. Me," Hunter clipped out in aggravation. He knew he wasn't going to like what he was about to hear.

"They vary anywhere from half an hour to two hours."

Hunter slammed a large hand down against his steering wheel and cursed. "That sick motherfucker!"

He had to will his mind to stop from considering the possibilities of what that psycho was doing during that long of a time alone in a house with his angel. The thoughts his mind was coming up with had him tightening his grip around the wheel until his knuckles were white. *I'm going to enjoy torturing and slowly killing this son of a bitch.*

He had to take a moment before he accidentally took his rage out on his friend. Hunter closed his eyes and forced himself to take a few slow calming breaths through his nose before he continued.

"Let me know the moment you find out anything on those notes."

"You got it, Bossman," Einstein said as he hung up the phone.

Hunter didn't exit his Jeep just yet. He needed a few minutes to collect himself before he walked inside and greeted his angel. She didn't need to see how worked up he was. He needed to be the strong one for her. Once he got his emotions under control, he exited the vehicle, said bye to Doc, and rang her doorbell.

Serenity practically ran to the front door and threw it open. She didn't bother checking to see who it was. She knew Doc wouldn't let her intruder walk up and ring her doorbell. The moment she opened the door, Hunter took two steps into the home and hoisted her up by her ass. Her legs instinctively wrapped around his waist as he buried his face in the crook of her neck.

"I missed you!" She hugged him back tightly. "Are you hungry? I made dinner."

He shut and locked the door without breaking their hug. "You're my dinner," he growled in a lust-filled voice as he climbed the staircase, two at a time. Pure need and arousal flooded every vein in her body, causing an ache to pulse between her legs.

She was tossed, landing flat on her back atop her bed, causing her nightgown to rise and reveal a red-laced thong. His eyes darkened as he took in the sight before him, his beautiful angel laying atop a bed, her long legs parted wide, welcoming him home.

He kicked off his boots and shredded his clothes in record time. She enjoyed the view as each piece of discarded clothing revealed nothing but muscular, tattooed, and scarred beauty.

She sighed dreamily. "I'll never get tired of looking at you."

"That makes two of us, Angel." He gave her his famous wicked grin that caused heat to warm her core and butterflies to swarm erratically.

Before she could close her legs, he grabbed her by the ankles and dragged her to the edge of the bed where he knelt before her, pulled her thong down her legs, and tossed it aimlessly aside. His mouth was on her entrance before she could blink and her hands went straight for his hair, undoing the knot in the back and releasing his long brown strands.

"Oh, God!" she moaned as he ate her with such intensity, such primal need, like a man who was poisoned, and the antidote lay between her legs.

He licked, sucked, and fucked her tight cunt with his tongue. She could feel an orgasm start to build in the base of her spine and at the rate he was going, she would be coming undone rather quickly.

Abruptly he stopped and stood, wiping his mouth and beard clean with the back of his hand. Such a simple action had her ready to burst. The thought of her arousal all over his face turned her on immensely. He hooked his hands behind her knees and yanked her further toward him, elevating her hips up to meet his height as he aligned the tip of his swollen head at her welcoming entrance. The elevation caused her nightgown to slide and pool around the base of her breasts.

In a single thrust, he buried himself completely inside of her, the action causing her to half-scream and half-moan at the sudden fullness she felt.

He grunted in pleasure. "Fuck, I've missed you!"

He kept her hips elevated and held her by the back of her knees as he began to thrust in and out of her. The sight of her beneath him had him already wanting to spill inside of her. But he restrained. He wouldn't come until she was clenching around his erection.

"God, yes! Keep doing that," she moaned as he moved inside her in rough, animalistic pumps.

This angle allowed him to reach deeper inside of her than she ever thought possible. Her orgasm built at a faster rate and before she knew it, she was fisting the covers and screaming in ecstasy.

"That's it, Angel. Come all over my fucking dick. Let me hear how good it feels," he growled, never once letting up on his assault.

With each harsh thrust, she felt her finish extend a little more, allowing her to ride the waves of her high as long as possible. Once it passed, she was a panting mess and yet, he still didn't let up. His pace increased and his movements became more erratic as he chased his own finish, which wasn't far behind hers. With another full thrust, he was spilling inside of her.

He moaned her name as he kept pumping into her, milking every drop deep into her core. Hunter slowly pulled out and set her hips back down as he dropped on the bed next to her, breathing heavily.

"I think I might like you going out of town more often if you fuck me with such intensity each time you get back," Serenity joked as she nestled into his side and rested her head on his strong chest.

He laughed as he wrapped an arm around her and kissed the top of her head. After they got cleaned up, he changed into a pair of black and grey flannel pajama pants before they went downstairs, ate some dinner, and curled up on the couch to watch TV.

CHAPTER 28

WEDNESDAY – 1 DAY TILL DEPARTURE

Addi was dancing around her room as she grabbed various clothes from drawers and off hangers, folded them, and started packing her suitcase. Her phone was Bluetooth connected to a wireless speaker that she had cranked up to max volume as she sang along with each passing song. She was getting married in a few days, and she was on cloud nine. The long white garment bag that hung off her closet door was a constant reminder, and she couldn't stop smiling each time she saw it.

Every woman has dreamed about their wedding day since they were little girls and hers was so close that she could reach out and almost touch it. She always hoped that one day she would find a good man who would treat her right and take care of her. Not that she needed a man in life, but rather she *wanted* a man to do life with.

The afternoon that Jack had walked into her life changed her world forever and she's been thankful each and every day for the blessing of such a gem. He was smart, caring, and passionate. He had a wonderful job that brought in great money. Even though that job was rather demanding and consumed a vast amount of his time, when he was with her, he gave her his full attention and made her feel special.

Their flight to Hawaii was departing early in the morning and she always had been a procrastinator when it came to packing. That explained why she was just now gathering her belongings and trying to neatly Tetris everything into her large suitcase. She turned around and saw the form of a tall man with his arms crossed over his chest, leaning casually against the doorframe of her bedroom.

"Oh, shit!" She clutched her hand to her chest, trying to calm her racing heart.

Jack wore an amused expression across his clean, angular features. "Did I scare you?"

"Yes, don't do that!" She threw a pair of socks at her fiancé. "I didn't hear you come in."

"You wouldn't have heard a nuclear bomb go off with how loud your music is," he teased as he bent down, picked up the pair of socks, and placed them in her suitcase alongside the others.

"Shush it." She turned down the volume to a low murmur before stepping in front of him and wrapping her arms around his neck. Her voice was sensual as she asked, "So, do I officially have you all to myself for the next two weeks?"

They planned on staying in Hawaii after their wedding to honeymoon around all the islands.

"Yes, ma'am. All my work is caught up and has been handed over to my colleague to handle while I'm gone." He wrapped his strong arms around her waist and gave her round ass a good squeeze. He nodded toward the long white garment bag hanging up. "Is that your dress?"

"Yep!" She beamed. "Are you excited to see me in it?"

"Mmm, I'm more excited to get you out of it." His voice was husky as he captured her lips with his.

Instantly their mouths parted as their tongues explored familiar territory. He hooked his fingers on each side of her grey shorts and underwear as he began to pull them down her thick legs. She stepped out of them as he cupped her bare ass and hoisted her up, turned, and set her atop their dresser.

Jack stepped between her spread legs as they resumed their kissing and Addi reached down blindly as she unbuckled his belt and pants. He assisted her by pulling his slacks and boxers down just enough to free his throbbing erection. He didn't need to test to see if she was ready for him. Her body had always responded well to the sight and touch of him.

He took himself in his hand and rubbed his swollen tip along the length of her folds a few times, teasing her. She leaned back on her hands as she moaned in pleasure and waited with anticipation for him to give her what she wanted, what her body craved. With a single thrust, he was buried deep inside the heat of her center.

"Shit!" He grunted then murmured, "Always so damn tight."

Addi gasped at the sudden fullness, and he didn't allow her time to adjust before he had one arm gripping her thick thigh and the other wrapped around her torso, pulling her into his front, eliminating any space between them. He buried his face in the crook of her neck as he began thrusting violently into her, sending the dresser shaking with each connection of their hips and causing the objects resting on top to fall over and land haphazardly on the carpeted floor.

She always loved this angle. He reached sensitive spots inside of her that never failed to bring on a quick and powerful release.

Though, most of the time they had sex, it was hot, powerful, and quick like this. In their years together, she could count on one hand the number of times they took it slow, fully exploring each other's body, and made love.

"Oh, Jack!" she moaned as she wrapped both arms around his broad shoulders. "Don't stop! I'm so close!"

"I won't stop until I come inside what's mine," he growled.

That possessive statement sent her over the edge as she screamed in pure bliss. Her finish flooded through her, sending every nerve in her body into an explosion of ecstasy. She dug her nails across his back and was thankful he still had his shirt on. If he didn't, she would've left deep red trails across his tanned skin.

He didn't let up on his rough assault as he felt her core clench around him, making his own finish follow close behind hers. With another thrust, he came and didn't stop until he was sure she took all he had to offer. He paused as he kept his head still buried in the crook of her neck as they were both left panting heavily by the end.

He withdrew and helped her down off the dresser, only letting go of her once she got her shaky legs under control and regained the ability to walk on her own. After they both got cleaned up and finished packing everything that they were taking with them, they crawled into bed and fell asleep as they held each other.

THURSDAY – DAY OF DEPARTURE

The chirping of Serenity's alarm woke her up out of a peaceful, dreamless sleep. A heavily inked and lightly scarred arm was draped across her bare torso, an arm that belonged to the warm and solid form that was flush against her back and cradled into the soft curves of her legs. Still half asleep, she reached over, turned off her alarm, and scooted further back into that comforting form.

"Keep wiggling against me like that and we'll miss our flight." Hunter's groggy voice vibrated against her sensitive skin as he buried his face in the crook of her neck and placed gentle kisses along it.

The thought had her unable to stop her mind from focusing on the hard bulge that was pressed against her backside. A weapon that was sure to kill her from an overdose of pleasure.

"I'm tempted to hold you to that." She wiggled against him a little more, teasing him further.

The low rumble that emanated from deep in his chest sent vibrations throughout her body and an aching need straight to her center. In one fluid movement, he flattened her back against the mattress and settled between her parted legs. The movement was so fast, so precise that it could have only been mastered from years of training how to handle an opponent and make them move how he wanted them to.

Reaching over, he tapped the screen of her phone, forcing the time to illuminate. "It looks like you're in luck. We have a few minutes to spare."

Though his long brown hair draped over his face, she could see that his grin was wicked as one of his large hands slid beneath her underwear and tested her readiness. That grin only spread further when he found her wet and needy. He pulled the front of his boxers down just enough to free himself as he pulled her panties to the side and lined himself up.

In one swift motion, he pushed into her and didn't stop until his hips met hers. His movements were slow and precise, filled with so much emotion and need for her. Serenity placed her hands on his ass, over the fabric of his boxers as she tried to pull him further into her, rocking her hips to match his deep, slow, and sensual thrusts.

"Come for me, Angel. I need to hear how good I make you feel." He coaxed her in a tone that told her he needed her finish just as desperately as she did.

With him kneading her breasts and steadily pumping into her, she felt her orgasm come on fast. Before she knew it, she screamed his name as she came. This one was different. Normally, his quick and hard thrusts brought her to a fast and powerful finish that always caused her eyes to roll in the back of her head and make her temporarily forget her name, but not this one. She felt so much emotion, a deep connection toward him that bound her heart with his, as scary as that might sound given how horribly her last relationship ended. She had to pull all the strength within her to not cry from the deep affection she was beginning to feel for him.

Hunter must have felt it too because he held her gaze as he spilled into her. The expressions he normally kept masked into a calm and observatory demeanor were torn down, revealing something terribly vulnerable in the hands of the wrong person. But she was different. She was one of the good ones and deserved to see exactly how she made him feel. He dipped his head down and claimed her mouth passionately.

As he pulled out, a spark of loss flashed through his eyes as if he immediately missed the warmth of her center. A look that mirrored her own. Reluctantly, they got cleaned up and dressed. Since they had close to a ten-hour flight, she dressed comfortably in a pair of black leggings and a bright blue workout tank top. She threw her raven hair up into a high ponytail and did her makeup light as usual.

Hunter groaned in frustration, causing her to stop dead in her tracks at the foot of the stairs. "Fucking hell, Angel."

She pinched her brows and cocked her head. "What?"

"You're going to have every man looking at that tight ass of yours." His heated gaze took in the vision in front of him. "Trust me. I know this because I'll be one of them."

"Let them stare." She shrugged, and called over her shoulder as she made her way into the kitchen. "Let them be jealous of what only you get to touch."

His laughter followed her, a sound that warmed her heart. Subconsciously, her bright green eyes darted to the table, dread trying to take over her emotions. Luckily, the table was empty this morning. There had been no sign of her intruder coming around since Doc scared him off a few nights ago.

She made her last rounds around the house, doing a mental checklist as she made sure everything was turned off and that she packed everything she needed for the weekend.

He stood beside the door with his duffle bag slung over his shoulder and her suitcase in his other hand. "Ready to go?"

Her suitcase wasn't light either. She tried carrying it down the stairs herself only to be stopped two steps in by him with a glare that rooted her to the floor. He took it from her, lifting it as if it weighed nothing to him.

"Yep!" She beamed.

She found herself in a rather good mood this morning. Her best friend was getting married. They were about to go to a tropical island for a long weekend. She had a wonderful man to bring with her and the sex that morning was the perfect way to start her day. Despite the darkness, fear, dread, and paranoia her intruder tried tainting her with, how could she not be good spirited?

Hunter opened the front door for her and carried both their bags to his Jeep as she locked up the house. She would be lying if she said she wasn't glad to get out of there for a few days. A long break from the dangers of her intruder was just what she needed. Hopefully, Einstein would have some news or even a lead on who the intruder might be by the time they got back.

The twenty-minute drive to the airport went by rather quickly as Hunter and Serenity rode in comfortable silence. The only noise that filled the vehicle came from the radio that played at a low volume.

He had rested his large hand on her thigh the whole drive and it was driving her hormones wild. How could a simple, innocent touch from a man drive her body that crazy? She hoped it would never change, that if things went well, thirty years from now his simple touch would still have this effect on her. After they parked in the long-term parking garage, they made their way through the automated doors of the airport and into the check-in line. Hunter placed their bags on the scales one at a time as Serenity spoke with the attendant behind the counter, giving the lady all their information as she typed away on her computer.

The attendant printed their boarding passes and pointed them in the direction of the security checkpoint. They filed through the line, stepped through the metal detectors, and started their trek to their terminal.

"Renny!" Serenity heard her name squealed in an excited pitch.

Addi jumped up from her seat beside Jack at their terminal as she threw her arms around her friend in a warm embrace.

"Hey, Addi!" Serenity returned the hug to her bubbly friend.

"Are you excited?"

"For the flight? No. For Hawaii? Hell yeah!" Her chocolate eyes were wide with anticipation.

"It's a good thing we decided to splurge on first class, huh?" Serenity laughed as Jack stood from his seat and walked over. "Hey, Jack."

"Hey, Renny." He pulled her into a hug.

She felt Jack's body tense for a moment before he let her go and stepped back. She looked up at him and followed his gaze toward Hunter. *That's right. They haven't met yet.* She could see why he would tense up for a second.

Jack was a tall man, but Hunter had a few inches on him and was broader, bulkier, and packed with more muscle. Muscles that were scarred in places and covered in ink. Not to mention the scar that bisected his left eyebrow and the brown hair he had half up in a knot on top of his head and the rest flowing freely across his shoulders. Even though his beard was trimmed close to his face, and he was dressed in a black T-shirt, jeans, and boots, he was terrifying at first glance.

"Oh, I'm sorry. Jack, this is Hunter. Hunter, this is Jack."

Jack stepped up and held out a hand, but Hunter didn't shake it. He merely stood there with an unreadable mask across his face. *Well, this is going lovely so far,* she thought.

An airport worker's voice sounded over the intercom and started calling passengers to board. As they all filed down the ramp and into the first-class section of the plane, Addi asked if a flight attendant could take their photo. They all scooted in close, and the flight attendant snapped a few photos with Serenity's phone before she handed it back.

"Send those to me," Addi said as she and Jack took their seats in the very front row while Hunter and Serenity's seats were just a few rows back.

"Do you want the window seat?" Serenity asked as she approached their chairs.

"No, I prefer the aisle," Hunter motioned for her to sit before he did.

She took her seat and got situated before she pulled out her phone so she could send her friend the photos before takeoff. She pulled up her camera roll, selected the images, and sent them. She was about to close out when a photo caught her attention.

Two deep lines formed between her brows as she clicked on it. It was a photo of her sleeping on the couch. All the color drained from her face and a mixture of emotions tore through her like a violent tornado. Fear, panic, disgust, violation, and mortification were only a few of them.

"Oh... my... God..." she whispered and nearly dropped her phone from shock.

CHAPTER 29

THURSDAY – DAY OF DEPARTURE

"What is it?" Hunter asked in a serious tone as he shifted his body toward Serenity's. The fear in her voice sent him on high alert. She turned her phone toward him with a trembling hand and showed him the photo.

"I... I didn't take this..." She trailed off, fear holding the rest of her words hostage.

He took the phone from her and examined the photo more closely. His face was unreadable but the emotions that raged in his eyes were like none she had ever seen. He swiped to see if there were any more.

She watched in horror at every new photo and each video that played, videos that showed someone touching her in very inappropriate places while she slept and one of her while she showered.

"This can't be happening..." she muttered in disbelief.

The violations her intruder had done to her were unforgivable. *What else has he done that wasn't captured on camera?* That thought sent her head spinning and her thoughts spiraling to a very dark place. She couldn't think of that, she *wouldn't*. It would only drive her fear further, to the point of a full-blown breakdown. And since they'd be trapped for hours on a plane flying thirty thousand feet above the earth, this wasn't the place for such an episode.

"I think I'm going to be sick," she choked out.

"Head between your knees, Angel," he instructed in a calm voice.

She did as she was told and took deep breaths through her nose and out through her mouth as he rubbed soothing circles across her back.

"How... How are you so calm right now?" she whispered.

"Years of practice," he gritted through his teeth. "I'm going to send these to Einstein, alright. Hopefully the lunatic was careless and caught his reflection on camera somewhere."

All she could do was nod, her body beginning to tremble as she fought hard to steady out her breathing before takeoff.

Hunter kept eyes on Serenity through both their flights. She didn't utter a single word though. She merely pulled her knees to her chest, wrapped her arms around her legs, and kept her gaze out the window. During their layover, Addi tried to chat with her, and he was proud of Serenity for putting on a brave face, but he could tell that mentally, she just wasn't there.

On their next flight that would put them in Hawaii, she did the same thing, curled up in her chair, and stared out the window for the full seven hours. It killed Hunter to see her that way. When he saw those photos and videos on her phone, the primal beast within him was raging, begging to be set free to feast upon the fucker who did this to her. He wanted nothing more than to kill her intruder and bring her his tortured, lifeless body so she could have peace of mind in knowing he would never touch her or cause her pain again.

He had his own list of suspects and right then, his number one was looking more promising, but he needed solid proof before he made an accusation of that magnitude.

By the time they landed and took the shuttle to their resort, Serenity was starting to come back out of her shell. Thank fuck. They parted ways with Addi and Jack when they reached the top floor of the resort and made their way to their room. Hunter swiped the keycard and held the door open for Serenity.

He watched as her jaw hit the floor when she saw their room, or maybe mini-suite was a more appropriate title for it. A small kitchenette equipped with a fully stocked mini-fridge filled the corner of the space to the left and a large leather sofa was positioned in front of a mounted flat-screen TV to the right. Beyond that was the king-sized bed, a door that must lead to the bathroom, and a large wooden armoire for storage.

All the furniture was whitewashed and weathered while a tanned sand color painted the walls. But he noticed that what truly drew her attention was the line of floor-to-ceiling windows straight back that gave them an unobstructed view of the crystal blue waters and white sanded beach down below.

"Oh wow! This place is beautiful." Serenity sighed happily as she took in the sights before her.

He placed their bags beside their bed before he walked up to her, pulled her back against his front, and wrapped his arms around her snuggly as they gazed out the window together. "It's pretty amazing," he agreed but concern filled his voice. "How are you doing?"

"Better." She tilted her head back and rested it against his strong chest. "Thank you for giving me space to work through everything."

"Good, because I don't plan on giving you much space while we're here." His lips connected to the sensitive skin of her neck. "The flight was miserable. I couldn't stop thinking about you in a bikini."

"Oh, yeah? Well, maybe we can sneak down to one of the pools or the beach tonight and ditch the suits," she said sensually.

"You dirty girl," he growled against her skin, the vibrations sending goosebumps pebbling across it. *Yep. This woman will be the death of me.*

"Come on, we need to meet Addi and Jack in the lobby to greet the wedding planner." Serenity turned in his arms and kissed his full lips quickly. He groaned at the sound of Jack's name. "Hey, be nice." She laughed.

Serenity and Hunter exited the metal elevator doors and met up with Jack and Addi who were already there with a woman Serenity didn't recognize. Throughout their travels, Serenity had plenty of time to fully process everything that had happened to her over the last week since her house burnt down, and she moved. She was thankful that Hunter gave her the space she needed to file through her emotions and come to terms with the new evidence they found that her intruder so generously left for her.

The violations done to her made her feel like she needed to scald her skin off in a hot shower to remove any trace of his touch from her body. Her overthinking mind fought her on trying to run wild with theories of what he may have done off camera, but she quickly stopped those. There was no reason to come up with scenarios that might or might not even be real and get herself all worked up about them.

Maybe it was the fresh island breeze or maybe it was the strong and wonderful man she had by her side that made her feel like everything was going to be ok. The lobby had its full glass accordion-style windows fully open, allowing a wonderful breeze to blow through the large open space.

"Hey! Did y'all get settled in ok?" Addi asked as Serenity and Hunter approached.

"Yes." Serenity smiled. "The room and view are breathtaking."

"Aren't they!" Addi practically squealed. "Guys, this is Nina, the wedding planner. She's going to show us around."

The short, Hawaiian woman smiled brightly. She had her long black hair tied back in a perfect bun at the nape of her neck and there was not a speck of lint or a wrinkle to be found on her maroon blouse and black slacks.

Nina spoke in a gentle voice. "Aloha! I am so glad you all had safe travels, and I couldn't be more excited to be a part of your special day. If you would follow me, I will show you all around the resort and to where the ceremony will be held."

Nina led the way through the open accordion doors and out to the rest of the resort. Jack and Addi followed close behind, hands intertwined and heads on swivels as they peered around. Hunter and Serenity trailed behind them; hands intertwined as well.

Nina showed them the multiple restaurants and bars the resort had to offer, the three large in-ground pools, all with a fully stocked swim-up bar, and then down to the beach to a private section where the wedding would take place. The space was bare though, they wouldn't set everything up until the morning of, to ensure nothing would get damaged by the weather or stolen.

Nina talked with the group about what to expect, the timeline of events, and walked them through a quick rehearsal. Most of Jack and Addi's family would be flying in tomorrow for the big day on Saturday.

"All the rooms are reserved and ready to go as your family comes in and everything with the wedding has been sorted out, so you all are free to enjoy the vast amenities the resort has to offer. Please, don't hesitate to find me or call me if you have any questions or concerns," Nina informed them before she departed.

"Well, I don't know about y'all but I'm starving. Airplane food isn't exactly filling." Addi laughed as she turned to the rest of the group.

"We could stop by one of the restaurants inside the resort?" Serenity offered.

"Yes! Lead the way!" Addi smiled brightly as she interlocked her hand with Jack's as they walked.

After dinner, Jack and Addi went off to do their own thing. Everyone agreed to meet for breakfast, and they would spend the day tomorrow doing different activities and excursions. Hunter and Serenity spent some time at the pool, had a few drinks, watched the sunset as they walked the beach, and, of course, later that night when the resort was deserted and everyone was asleep, snuck back to skinny dip and made love in one of the pools.

CHAPTER 30

FRIDAY - 1 DAY TILL WEDDING

Friday's schedule kept the team of four pretty busy. Hunter and Serenity met Addi and Jack at a cozy diner in the restaurant that dealt strictly with breakfast foods and was only open for a few hours each morning. The group laughed and chatted as the girls skimmed over brochures about excursions the resort offered.

By the time they were through eating, the girls had organized a fun day that started with snorkeling. The couples swam over the reef, observed the absolute beauty of Mother Nature, and did a snorkeling scavenger hunt the resort had set up. The resort would occasionally sink full bottles of wine to the ocean floor and anyone who found and recovered the bottles got to keep them.

They ended up finding two bottles while exploring. Swimming with sea turtles was next and Addi was in absolute heaven. They stopped for lunch, and after which, they rented a couple of jet skis and tore through the waves on pure adrenaline and speed. To finish off the day, they reserved a catamaran for a romantic sunset dinner.

Addi, Jack, Hunter, and Serenity were taken offshore where

they gently floated in calm crystal-clear waters and were waited on and served a fancy three-course meal with endless champagne as they got to view the most beautiful sunset they would ever witness firsthand.

Serenity would call the day a success. Although the men didn't really talk to each other directly, they were cordial. When they returned from dinner, Addi and Jack decided to retire to their rooms since tomorrow was their big day. Serenity and Hunter were just returning from a calming walk along the beach when someone called out her name from somewhere in the lobby.

"Renny!"

She turned around and narrowed her vision from someone using her nickname. Her green eyes scanned the space, and her body locked up when she found the source of the voice. Noah brushed his shaggy red hair back with his fingers and gave her a big smile as he walked over, his long legs putting him in front of her too quickly for her liking.

When she finally found her voice, she questioned, "Noah? What are you doing here?"

I must be dreaming, she thought as she casually pinched a spot on her arm, trying to wake herself up from this nightmare. Unfortunately, this was a living nightmare she wouldn't escape from that easily.

"Addi and Jack are still getting married tomorrow, right?" he questioned as he flashed her a freckled smile.

"Yeah?" Her answer was hesitant, unsure of where he was going with that.

"I figured you wouldn't want to attend alone so I'm here as your date." He spoke confidently.

She watched as Noah glanced over her shoulder to Hunter.

His vision looked Hunter up and down as he pulled his fiery brows together in confusion before returning his stone gaze to her.

"So, you assumed I wouldn't have found a new date?" she questioned him flatly. He opened his mouth but closed it, unsure of how to respond. "Hunter, this is Noah. Noah, meet Hunter, my boyfriend."

Hunter waited patiently and observed the interaction, knowing she could handle it on her own. She knew he only stepped up when she made it a point to introduce him, giving him the green light to enter the conversation. Which she both respected and appreciated.

"Boyfriend?" Noah inquired.

Noah appeared shocked at first, his stone eyes going wide as he took in the frightening man standing next to her. Then he scowled in anger.

"Yes. I'm sorry you wasted the time and money to come all the way out here, but you need to leave, Noah." Serenity forced sternness into her voice that didn't match the chaotic feelings swirling around on the inside.

"But Renny... I came here to get you back," he confessed. "I still love you."

"If you truly loved me, you wouldn't have fucked another woman in your bed." Hurt filled her voice with the painful reminder.

"It was a mistake. A moment of weakness that will never happen again, I promise. I fucked up, Renny, and I'm so damn sorry. Please, give me another chance," he begged.

"I honestly believe you're sorry, and I appreciate you owning up to your mistake. I truly hope you've learned from it, but there is no *us* anymore, Noah." Her voice cracked. She was pulling every ounce of strength within her to not break down and cry at that moment.

"But we were so fucking good together. We can get back to that again. I had plans to propose," Noah continued.

"We were pretty great," she agreed. "But you blew my trust, and I'll never be able to give it back to you. You know how much I value trust more than anything in a relationship. You have to let go and move on, please."

Serenity broke it to him as easily as she could. A part of her would always care for the man and despite the pain he caused her, she didn't want to hurt him, but he needed to know the truth.

Noah's gaze raked up and down her front, then shifted over to Hunter as if he were studying them. She watched as his eyes met with Hunter's and Hunter held the gaze, boring a hole through Noah in a silent warning. Noah must've understood because he quickly averted his gaze to the floor before he spoke again.

"Ok." He admitted defeat as his shoulders slumped. "I understand… I'll catch the next flight out in the morning." He finished and walked off toward the elevator, not giving her the chance to reply, not that she planned to.

She took a deep breath and released it shakily as she turned toward Hunter. "I'm so sorry. I had no idea he would physically come here."

"You have nothing to apologize for. You gave that man no reason to think there was a chance he could get you back. Coming here was his own doing." He kept his tone gentle as he pulled her against him and wrapped his arms around her. "Are you alright?"

"I will be. It was unexpected but I feel like we finally have the closure we both needed."

She didn't have to specify that she was talking about closure for her and Noah. She knew Hunter understood.

"Come on, let's get you to bed." He laced his fingers through hers and tugged her toward the elevators. "The maid of honor needs her beauty sleep, and I plan to keep you up for at least another hour."

"An hour, huh?" she teased, but she could already feel her body waking up for him from his delicious sinful threat alone.

"At least." He winked, and excitement exploded within her.

CHAPTER 31

Serenity entered one of the bridal suites tucked away in a private section on the main floor of the resort. A midsize room with light sandstone-colored walls and plush cream-colored carpet covered the floor, giving the space a cozy feel. Multiple large vanities with oversized mirrors lined one full wall, giving everyone enough space for hair and makeup applications. Large windows let in a vast amount of natural light and offered a wonderful view of the clear ocean.

"Oh my, look at you! You're practically glowing!" she said to Addi as she entered the room. Happy tears threatened to fall from her eyes, but she forced them to stay put.

"Renny!" Addi squealed as she embraced her friend in a warm hug.

Both girls were in their pajamas with their hair pulled up into messy buns. They planned on helping each other get ready for the ceremony. Serenity walked over and hung her garment bag next to Addi's before taking a seat at one of the vanities.

"You don't think he'll get cold feet, do you?" Addi asked apprehensively as Serenity started on her makeup.

"Who? Jack? Hell, no! That man loves you. You know that." Serenity began blending in the foundation with a brush.

Addi tried her best to hold still so her friend could work her magic. "I know, just pre-wedding jitters and all."

"Besides, we're on an island. It's not like he could go anywhere that you or I wouldn't catch up to him quickly and beat the snot out of him." She laughed as she began to apply a trio eyeshadow pallet that would make Addi's chocolate eyes pop.

Addi joined her. "True!"

They continued chatting as they took turns dolling each other up before starting on their hair. Before they knew it, it was time to get dressed. Serenity unzipped her bag and removed her dress from its hanger. Faint tan lines from her bathing suit were unobstructed by the beautiful A-line, one-shoulder, floor-length dress in a bright coral pink that popped against her olive complexion. A long slit ran up the left side that stopped mid-thigh.

She turned her back toward her friend. "Can you zip me up?"

Addi did and Serenity stepped in front of the trifold full-body mirror as she twirled in a circle, allowing the sheer fabric of the dress to flutter around before gracefully falling back into place.

"Damn, I did good when I picked this dress." Addi took in her maid of honor.

Serenity couldn't look away from the goddess staring back at her. She felt unbelievably beautiful at that moment.

"Your turn," Serenity sang, wiggling her brows mischievously as she walked over to the white garment bag that held the wedding dress.

She removed a floor-length, spaghetti-strapped dress full

of elegant white lace that flowed exquisitely to the ground. The V-neckline allowed a decent amount of Addi's voluptuous cleavage to be ogled over. She helped her friend step into the masterpiece as she zipped it up and secured the back.

"Damnit!" Addi began to fan her face with her hands, forcing the tears to vanish before they ruined her makeup. "I promised myself I wasn't going to cry until after the ceremony."

"Addi, you look absolutely stunning!" Love and admiration welled inside of Serenity as she took in Addi's glowing sun-kissed complexion. "Like Aphrodite about to greet her worshipers."

A knock sounded at the door and Addi's parents walked in. Her mother was a little shorter than her but had the same big brown eyes, rounded features, and brown hair just with hints of grey around her temples. She got her height from her father, who was right at six feet. Her father was a slim man with a shaved head and a thick caterpillar of a mustache that he was very proud of.

"Oh, my baby girl!" Debra, her mother, said sweetly as tears began to fall down her cheeks.

As if on cue, Roger, her father, pulled out a blue handkerchief that was resting in the chest pocket of his black suit jacket, and handed it to his wife. Debra took it and began to dab lightly at her wet cheeks.

"Don't they both just look lovely?" she asked after she composed herself.

"True visions," Roger agreed and immediately cleared his throat, trying to hide the emotion in it. "Well, let's not keep that man of yours waiting too long. Don't want him running off," he joked.

"Don't you dare say something like that to a bride on her wedding day," Debra chastised as she play-slapped her husband's arm.

Roger chuckled deeply and extended his right arm out toward his daughter. "Ready when you are."

Addi took a deep breath as she looked herself over in the mirror one last time before looping her left arm through her father's. Debra handed her daughter a large bouquet of bright pink lilies as she and Serenity followed them out of the bridal suite.

The ceremony was a small and intimate gathering of close family and friends from both parties. Forty white folding chairs were separated down the middle, creating an aisle that was littered by a path of bright pink lily petals. A dark wooden arbor was constructed at the head of the aisle and wrapped with beautiful white lace with more pink lilies sticking out of it.

They came to a stop where Nina was waiting by a wall that kept them hidden from sight. She instructed the music to begin playing as she motioned for Debra to walk out first. Serenity looped her arm through Jack's best man as they walked out next. She gasped at the beautiful and elegant setup the resort constructed for Addi and Jack's special day.

Her eyes darted around, trying to take in the masterpiece until her vision met a gaze of ice-blue and hazel. *Holy hell!* If it wasn't for the pounding in her chest, she would've thought her heart stopped beating at the sight before her. Hunter was dressed in a blacked-out tux that made him look godly as if he should be standing at the gates of the Underworld, waiting to greet new souls, or as if he should be the one reaping those fresh souls, not casually standing on a beach in Hawaii.

His long brown hair was half tied up in a knot behind his head while the rest was down, flowing gently with the sea breeze. His beard was freshly trimmed and the scar that bisected his left eyebrow made him look like divine death.

She noted the heat in his eyes as his gaze bore into her, promising nothing but sinful pleasure as he raked down her front and back up again. Her body reacted instantly as her core clenched with primal need, wanting nothing more than for him to deliver those unspoken sinful gifts upon her body.

She felt his gaze follow as she passed, released the arm of Jack's best man and came to a stop at her place to the side of the arbor. She glanced over at the groom, wondering if he was more nervous than she was at that moment. Jack met her stare and briefly dipped his gaze down her front and back up as he gave her a full smile before looking away down the aisle where his bride would shortly emerge. The music slowly faded out and there was a brief moment of silence before a slower, more intimate remixed version of "Kiss the Girl" by Brent Morgan started to fill the air around them.

Everyone stood up and turned toward the back as Addi and her dad exited from behind the wall. Everyone always looks to the bride for her reaction, but Serenity looked toward Jack. He stood there in his tux with his hands clasped in front of him with a huge smile on his face as he kept his emerald gaze on his bride.

Addi looked radiant as she glided down the aisle next to her dad, her lace dress lightly blowing in the ocean breeze. They came to a stop in front of the arbor as the officiant started to speak.

"Who gives this woman away to be married today?" the man said in a deep voice.

The officiant, dressed in a tailored grey tux, was an older man in his mid-fifties, a native Hawaiian with his tanned skin and long black hair braided neatly back.

"Her mother and I do," Roger said as he placed his daughter's hand in Jack's outstretched palm. He gave his daughter a quick kiss on the cheek before he turned and took his seat next to his wife.

"You may be seated," the officiant instructed the crowd. "Dearly beloved, we are gathered here in the sight of God and in the face of this company to join this man and this woman in holy matrimony. If anyone has just cause why they should not be joined together, speak now or forever hold your peace."

The crowd of seated guests remained silent as Jack glanced over Addi's shoulder to Serenity for a heartbeat, meeting her gaze before locking eyes with his bride again. *That was weird,* Serenity thought. *Did he fear I would object to my best friend marrying him?*

When no one objected, the officiant continued. "Marriage is the union of husband and wife in heart, body, and mind. It is a means through which a stable and loving environment may be attained. If you two will hold hands, we will begin the vow exchange."

Addi turned and handed Serenity her bouquet and gave her a quick wink before turning back to Jack, placing her hands in his.

"Addison Thatcher, do you take this man to be your husband, to live together in holy matrimony, to love him, to comfort him, to cherish him, and to keep him in sickness and in health, forsaking all others, for as long as you both shall live?"

"I do," she said without hesitation, her tone filled with so much love as she smiled brightly at Jack while slipping a silver wedding band on his ring finger.

"Jack Maddlen, do you take this woman to be your wife, to live together in holy matrimony, to love her, to honor her, to comfort her, to cherish her, and to keep her in sickness and in health, forsaking all others, for as long as you both shall live?"

Jack took a deep breath before he winked at Addi and said, "I do," as he slipped the silver wedding band around her ring finger.

"By the power vested in me under the laws of the State of Hawaii, I now pronounce you husband and wife. You may kiss the bride." The officiant concluded the ceremony as the crowd erupted in cheers and applause as Jack pulled Addi into a passionate embrace, kissing her, and confessing his love in front of family and friends.

He twined his fingers with his wife's as he escorted them down the aisle as husband and wife. Serenity and Jack's best man exited down the aisle next before the rest of their family and friends filed their way toward the reception area.

The reception party took place on the edge of the beach, where the grass met the sand. A large, stone patio area with wooden posts on each corner served as anchors for the multiple strands of lights that criss-crossed over the space. They were off since it was daytime, but they still made the place appear magical.

Extra long tables draped with white cloth were lined with various foods and drinks and a DJ booth with large speakers lined another side. Everyone cheered as Jack and Addi entered the space, stopping in the middle as music played and they shared their first dance.

"May I have this dance?" A deep voice washed over Serenity.

She didn't need to turn to see who that voice belonged to. Her body could sense Hunter's presence. She turned and there her god of death stood, in all his devilish glory, with his hand extended, waiting for her to take it.

"I don't know. My boyfriend is pretty territorial," she teased and loved the way his eyes flashed with emotion at hearing her refer to him as such. "He wouldn't take too kindly to another man's hands on me."

"I'll deal with him later." His husky voice dripped with lust.

"My hands have been itching to touch you since the moment I saw you in that dress."

She flashed him a sensual smile as she gently placed her hand in his. The moment their skin made contact, he pulled her to him and started dancing in one expert fluid movement that shouldn't have been as hot and alluring as she found it to be. Other couples joined shortly after and soon, the dance floor was littered with couples twirling and moving their partners around the stoned space.

After a few more songs, Addi and Jack cut their cake, and the maid of honor and best man gave their speeches as everyone toasted to the new, happy couple. Shortly after, the ceremony wrapped up as Jack scooped up his wife bridal-style and hauled her off the dance floor, toward their hotel room. Everyone began to slowly filter out, going off to do their own thing, while some hung around a while longer.

Hunter pulled Serenity completely against his hard frame and bent his head down, till his lips brushed the shell of her ear. "I want to bend you over the couch in our room, hike that pretty dress up, and fuck you into the middle of next week," he whispered with such promise behind those words. Words that sent her arousal coursing through her heated body as her core began to throb with desire.

She closed her eyes as she whispered back, running her delicate fingers through his long brown hair. "I'd like that very much, sir." A sound of approval emanated from deep in his chest at her response.

"Mmm, you're going to call me that when I'm pounding into you from behind, understood?"

"Yes, sir," she practically moaned at the thought. Her body was on fire at this point, every nerve ending was on overdrive.

"Now let's get you back to our room before I change my mind and bend you over that table and take you in front of all these strangers."

That threat gave her core its own heartbeat. She wasn't one for voyeurism, but she would be lying if the thought didn't excite her further. Without hesitation, Hunter swept her into his strong arms as if she weighed nothing to him and carried her back to their room.

Serenity lay naked under the covers beside Hunter, her head resting against his chest and her fingers running through the light dusting of hair. They were both exhausted from exploring each other for the last few hours. He held up to his promise and the moment he got her to the room, he set her down behind the couch, lifted her dress, and took her from behind.

Both of their clothes were scattered throughout the room, with no rhyme or reason as to where they were thrown when they were removed. Her phone vibrated against the nightstand. She reached over to check it and was surprised to see it was a text from Addi. She figured they'd be locked away in their room until at least tomorrow, knowing that if this were her wedding, she wouldn't leave the room for days.

Addi: Hey girl! Want to get together for drinks tonight?

Serenity: I figured y'all would be "busy" until tomorrow. (Winky face emoji)

Addi: Trust me, we've been busy! Haven't stopped since we left the ceremony! (Tongue out emoji)

Serenity: Drinks sound great! See you in a bit.

"Addi asked if we wanted to get drinks with them," she informed Hunter as she set her phone back on the whitewashed nightstand and snuggled back into his warmth.

"Through already, huh? You won't be seeing the light of day for at least three days after our wedding." He winked at her as he flipped her on her back and nestled between her legs.

"Our wedding?" Her mouth parted in shock but the idea of marrying him sent butterflies soaring in her belly. "That's a little presumptuous of you, don't you think?"

"That's confidence, Angel. I told you I don't intend to let you go. We'll be married and after that, I'll watch as you grow, carry, and bring each of our children into this world. I'm thinking three." He traced light circles with the tips of his fingers across the planes of her flat stomach.

What he was saying should scare her off. They had only known each other for almost two weeks now and he was already talking about marriage and children. But there was something deep down, a small voice in the back of her head and a feeling in her heart that was telling her everything would be ok. That he was the one she was meant to be with. So, for now, she would listen to that little voice and not overthink this one.

"Three, huh? How soon do you want kids?"

She was only twenty-three, so she had plenty of time, but he was twenty-nine. Would he wait until she was ready, or would he want them sooner?

"Whenever we're ready. There's no rush. I want to be a little selfish and have you all to myself for a while before I share you with our kids." He laughed with a bright smile on his face, a smile that made her heart stop and fall for him just a little bit more.

"Well, if we keep having this much sex without using a condom, then our odds of an accidental pregnancy are pretty high."

"And if that happens, I'll be the happiest man alive."

He leaned up and positioned his swollen head that was beaded with pre-cum at her entrance. Serenity gasped as he slid inside, burying himself to the hilt as he crushed his lips to hers in a passionate kiss. He kept his movements slow; each thrust was deep, meaningful, and filled with love for her. She placed her hands on his toned ass as she pulled him into her, needing all of him in that moment. When they came together, their cries of passion filled the room.

CHAPTER 32

Hunter and Serenity got cleaned up and made their way to one of the numerous bars located on the grounds of the resort.

"Renny, over here!" Addi called out as she waved her hand in the air from the table she and Jack sat at.

Hunter placed his large hand on the small of her back and escorted her through the crowd of people.

"Hey, newlyweds!" she squealed as she hugged her friend. "How does it feel to be married?"

"Like a dream!" Addi swooned.

"Better than I could've imagined," Jack added.

They ordered a round of beers as they chatted. A song came on that had both women pulling each other toward the dance floor, leaving Hunter and Jack to watch their drinks. Though he would rather shoot himself in the foot than hang out with Jack, Hunter entertained Jack's attempt at friendly small talk. He did, however, keep one eye on Serenity and Addi as they danced, wanting to make sure they were both safe and free to have a good time. After dancing for three consecutive songs, the women made their way back, most likely needing a drink.

Jack laughed as he took in both exhausted women panting for

air. "I think we need more beers."

"I'll get the next round." Hunter turned and zigzagged his way through the crowd of people.

He flagged the bartender down and ordered another round. As he waited, a woman he had never seen before walked up next to him. He glanced at her through his peripherals, but ignored her.

"Excuse me?" The woman tapped on his shoulder lightly to get his attention. He peered down at her.

"Can I help you with something, ma'am?" Confusion filled his tone. His looks don't exactly scream "approachable" to strangers. They generally steer clear of him, which he preferred.

Without any warning, she cupped his bearded cheeks with both hands and kissed him. Hunter froze, the action taking him by complete surprise. He had guessed she was going to try and flirt or possibly need help, but not do something that forward. The shock quickly faded, replaced by his years of training in how to remain calm and get himself out of any situation. That training wasn't exactly meant for this type of situation, but it worked just the same.

He snapped out of it and pushed the woman off him. Not forceful enough to send her falling backward, but enough to get her away. He turned to leave, but froze when he saw his angel standing a few feet from him. Shock marred Serenity's angular features and devastation swam in her mossy eyes, and fuck if that didn't make him want to rip his beating heart right out of his chest. Before he could say anything, she pivoted on her heel and stalked off.

He wanted to go after her, but he quickly lost her in the crowd of people. Not sure where she went, his only option was to get to the bottom of what just happened. So, he turned all his barely contained rage toward the woman who caused his angel unnecessary pain.

"What the fuck is wrong with you?" Hunter growled in a tone that had the woman stepping back with fear in her eyes.

"I'm sorry… I-I didn't…" She fumbled over her words.

She should *be fucking scared,* he thought.

"Use. Your. Fucking. Words." He gritted each word out slowly, menacingly. "Why the hell did you just kiss me?"

He had to use every ounce of his restraint to not scream at the now-trembling woman. Her face had drained of color. Apparently, him not screaming was more frightening.

"Some guy paid me to. I thought it was a prank or something. I didn't mean to cause any turmoil," she pleaded with him.

"Yeah, well you fucking did. Thanks." He ran his large hand through his long hair in frustration. Then he stopped and shot his gaze back toward the woman. "Someone paid you to kiss me? Me specifically?"

Some of the color finally started to flood back into her face. "Yeah, he gave me two hundred dollars. I thought it was a joke until he handed me the cash."

Hunter prodded further, furrowing his brows in determination. "What did the guy look like?"

Someone paid a random stranger to kiss him, knowing Serenity would see. Whoever the mystery man was, he was about to have a little chat with him, a chat that wouldn't consist of too much talking. The thought sent a grin trying to pull at his lips.

"I'm not sure. I only spoke to him for a few seconds, and it was pretty dark. I know that he was tall."

He removed his phone from the back pocket of his jeans and pulled up the photo the flight attendant had taken of him, Serenity, Addi, and Jack. "Did he look like him?" He pointed to Jack.

"Maybe? I'm sorry, like I said, it was really dark. I'm sorry about your girl too. I can find her and talk to her for you if you want," she offered hesitantly.

"No, thanks. You've done enough damage already. I hope the money was worth it." He turned and walked off, leaving the woman with her mouth hung open in shock.

Fuck, he thought. *This is a shit show.* Serenity valued trust more than anything in a relationship, as much as he did, and after what happened between her and Noah, seeing that must have shattered her. He needed to find her fast so he could explain himself.

The horrific sight before Serenity shattered her newly healed heart all over again. *No... Not again...* she thought as she watched the kiss between Hunter and some woman. Someone could have had a gun to her head saying that if she didn't talk, they would shoot, and that still wouldn't be enough motivation for her body to get words out.

So much flashed through her in those few seconds: pain, heartache, disbelief, agony, and anger. There were things she wanted to scream at him, questions she wanted answers to. Hell, a part of her even wanted to hit the man, but she didn't do any of that. Pure betrayal filled her gaze before she turned and stalked off.

I have to get out of here. I need some air. She could feel her eyes dropping a river of tears down her cheeks. The night ocean breeze felt amazing against her heated skin.

She heard a man shout for her. "Renny!"

Her heart skipped a beat, thinking it was Hunter. She couldn't face him, not yet. She needed another minute or two to collect herself and get her emotions under control. Then her brows furrowed. Hunter never called her Renny. He always called her Angel. She turned as Jack rounded the corner and came up to her with concern on his face.

"Hey, I saw you rush out the door. Is everything ok?" he prodded gently.

She still couldn't form words. All she could do was shake her head from side to side as more tears fell down her face.

"Oh, Renny," he cooed softly as he pulled her into him and wrapped his arms around her tightly. "What happened?"

"I saw... Hunter ki—kissing... another woman," she choked out between sobs.

He held her for a moment, resting his chin atop her head. "I'm so sorry."

"Why does this keep happening to me?" Her words were a little muffled from speaking into Jack's chest. "First Noah, then Hunter. I thought he was different. I *never* expected him to do something like that."

"You can feel like you truly know someone and never see the real them. I wish that never happened. I hate seeing you hurt like this." Sympathy laced each of his words. "Tell me what I can do to make it better."

Serenity stepped out of his embrace, and he didn't fight it. "I just need some time alone. I'll be ok, I promise." She gave him a weak smile that didn't reach her eyes.

"Ok. If you need anything, just let me know."

"Thank you." She wiped her cheeks dry with the back of her hands. "You're a good friend, Jack. I'm glad Addi has someone like you."

An unreadable emotion flashed through his eyes, but it was

gone just as fast. Jack made his way back inside, leaving her there with nothing but her thoughts, and for an overthinker, that was never good. She slipped off her shoes and started walking toward the beach.

CHAPTER 33

Hunter searched around the entire bar and couldn't find his angel anywhere. "Hey, have y'all seen Serenity?" he inquired as he approached Jack and Addi sitting at their table.

"No, I thought she was with you. Is something wrong?" Addi's eyes went wide.

She went to stand up, but Jack's hand on her shoulder halted her. Her gaze shot to her husband's in question.

He spoke to Hunter, looking him dead in the eyes. "I saw her looking pretty upset as she made her way outside. I followed and asked if everything was ok. She told me she saw you kissing another woman."

"What?" Addi shouted, turning toward Hunter with horror in her big brown eyes.

"I didn't fucking kiss anyone. Let's get that shit straight right now. Apparently, some dick paid her two hundred dollars to kiss me for reasons unknown," Hunter shot back at Jack, holding his gaze.

Like hell if he was going to show any kind of weakness or back down from a lesser man like Jack. A spark of surprise flashed through Jack's emeralds.

"Did she say who it was?" Addi's gaze shifted frantically between the men as they stared each other down.

"No," Hunter gritted through clenched teeth.

The surprise in Jack's vision was replaced with what might be relief or cockiness, but he wasn't sure. *You think you're so fucking clever, don't you?* Hunter thought.

"We should go look for her," Addi offered.

Still without breaking eye contact, Jack spoke. "She told me she needed some time alone."

"Like you know what the fuck she needs," Hunter rebuked, holding strong.

"I'm her friend! Of course, I do!"

"I'm more than that to her," Hunter shot back. *Something you'll never be.* "Don't you fucking tell me what *my* girlfriend does or doesn't need." Hurt flashed in Jack's irises as he finally looked away. *Pathetic fuck.* Hunter shook his head disappointingly. "Don't worry about it. I'll find her on my own." He turned and began weaving through the crowd of partiers before anyone could utter another word.

"That was bizarre." Addi loosened a heavy exhale and leaned against their table. "What would be the point of someone paying a girl to kiss Hunter?"

"Only thing I could think of is someone who doesn't want them together," Jack suggested, his lawyer brain kicking in.

"I can see that, but who would want that? We're far from home. No one knows us here." She paused, lost in thought. "Noah!" She practically shouted as she sat straight up. Jack's head snapped up and started scanning the room. "No, silly, I mean he's the only one

I can think of that would want those two apart. We know he was here this morning. What if he hadn't left yet?"

"That's a good theory. You would make a pretty good lawyer," he joked, nudging his shoulder into hers playfully.

"Nah, I'll leave that to you. You're one of the best." Admiration filled her round eyes as she looked at her husband. "Honey, maybe we should go look for Renny. Three people would be able to find her faster than one. Besides, I don't like the thought of Noah possibly still being here and her out there all alone."

"Yeah, I think you might be right." He stood up from his chair with his wife following. "I'll go look inside the hotel area, you look around the pools and beachfront. If you find her, call me." He placed a quick kiss on his wife's lips and then parted, the two going in separate directions.

Addi searched the beach first. If she were in Serenity's place, that's where she would go to be alone, but she wasn't there. She made her way around the pools, scanning left and right as she went. An uneasy feeling settled over her as she rounded the third pool, off to the side of the resort. She paused and scanned the area for the source of it and found it.

Two men veiled in darkness were walking right toward her. They appeared to be lost in conversation with each other, but they spoke so low that she couldn't make out what they were saying. Something about it felt off. Wrong. She turned back around and withdrew her phone as she continued her walk, trying to act as if nothing was wrong, but quickening her steps slightly.

"Hey, did you find Renny?" Jack asked as he answered his phone.

"No," she whispered as she turned back toward the lobby. "But I think there are some men following me."

"Where are you?" His tone turned serious and was laced with worry.

She tried to will herself to stay calm, but panic started to creep into her voice. "Passing the pool off to the side of the hotel. I'm heading toward the lobby now."

"Get inside the lobby as fast as you can. I'm on my way—" Jack was cut off when he heard a commotion on Addi's end of the line. She began to scream but it was quickly muffled. "ADDI!" he roared through the phone, but there was no answer.

Hunter was growing frustrated and worried simultaneously. He checked their hotel room, all the restaurants and bars, around the pools and along the beach but Serenity was nowhere to be found. He'd tried calling her numerous times, but it kept going straight to voicemail.

A bad feeling started to form in the pit of his stomach. A sign he knew all too well to pay attention to and listen to closely. A sign that had saved his and his team's lives more than once while out on operations as a Navy SEAL and while on protection details with clients.

"Hey, Bossman, what's up?" Einstein greeted after the second ring.

"Are you at your computer?" Hunter inquired.

"Always." Einstein laughed.

There was a brief pause before he questioned, "Were you gaming?"

Einstein hesitated. "No."

"Don't let him lie to you, Boss. I saw it with my own eyes," Hunter heard Fuse call from somewhere in the background.

"Fuse? What the hell are you doing in Einstein's office this late at night?"

"We're all in here watching the game, Big Daddy." Sweeney's playful voice sounded faint through the phone. "The evil genius got us the NFL package for free."

"Jesus, I work with a bunch of kids," Hunter muttered as he ran a hand through his hair.

"How's Hawaii?" Doc called out.

"You sound wound up tight, Big Daddy. You should go find that angel of yours and relieve whatever stress you've got bottled up," Sweeney joked.

"I would love to, if I could fucking find her!" Hunter growled at his men in frustration.

There was a hesitant pause before Fuse questioned, "What do you mean?"

Hunter knew that every man in Einstein's office was now on high alert. They all have similar backgrounds. Fuse was a former Marine, Doc used to be in the Army, and Sweeney used to work for a private military contractor. Their particular abilities is what drew Hunter to hire each one when he founded Red Sky Security. He knew each man was now alert, dissecting this entire conversation, and ready to fight at a moment's notice.

Hunter softened his tone slightly. "It's a long story. Look, Einstein, if I give you her number, could you locate her phone for me?"

He was frustrated but he knew taking it out on his men was wrong. No, he would channel all that frustration and rage and direct it at the man solely responsible. A wicked smile curled his lips up at the thought.

"You don't even have to ask, Bossman." Hunter heard quick

typing through the phone. "What's her number?"

"555-0397." He forced himself to memorize it the night she put it into his phone.

"The phone is off. I can't trace it." Einstein's voice was filled with remorse. "I only have its last known location, which was the resort."

"Does this have to do with her intruder situation?" Doc inquired. "You don't think he followed y'all out there and got to her, do you?"

"Maybe," Hunter said hesitantly. He had limited his suspect pool down to two men, both of whom were at the resort that day. "What about these two numbers? 555-0011 and 555-5222?"

There was another brief moment of silence between all the men as if everyone waited with bated breath. The only sounds that could be heard were the erratic clicking of Einstein's mouse and keyboard. "Both are turned off as well, Bossman."

What the fuck? Why would both Jack and Addi's phones be off?

"Alright, one last number. 555-7714?"

Another pause before Einstein said, "That one appears to be on a plane somewhere over Colorado, heading this way."

It has to be him. Everything adds up and points right to him like a flashing neon sign.

"Still no word on the handwriting match?"

"Not yet, Bossman, but I'm close. Real fucking close," Einstein reassured him.

"Do you need us out there?" Sweeney offered, ready to leave at a moment's notice.

"If my gut feeling is right and it's who I think it is, then shit is going to get ugly, real fast. But I won't be able to confirm my suspicions until I have actual proof from the handwriting match.

Fuse, Doc, y'all have an assignment in the morning so y'all hang back."

"Alright, Boss." They both spoke with deflation heavy in their voices.

"Einstein, I need you at your computer. You might need to pull an all-nighter and make sure to keep your phone close in case I call."

"You got it. It wouldn't be the first time I've slept in my office. I keep spare clothes here for a reason." He laughed.

Hunter knew that was also the main reason Einstein had a couch in there as well. The kid had slept on it too many times to count when the rest of the team was out on assignments and needed him close by.

Hunter continued giving orders to his team. "Sweeney, I need you to pack up some gear, get on the company jet, and come straight here."

"I'm leaving now. I'll call you when I land."

"I'm going to keep searching here. Einstein, call me the moment any of those numbers pop back online or you finally get a match on the handwriting," Hunter instructed and then hung up.

He tucked his phone into the back pocket of his jeans as he took off in search of his angel again. *Come on, baby. Where the hell are you?*

CHAPTER 34

Serenity stirred in a groggy state, her eyes feeling like lead as she tried and failed to lift them. She pulled her brows together as she tried to recall what happened, but her mind was hazy as if a thick fog had rolled in, shielding her from her memories. She gave up on opening her eyes and began to use other senses to focus on her surroundings.

The flooring beneath her was soft against her skin with a fuzzy texture. A rug or carpet maybe? There was a hint of salt in the air, and every now and then she would catch a whiff of fish. *Is the building moving?* She focused harder. The movement, she quickly realized, was a gentle swaying. She wasn't in a building. She was on a boat.

She didn't remember boarding a boat. Her eyes felt less heavy as she tried again to pry them open. She was successful this time as she blinked rapidly to clear her blurry vision.

Her gaze roamed around the small space—a bedroom of some kind. There was a full-sized bed, a nightstand on each side, accordion doors that must open into a closet, and another door on the opposite wall. *How long have I been out?* She observed a small window, not even a foot wide or tall, revealing clear blue skies.

She was lying on the floor by the closet when she noticed a foot sticking out from around the other side of the bed. *What the hell? Who is that?* Her body felt heavy, but she forced herself up on her hands. That's when she noticed it. Her wrists were bound together with thick brown rope.

She gave the bindings a few tugs, but they didn't budge, and she let out a hiss as they bit into her sensitive flesh. Her memories came flooding back to her like a damn that had burst. She remembered walking along the beach when someone came up from behind and grabbed her as they covered her mouth with cloth. She tried kicking and screaming, but in a matter of seconds, everything went black.

Oh shit, she thought as the reality of being kidnapped hit her. *I have to get out of here. I have to find a way to get ahold of Hunter and let him know where I am.*

The foot across the room started to stir, pulling her from her thoughts. Was it her kidnapper?

"Addi?" Serenity asked, barely above a whisper, as she took in her best friend sitting up across the room.

"Oh my God, Renny!" Her friend sighed with relief and then groaned. "Where the hell are we? What happened?"

"The last thing I remember is someone grabbing me from behind," Serenity recalled. "Then I woke up here. You?"

"I went looking for you, when I noticed two men following me." Addi kept her voice low. There was no way of telling if they were alone on the boat. "I was on the phone with Jack when they grabbed me."

"That's great!" she shouted no louder than a whisper. Addi's rounded features scrunched up in question. "Not the getting taken part, the part where you were on the phone with Jack. He would've heard them take you. Hopefully, he found Hunter and told him what happened. I'm sure they're looking for us as we speak."

Though their odds weren't looking promising, she tried to remain hopeful.

"But why would they take us both?" Addi's face quickly drained of color. "Oh, fuck… You don't think they're… sex traffickers, do you?"

A little of that hopefulness fled from Serenity at that startling possibility. "I really hope not."

Just then, the door to the small bedroom swung open, revealing a large scary-looking bald man with tattoos creeping up his neck and across his face.

"Good, y'all are awake," he said with a creepy smile that sent Serenity's stomach churning.

It was now early Sunday morning and Hunter hadn't gotten a lick of sleep. He searched the resort for hours until everything shut down for the night. With each passing minute, Serenity could be getting further away from him and there was nothing he could do.

Throughout the night, a roller coaster of emotions tore their way through him. When he first realized his angel was missing, fear took over. Fear of the unknown. Fear for her safety. Fear of never seeing her again. Then frustration took over after hours of searching with nothing to show for it. The closer the night drew to sunrise, desperation kicked in.

He'd give anything to just know where she was, who had her, and if she was ok. The thought of the slightest bit of harm befalling her was enough to churn his insides. Now that the sun was beginning to paint the sky, rage was trying to consume him.

It was almost enough to have him searching every building on this island and burning it to the ground until he found her. Though the thought of violence was pleasant, he fought with every ounce of strength he had to keep it together.

He had to if he was going to get his angel back. The horrifying thought of never seeing her again tried to take root in his aching heart. In his former line of work, he was no stranger to torture. But at the thought of living this life without Serenity, he'd rather die. The moment he saw her leaning over him as he lay on the road after his motorcycle crash, her beauty had captured his heart in a death grip.

Hunter had thought he'd lost her when she left. He'd kicked himself for not getting her number and he almost had Einstein find her, but it felt wrong to track her down like that. The next day, as if fate were smiling down upon him, a message waited in his inbox on a dating site he'd been forced to use after losing a bet with Sweeney. It was her. He'd recognize those bright green eyes and that stunning smile anywhere.

When he saw her enter the restaurant, he knew he was done for. Now that life was giving him a second chance with her, he wasn't about to waste it and let her go again. Even though she was taken from him, he would give his last breath to get her back. Determination settled in. A determination that wouldn't stop until she was safe and back in his arms again. Where she belonged.

A single knock sounded at his hotel door, followed by a pause, then two quick knocks, another pause, and one last knock. Sweeney had finally gotten there. He felt a little better knowing he had backup he could count on, and a bag full of gear. He opened the door and motioned for his friend to enter.

"You look like shit, Big Daddy." Sweeney observed him as he

entered the room. "Any news?"

"Nothing yet. Einstein said he should have some kind of results within the next hour or so."

His friend placed a black duffle bag on the couch. "Did you get any sleep?"

"Fuck no," Hunter clipped out.

How the hell was he supposed to sleep when his angel was missing? He didn't even know if she was still alive. *No, don't think like that. He wants her alive.* That thought pissed him off to no end but also made him feel relieved. At least he knew she was safe, wherever she was.

"Alright, well I'm here now, so get some shut-eye," Sweeney said. "I'll wake you the moment either of us gets a call."

"Like hell, if I'm going—"

"With all due respect, Big Daddy, get some fucking sleep. You and I both know that Serenity is going to need you at full strength, not falling asleep halfway through her rescue."

Hunter wanted to protest again but he knew his friend was right. He needed to have a clear head and for that, he needed some sleep. He gave Sweeney a curt nod as his jaw ticked in annoyance and he turned, making his way to the bed.

"Big Daddy," Sweeney called out.

Hunter jolted upright, shaking off what little sleep he got. "How long was I out?"

"About two hours or so. Einstein's on the phone." Sweeney held his phone in the air for his friend to see.

That snapped Hunter out of whatever sleep-deprived daze he was in. He was fully awake and had reverted to fight mode. "Please tell me you've got good news," he called out, knowing Sweeney had it on speaker phone as he stood up and stretched before striding over to his friend who was sitting on the couch with his forearms resting atop his knees.

Einstein let the excitement in his voice flow loudly. "Damn right, I do! I finally got a match on the handwriting."

This was it—the moment Hunter would know if his suspicions had been right. Although his composure was collected and masked on the outside, he was a raging river of emotions on the inside.

"They belong to Jack Maddlen."

"I fucking knew it!" Hunter fought hard to not throw something as he clenched and unclenched his fists at his sides.

He had his suspicions from the very start. Jack had always been too friendly with Serenity. He tried to chalk it up to them knowing each other for years, but something didn't settle right with that. Jack was his number one suspect. Jack and Noah both.

However, Jack checked off more boxes than Noah. He had access to the house, access to the cameras, a past with Serenity, and an excuse to be out late with no one checking in on his whereabouts.

"That son of a bitch!" Sweeney growled. "He fucking played both of them."

"What do you mean?" Einstein inquired.

"Jack is Addi's fiancé. Sorry, husband now." Sweeney corrected himself, unable to hide the hurt in his voice. "But apparently he's had the hots for her friend the whole time." He tried hard to not crush his phone in his strong grasp. "But what I can't figure out is why. Why not break up with Addi and shoot his shot with Serenity? Why follow through with a wedding if he loves another?"

Hunter began to pace the small room. "He must have a reason to keep Addi around. Einstein, can you do some digging on her, see if she comes from money or anything like that?"

"Yeah, give me a second." Einstein's fingers flew over his keyboard with lightning speed.

"I want nothing more than to slice up that fucker," Sweeney clenched his jaw together. Any tighter and he would risk cracking a tooth.

"That makes two of us. I'm sure the girls will want a piece of him as well." A hysterical half-laugh left Hunter's lips.

A wicked grin pulled at one side of Sweeney's mouth. "We can share the fun."

"Addi doesn't come from money, but—" Einstein stopped mid-sentence. Both Sweeney and Hunter glanced toward the phone to see if the call dropped.

The bad feeling in the pit of Hunter's stomach grew worse. "What is it, Einstein?"

"Addi has a life insurance policy," Einstein said.

"That's not that unusual. A lot of people have them," Sweeney replied with a confused expression.

"Yeah, but she didn't set it up, Jack did. It's not just some measly amount either. It's a two million dollar policy with Jack as the sole beneficiary." There was a brief pause before Einstein continued. "I fear that he did this and went through with the wedding to take some of the heat off himself."

"Heat from what?" Sweeney asked hesitantly, as if deep down, he already knew the answer.

Hunter spoke next with nothing but full sympathy in his words. "The heat the cops would be bringing down on him if he off'd his wife to get her life insurance money." He knew Sweeney had a thing for Addi, and that had to be hard for him to hear.

"We need to find them. Right fucking now!" Sweeney gritted

out.

"Now that I know who we're looking for, I have a facial recognition software I can use." Einstein continued clicking furiously on his keyboard as he worked. "If he passes in front of any active surveillance camera, I'll be able to find him."

"You probably shouldn't admit that over the phone," Hunter suggested.

"You really think I don't secure my calls? Come on, Bossman, you know me better than that." Einstein laughed. "Oh shit, that was fast. This dude doesn't like to waste time."

"What do you got?" Hunter peered into the phone as if he could see Einstein's monitors through it.

"He just purchased a car from a local dealership on the island. There are no new charges to his bank, so he must've paid in cash."

"Can you follow where—" Hunter stopped himself. "Never mind. Of course, you can. Just let me know where he goes."

"You're catching on quick, Bossman." Einstein laughed. "Once he stops, I'll text you the address."

"Alright, thanks," Sweeney said as he ended the call.

CHAPTER 35

"Where are we?" Addi asked their kidnapper.

Fear was thick in her voice as she scooted across the small bedroom, coming to a stop next to Serenity. Serenity noticed her friend's wrists were also bound with the same thick rope. She didn't blame Addi, she wanted to put as much distance between herself and that man too, but there was no further for her to go in the small bedroom.

"On a boat," the dangerous bald man said as a wicked grin spread across his tattooed face.

His large, round body consumed almost the entirety of the doorway. She could barely see the rest of the cramped cabin beyond him.

"So, if you planned on trying to escape, I wouldn't. Unless you can swim a mile in shark-infested waters with your hands bound together. Oh, and don't bother trying to shout for help, there's no one around to save you. All it will do is give me a headache and make me angry, at which point I will be forced to shut you up."

Stay calm, Serenity repeated to herself. "There are people who know we're missing." She tried to force her voice to stay steady. To her surprise, it held a mostly even tone, and she sent up a silent thank you and a prayer that she would continue to keep a level head. "They're looking for us and they'll stop at nothing to get us back."

The man bellowed in a deep, sinister laugh, and the sound sent the hairs on the back of both girls' necks standing up and goosebumps prickled up their arms.

"I wouldn't hold your breath, sweetheart."

The sound of that name coming from his thin lips sent a chill down Serenity's spine, and she resisted the urge to shudder. "What do you want with us?"

She tried to hold the criminal's black gaze, but his intimidating demeanor caused her to shift hers to the floor. His cruel eyes raked over their bodies, enjoying the view as evil thoughts crossed through his mind. Both girls leaned into each other as they watched him.

"Nothing. Well, I can think of a few things, but it's the guy who hired us that wants you so badly. And after seeing the two of you, I don't blame him."

"Who… Who hired you?" Addi fumbled over her question.

Serenity draped her bound hands over her friend's and pulled her tightly into her, trying to comfort her as much as possible.

"And spoil the surprise? Where's the fun in that? You'll see soon enough when we deliver you both to him." With that, the large man turned and walked back through the cramped cabin and up a few stairs that led to the deck of the boat.

"This is bad." Addi let out a large sigh, relieved that their kidnapper left them alone.

"Very bad," Serenity agreed, barely above a whisper.

The women could hear their kidnappers conversing above deck.

Unfortunately, the sea breeze carried off with the majority of their conversation. The women heard a cell phone ring from up top as one of the men answered it. Shortly after, the boat's engine roared to life and the girls felt the gentle sway shift as they started to cut through the water.

"What are the odds that they are taking us back to the resort?" Addi asked sarcastically, but Serenity heard the fear and worry lining her words.

"Unfortunately, we aren't that lucky," she answered with a deflated tone.

They sailed through the water for what felt like an eternity, but thirty minutes later they felt the boat slow down before it eventually came to a stop as the engine was cut off.

"Let's go," Baldy said as he came down to the small bedroom where the women still sat.

They couldn't get themselves to go above deck. They wanted to try and keep as much distance between their kidnappers and themselves as possible. Addi and Serenity shared a worried glance before turning their gaze back to the large man.

"Now!" he shouted.

That got both women to their feet quickly as Serenity took the lead and slowly emerged from the cabin. As she topped the stairs and stepped onto the white deck, she finally got a good look at their other kidnapper.

He was a lanky man with every bit of skin covered in cheap, chicken-scratch ink. His black hair was buzzed close to his head, and he kept wiping at his nose. *Great, a druggie,* she thought. *Just what we need right now.* Serenity looked around and noticed they had docked at what looked to be a private residence, surrounded by woods with no neighbors in sight.

The two-story home was painted a calming cream and was lined with numerous large windows that were meant to capture as much ocean view as possible. It was topped with a black-shingled roof and surrounded by a variety of beautifully tropical plants and shrubs. Palm trees littered the property, creating a picturesque scene one would find on a postcard.

Baldy spoke as he gripped Serenity's bicep rather tightly. "I'll take this one, T. You escort the other. Can't have you trying to run off."

She fought off the wince that wanted so badly to escape. She wasn't about to show these men any weakness if she could help it. She tried to keep up with Baldy's long strides, but it took her two for every one of his. They walked up the well-manicured lawn and stepped under the shaded lanai. Baldy reached for the back door, opened it, and practically shoved her inside the home. T and Addi stepped through right behind them.

The main floor of the home was beautiful, open, and bright with natural light as the ocean breeze flowed through the space. Dark wood tiles covered the entire bottom floor, helping to keep the house cool during the warm summer months. It was updated, clean, and looked expensive.

"Ah, there y'all are. I was starting to wonder if you got lost."

A male voice sounded from the living room. Addi paused next to Serenity in the kitchen as they shared a look that said they both recognized the familiar voice.

"No, everything went smoothly. You got a couple of obedient girls here," T said as he walked to the girls and flashed them a creepy grin. This time they both visibly shuddered, unable to fight the uneasy feeling he gave them.

"That I do," said the familiar voice as footsteps sounded from the other room. Both girls waited with bated breath as those steps drew closer. A tall, lean man rounded the corner as he stopped and smiled brightly at both women. "Good afternoon, ladies."

"Jack?" both girls asked in unison, each bearing their own shocked and horrified expressions across their faces.

"What's up, Einstein?" Hunter asked as he answered his phone that sat on the coffee table of his hotel room.

"I lost sight of Jack as he left the city, but he turned his phone back on. I tracked his location to a few square-mile radius. I did some digging, and he owns a property in that area. Looks like he bought it last week and paid for it in cash. I'll bet money he's there with the girls. I already arranged a rental car at the resort for y'all to use."

"Send me the address, we're leaving now. And Einstein?" Hunter said as he grabbed the duffle bag and left with Sweeney following close behind.

"Yeah, Bossman?"

"You're awesome. Drinks will be on me when we get back." He didn't know what he would do without that little genius.

"All in a day's work. Now, go get those girls and bring them home safely," Einstein ordered as he hung up the phone and texted Hunter the address.

CHAPTER 36

"Jack? What's going on?" Addi asked in disbelief, and her body visibly began to tremble.

Her husband stood there with his legs spread apart and his hands tucked casually into the pockets of his slacks. "Isn't it obvious?"

"No... it can't be," Serenity mumbled. If it hadn't been so quiet you could hear a pin drop, no one would've heard her words. "You're my... intruder?"

Both kidnappers filed into the living room, removed the bindings from the girls' wrists, and took a seat on the couch. They leaned back and watched the scene unfold in front of them as if they were watching a movie and not two people's lives being torn apart at the seams.

Addi whipped her head toward her friend, her eyes wide at the accusation. "Of course not! Honey, tell her she's wrong." When Jack didn't say anything, she snapped her head back toward her husband. Any faster and she would risk a broken neck. "J-Jack? Renny's wrong... right?"

"She's not wrong." Jack shrugged, acting as if he didn't just rip out and stomp all over his wife's heart.

Addi remained silent, her mouth slightly parted, a war between her heart and head waging inside her. If it wasn't for the slight rise and fall of her chest, Serenity would've thought her friend stopped breathing altogether.

"Why?" Serenity shouted at him. "How could you do this to her?"

His emerald gaze held her bottle-green eyes prisoner. "Because it's you, Renny. It's been you from the start. She was just a means to an end."

Serenity closed the space between herself and Jack and slapped him, the sound echoing in the otherwise silent space. She heard Addi gasp in shock. *Good, she's still with me,* she thought.

T went to stand up, but Jack held out his hand, stopping him. "It's alright. Emotions are high right now." He gently rubbed his clean-shaven cheek, smoothing out the sting from the slap.

"How could you say that about your wife? My best friend!" She balled her fists at her side, rage boiling up inside of her. Rage for what Jack put Addi and her through from his sick little games.

"It is what it is," Jack stated calmly. "I won't sugarcoat anything, and I won't lie."

"But... I love you, and... I know you love me." Addi's quiet voice was filled with disbelief.

"Jesus, you must have those rose-colored glasses glued on, don't you? I never loved you." He had the audacity to laugh. Serenity swung to slap him again, but Jack caught it this time. "I allowed the first one, but you *will not* hit me again."

She yanked her arm out of his grasp and took a few steps back, coming to a stop beside Addi again.

"That's a fucking lie!" Addi shouted in denial. "You wouldn't have married me if you didn't love me."

"I was only with you to get close to Renny," he confessed, keeping his calm demeanor.

"Explain yourself. Now!" Serenity gritted out through clenched teeth.

"When I first saw you, your beauty lured me into a trap like a siren's sweet melody. I knew immediately that you were the one I wanted. Unfortunately, I realized you were otherwise… unavailable at the moment because of Noah." He locked eyes with Serenity again. "When I learned the two of you were as close as sisters, I saw an opportunity that Addi could provide for me, so I took it. By pretending to date her, I got to be around you all the time. Each time we hung out, I fell further for you. Your beauty, your intelligence, your wit, your kind heart. I loved it all. I thought Noah was a fling, but when I realized how serious the two of y'all were becoming, I knew I had to get him out of the picture."

A sick feeling churned in Serenity's stomach. "What do you mean you had to get him out of the picture?" she inquired wearily, not liking where this was going.

His grin turned ominous. "I paid a prostitute to sleep with him. Knowing how big trust is to you, I knew you would dump him, and boy was I ecstatic when you did."

"But we were already engaged at that time? How do you explain that?" Addi threw in.

"We had reached the point in our 'relationship,'" he used air quotes for the word as if none of it was real, "where it was time for me to propose if I wanted to keep you around. If I lost you, I lost her." He motioned his head toward Serenity.

Serenity kept up her interrogation. "Then why go through with marrying her? Why not find a reason to postpone it so you didn't get locked in?"

His eyes darkened as a wicked expression crossed his pointed features. "Because it would look less suspicious to the cops."

"Wh—what?" Addi stuttered and staggered back as if his words physically struck her.

"I took out a multi-million dollar life insurance policy on you, my dear wife. I married you so I would look less suspicious to the cops when I hired people to kill you the day after our wedding. You would be surprised at the number of criminals I've defended who had killed their partners for the money. I learned from their mistakes and formulated an airtight plan that would not tie anything back to me."

"You sick fuck!" Serenity shouted. "Why would you ever do that?"

"For us," Jack's voice rose slightly with desperation, piercing Serenity with his heated gaze. "I quit my job at the firm and bought this house. Our house, Renny. After the authorities discover my poor wife's body, I'll collect the money so we can live here comfortably, just the two of us. I wanted enough time alone with you to help you adjust and to make up for all the lost years we should have been together." He took a step toward Serenity, but her cringe had him pausing.

"What makes you think I would ever be with you? Especially after I knew what you did to my best friend."

"You don't have a choice, Renny. Given enough time, you'll warm up to me. I'll prove that I'm nothing like those cheating men you keep getting involved with," he threw at her, knowing the fresh memory of Hunter's betrayal still stung.

"But you paid another woman to kiss Hunter last night. He didn't do anything wrong!" Addi defended Hunter.

Serenity gasped at the new bit of information. "What?"

The realization that Hunter didn't betray her was a breath of fresh air in this storm of ugly confessions. But before she could linger on that relief, Jack spoke again.

"It was to prove that if the temptation presented itself to them, any man would give into it. I would *never* do that to you, Renny. I've been loyal to you from the start, and I always will be." Confidence laced each of his words.

"Loyal to me?" Serenity scoffed. "Jack, you were living and sleeping with my best friend, just to get to me. How is that loyalty?"

"Because every time I was with her, I pictured it was you!" His voice rose another octave. Noticing it, he took a deep inhale and released it slowly, helping to calm himself back down.

The confession hit the women like a bird flying into a windshield. Hard and ugly.

"What the fuck!" Addi shouted now that she had some time for the shock to wear off. From the expression contorting her rounded features, Serenity knew her best friend was beyond pissed, and rightfully so.

Jack turned to his wife and spoke calmly. "Didn't you ever wonder why I never said your name during sex or usually buried my face in the crook of your neck?"

"I thought it was weird at first, but I just figured it was one of your quirks."

"It's because if I said a name while coming, it would have been Renny's name on my lips, not yours, and there was no getting around trying to explain that one. Anytime I entered you, fucked you, came inside of you, I pictured it was her I was doing all those things to. You were just a hole to use."

"You fucking bastard!" Addi stormed toward him and slapped him. He allowed the first one but caught her wrist when she went to swing a second time. "Did a part of you ever love me?" Her voice broke as tears fell in rivers down her cheeks. "Was there any part of this that was real?"

"No." His voice was cold, and a bit of Serenity died for her friend. "I think we're done here. Gentleman," Jack called to the two men still sitting on the couch, "she's all yours. You know what to do."

"Addi!" Serenity yelled as Baldy bent down and threw Addi over his shoulder as if she were nothing but a measly sack of potatoes to him.

Serenity wasn't sure how she planned to stop three full-grown men, but she had to do something. However, Jack quickly blocked her path as she tried to run toward her friend and pulled out a gun he had tucked into the waistband of his slacks behind his back. Serenity stopped dead in her tracks as her eyes widened at the sight of the weapon.

"Don't fucking touch me! Let me go!" Addi screamed as she flailed around in Baldy's grasp. She used every ounce of strength inside of her to kick her legs and pound her fists onto his meaty back. She might as well have been a child for how little her struggle affected him. "Renny!" she screamed as he hauled her to their car with his partner shutting the door behind them as they left.

CHAPTER 37

Hunter and Sweeney pulled over to the side of the road a distance back from the address Einstein gave them, climbed out, and made their way around to the trunk. He popped it and unzipped the black duffle bag, handing Sweeney a black bulletproof vest with pockets all down the front.

Sweeney slid it over his head and secured the Velcro sides, so it was snug against his muscular torso. Hunter pulled out a second one and slid it over his own body. Sweeney reached in and grabbed two pistol holsters, handing one to Hunter.

"So, there should be a total of five people in the house?" Sweeney asked as he snapped the top and bottom buckles around his thick right thigh, his charismatic attitude causing a smile to form across his lips at the thought of the battle that lay ahead.

"If what Jack told me is true, yes. He said two men kidnapped Addi. We can assume the same two men took Serenity as well." He secured his own holster to his muscular right thigh.

Sweeney pulled out a knife sheath and buckled it tightly against his left thigh. He grabbed a large KA-BAR knife, the long black blade glistening in the sunlight. He ran his thumb across the edge lightly, testing its readiness before he twirled it around in his hand and slid it in place as he secured the strap around the hilt.

Hunter withdrew two pistols and handed one to his friend. Each man checked and loaded a full magazine into their gun and racked it back, sending one bullet into the chamber, making it ready to fire before they secured them in their holsters. Sweeney pulled out four extra loaded magazines, handing two to Hunter as he slipped the other two into the pockets of his vest.

"Don't forget your babies," Hunter joked as he handed his friend a handful of solid black throwing knives.

"I wouldn't dream of it." Sweeney smiled wide as he took them. "You beauties ready to taste some blood?" He spoke to them in a lover's voice as he secured each one in various spots around his vest.

Hunter snorted and shook his head. "Game time." He closed the trunk and led the way through the woods to the private property on the other side.

As the men drew closer, shouting emanated from the home, causing Hunter and Sweeney to crouch behind nearby shrubs. They watched as two men emerged from the house with Addi in tow.

"You can kick and scream all you want, girly, but your fate has been sealed," a tall lanky man said as he placed a quick smack to Addi's ass as he passed by and popped the trunk of their car.

"Don't you dare put me in there!"

Hunter and Sweeney watched as Addi began kicking and pounding against the rock of a man, but he simply laughed and dropped her into the trunk. She landed with a loud thud.

"I'm going to kill you, you son of a bitch!"

Her screams were cut off when the guy who carried her slammed the trunk shut.

"Think rationally, Sweeney, not emotionally," Hunter warned

in a low voice when he noticed the shift in his friend at the horrid sight before them.

"I haven't thrown my knives, have I?" Sweeney gritted out through clenched teeth.

"That should leave only Serenity and Jack inside the home," Hunter whispered as the two kidnappers climbed into their vehicle. "It's your lucky day."

Sweeney perched a thick brown brow high on his head as he turned toward Hunter. "How so?"

"You've probably envisioned at least seven different ways to murder those men. Pick one and make it happen. Take the car and go get Addi back. I can handle Jack." Hunter tossed his friend the keys and gave him the green light he so desperately craved.

Sweeney's whisky eyes darkened as a sinister smile spread across his face. "With pleasure, Big Daddy." He quickly turned and began his trek back to the car.

Addi had to force herself to take deep breaths. She was on the verge of a panic attack, and she had to keep a level head if she wanted to live through this. However, getting her emotions under control was proving rather difficult. Everything Jack said, his cruel words, were still sharp daggers that were buried deep in her heart and refused to release their hold.

How could he do this? I gave him my heart and soul and he acted as if it were something to just throw away with yesterday's garbage. She tried hard to hold them back, but her tears betrayed her just like her husband had. All she wanted to do was curl into a ball and let her heartache and grief consume her, but she had a bigger problem at hand. She had to survive the two men her husband hired to kill her. Another round of fresh tears fell at the reminder of Jack's treason.

Nothing in this world would make Addi happier than seeing Jack dead for what he did to her, what he was still doing to her, and what he did to Serenity. Instead of wallowing in self-pity, she decided to turn that into anger. She let the rage consume and fuel her until she was filled with a fighting spirit. She *would* get away from these two criminals, then she would make her husband pay.

There must be something I can use in here. The darkness was so overpowering that she wouldn't be able to see her hand if it were right in front of her eyes. *The taillights!* She remembered watching a movie about a girl getting kidnapped. She had kicked out the taillights, causing the cops to pull the car over and she was rescued.

Addi felt around the pitch-black trunk, making sure to orient herself properly so that when she kicked, she was hitting the right spot. She peeled back the lining of the trunk and placed her foot against the spot as she listened. The criminals had the radio turned up loud, so she prayed it would drown out the sound of her kicking.

With a deep breath, she sent her foot flying against the taillight and paused. It didn't give and it appeared her kidnappers didn't hear either, so she tried again. With the next kick, she knocked it loose. A small beam of light filtered into the tight space. With one last kick, she knocked it out and a blinding light flooded the space.

She crawled her way toward the hole as she peered out at her surroundings. The two-lane road was boarded by woods on both sides. She cursed to herself when she noticed they were driving in a low-traffic area. There was one car behind them, but it was off in the distance. It wasn't close enough for her to stick her arm through the hole and try to get their attention.

She glanced up and saw the trunk release lever that was wrapped in black electrical tape and previously concealed by darkness. *That would be too easy,* she found herself doubtful as two creases formed between her brows. She was positive she wasn't these criminals' first victim to be locked in their trunk, surely, they would have disabled it. *It's worth a try anyway,* she forced herself to remain hopeful.

Addi padded around the floor of the trunk and smiled as she peeled back the carpet to expose the spare tire compartment. *Please let there be a tire iron in there!* She prayed as she scooted toward the edge of the trunk, allowing herself enough space to pull up the plywood lid and feel around. There was a spare in there, what felt like a small jack, and then her hand wrapped around a long piece of iron. She pulled it out, breathing a sigh of relief as she replaced the plywood and carpet.

With a tire iron in hand, she was ready. She knew that the moment she pulled that release, if it worked, the kidnappers would be notified and stop. She would have a small window in which to make her escape.

Addi took a deep breath and pulled the trunk release. To her surprise, it popped open. The driver slammed on the brakes, causing her to roll to the back of the trunk from the force of the sudden stop. Before the car came to a complete halt, she leaped from the trunk and sprinted off into the woods.

CHAPTER 38

"Hey! Get the fuck back here!" T yelled as he leaped from the car and sprinted after Addi.

She didn't have to look back to know that both men were now chasing her. Addi had to focus on where she was going. She ducked under low branches, weaved through the trees, and vaulted over fallen logs. She knew that if she spared a glance backward, she would trip, and the chase would be over.

Both men shouted vulgar expletives at her and threatened to shoot, but she didn't slow her pace. She would be dead if she did, this was her only chance at survival. The threat of them motivated her to move faster than she thought possible, but not fast enough. The force of what felt like a linebacker slammed into her, tackling her to the forest floor. She swung the tire iron with all her might and knocked T on the side of the head.

"Ah! You fucking bitch!" T shouted as he rolled off her, holding the side of his bony face.

Addi didn't spare him a second glance as she quickly got to her feet and took off running again. T caught up to her a second time, knocking her to the ground, but he was ready this time. She swung the tire iron at him, but he caught it with his hand, ripped it from her grasp, and tossed it to the side.

He rolled her to her back, straddled her, and sent a bony fist flying into the left side of her face. She cried out in pain as a second and third punch landed.

"Doesn't feel good when someone hits you, does it?" he spat at her.

Addi was dazed as Baldy finally caught up to them.

"Well, I guess here is as good of a place as any." Baldy's scratchy voice filled the quiet woods around them. "I doubt we'll be able to get her back to the car unnoticed."

"Hold her wrists down," T instructed his partner. The large man grabbed her limp wrists, placed them above her head, and knelt his knees into her palms, pinning them in place. She grunted from the pain, still dazed. "I don't know about you, but I want to have a little fun with this one first before we kill her."

"Burn in hell!" Addi spat a mouth full of blood at T, who still straddled her thighs.

"Tell me something I don't know, sweetheart. But until then, I'll relish in the joys of the living." T ripped the front of her tank top down to her navel, exposing the dark purple lace push-up bra that plumped up her already voluptuous cleavage. "Fuck, girl! God definitely blessed you."

T placed his slender, pale hands over each breast, giving them a good squeeze as he let out a groan of pleasure. She tried to turn herself from side to side, tried bucking her hips to get him off her, but she was held tightly in place. "Let's find out if you're wearing matching bottoms." T's voice was laced with hunger. Baldy grunted in agreement as his dark eyes watched his partner undo the button and zipper of her jeans.

"Get your filthy hands off me!" Addi screamed in frustration.

She used every bit of strength in her, but it wasn't enough to throw a fully grown man off.

T opened the front of her jeans and smiled wickedly. "You dirty girl." His tone deepened with want as he took in the matching underwear.

He hooked his calloused fingers in the pocket of her jeans and began to tug them down her hips. T didn't get them down further than half an inch before his body jerked and a loud gurgling sound emanated from his mouth. Addi shifted her gaze up at the skinny man and a bloodcurdling scream ripped from her throat. The tip of a black blade protruded from the middle of his long, slim, tattooed neck.

A crimson river dripped down, causing blood to soak into the collar of his shirt. T's dark brown eyes were wide with shock as his hands came up and numbly clawed at the blade, trying and failing to remove it. Within seconds, his lifeless body slumped over and covered Addi's torso, the weight of him knocking the air out of her lungs.

"What the fuck!" Baldy cursed as he quickly stood and drew his gun. "Who's out there?" He scanned the woods for any sign of movement.

She struggled but managed to finally push T's corpse off her as she quickly zipped and buttoned up her pants before sitting up and scooting her back against a nearby tree that was out of the way. Her vision scanned the forest for her mystery savior.

"Show yourself, you fucking coward!" Baldy shouted before a whooshing sound flew through the air, followed by a soft thump. "Ah, fuck!" he cursed as he dropped his gun from the impact, and his black eyes took in the knife jutting out of him, the long blade buried deep within the muscle and tissue of his right shoulder, immobilizing his arm. Before he could remove it, a second knife flew through the air and landed in the mirrored spot on his left shoulder, rendering that arm useless as well. The criminal screamed in frustration.

Sweeney spoke in a comedic tone as he stepped out from behind a nearby tree. "You're not as tough as you look, but I'll say, you are as *dumb* as you look."

Addi's head whipped toward him in disbelief. *What is he doing here?* she found herself asking, but quickly pushed it away. She didn't care how or why he was there, just that he was.

"That's a lot of talk for someone who doesn't fight fair," Baldy gritted out as he tried and failed to bring his arms up to dislodge the blades. He was only able to swing them a few inches before they couldn't go any further.

"Fair is why you've lost, and I've won." Sweeney laughed as he slid his index finger through the circled bottom of another throwing knife and began to twirl it around playfully. "In the game of death, only a fool fights fair." He casually strolled toward Baldy as embarrassment, anger, and frustration washed through the criminal at his carelessness. His thick face turned as red as an apple.

Sweeney turned his head toward Addi as he took in her ripped shirt and busted lip. She watched with bated breath as his playful demeanor vanished, replaced by a hard, unreadable mask, but a moment later, his expression reverted.

"Which one of them hit you?" Sweeney asked her calmly.

"That one." Her voice was barely above a whisper as she pointed a shaky finger at T's body.

"It's a shame he died quickly," Sweeney shook his head and shrugged a shoulder. He turned and flashed a sinister grin toward

Baldy. "Oh, well. I won't make that mistake twice."

Addi's eyes were glued on Sweeney as he tucked the throwing knife into a pocket of his vest and withdrew a larger knife from the sheath on the outside of his left leg. Her eyes widened as she took in the weapon that had a blade half the length of her forearm that was black as night and razor-sharp with a polished wooden handle. *How many knives does this man have on him?*

"My eyes are up here, sweetheart," Sweeney called playfully to her. Instantly, her brown gaze shot up from his knife and met his golden eyes. His deep laugh filled the quiet woods around them. "You have two options. Option one." He slowly stalked toward Baldy, casually tossing the knife in the air, where it flipped a few rotations before he caught it, over and over. "You close your eyes and cover your ears for what's about to come."

You mean while you kill him?

"Option two," he continued as he began to slowly circle his prey. Baldy followed the movements with his head, never letting Sweeney out of his sight. "You watch as I torture and kill this man."

His tone threw her off. He spoke as if that was normal for him, as if torture and murder were an everyday routine.

"I'll warn you though," he continued as he kept his voice light, still tossing the blade playfully into the air. "It won't be fast or merciful. So, choose now. Do you wish to blind yourself, to protect a false image of me you have created in your mind, or will you witness the nefarious acts I'm truly capable of?"

Addi was quiet for a moment as she pondered the ultimatum he presented to her. Should she shut her eyes? She wasn't a warrior; she wasn't used to seeing death firsthand. T's death nearly gave her a heart attack, but she didn't want to miss seeing the real him either, no matter how dark or scary that side of him might be. There was something about the man that drew her to him, like a moth to a flame, like a magnet to steel, and to see his true nature firsthand... The thought should terrify her, should send her running far away in those woods, but it did the opposite. She found herself intrigued.

"I will not look away." She spoke quietly, straightening her spine and lifting her chin slightly.

She would watch, no matter how gruesome it was going to be. That man had kidnapped both her and Serenity, hauled her out of the house, shoved her in a trunk, and was going to kill her after he and his friend had their way with her. No, a part of her would welcome the sight of his death.

Pride flashed through Sweeney's eyes at her answer. "Let's get this party started, shall we?" He smiled as he slashed the backs of Baldy's knees faster than lightning.

The large man dropped to his knees and groaned in pain. With knives still buried deep in each shoulder, and no possible way to get them out, he had accepted his fate. She never once looked away. Aside from occasionally blinking, she witnessed every lethal movement, every precise slice across the man's body, every cry of pain from the criminal that echoed off the trees.

She lost count of how many gashes now covered Baldy's mutilated body. His arms, stomach, back, and face were covered in deep crimson lines. Some were deep and others were mere surface-level cuts. Some were only an inch or two long while others stretched nearly a foot in length.

"Please," Baldy choked on his own blood. "Just kill me."

"Well, since you asked so nicely." Sweeney looked the man dead in his eyes and smiled. He slowly sliced his blood-soaked blade, inch by agonizing inch across Baldy's thick tattooed neck.

A loud gurgling sound echoed through the woods. Even the animals remained quiet, as if they too watched with bated breath as this man played judge, jury, and executioner. Seconds passed by like minutes as Baldy collapsed to the forest floor and Addi watched as the life left his black eyes.

Sweeney removed a rag from a pocket of his black cargo pants and slowly cleaned off his blade. The man didn't get so much as one drop of blood on himself as he dished out the criminal's punishment, which made her wonder just how many times he had done this before.

He slid his knife back in its sheath and turned his full attention to her. Addi never left her spot from the base of the tree and he didn't bother moving. It was as if he wanted to give her space until she made up her mind on how she felt about him after this new revelation.

Her mind was a mess. She was horrified as she watched Sweeney work, but not once could she get herself to look away. A part of her was mesmerized by the beauty of his art, despite how graphic and gory it was. A part of her was terrified that what she saw might make her fear him, but it didn't. To her, it proved just how much he cared about her and the extent he was willing to go to keep her safe.

Never once had she had a man willing to, let alone *actually* torture and kill another for the sake of her safety. She was incapable of forming words, so she did the only thing she could do. She got up, walked over to him, and threw her arms around his neck.

At that moment, she let herself go as she began to weep uncontrollably into Sweeney's strong chest. All the emotions flooded her body in a tsunami of confusion. Sadness, anger, relief, heartache, grief, terror, and joy fought each other in a losing battle for dominance. Sweeney wrapped his strong arms around her, bringing one hand up to gently stroke her brown and blonde strands between his fingers.

"With some time, you'll be alright." His tone was shockingly gentle as he held her tightly, letting her purge the emotions from her body the only way she could at that moment. After a while, she calmed herself down enough to be able to speak again.

"Thank you," she whispered, arms still wrapped tightly around his neck.

He continued to stroke her hair soothingly. "For what?"

She pulled back enough to gaze up at him. "For coming to rescue me."

"Even if you hate me after what you just witnessed, I will *always* come for you," he reassured her.

"I could never hate you," she choked out a half-laugh.

"So, what you saw didn't scare you off?" He held his breath waiting for her answer.

"Oh, it scared the shit out of me, don't get me wrong. But I'm not scared of *you*." Her confession hit him hard as he breathed a sigh of relief.

Slowly he cupped her face and claimed her lips with his. She didn't pull away or fight it, and she didn't try to deepen it. She merely closed her eyes and let it happen. He pulled back before he accidentally pushed her to a point where he knew she was nowhere near ready to cross yet.

"Oh my God, Renny!" Realization widened her eyes, and she cursed herself for letting herself get so caught up in what was happening that she forgot her friend was left alone with Jack back at his house.

"Don't worry," he laughed lightly. "I'm sure Hunter handled things quickly." Hurt flashed through her eyes. "Shit," he cursed at himself for what he let slip. "I'm sorry, I didn't—"

"No, you have no reason to be sorry." She took a deep breath. "I hope that piece of shit got what he deserved."

Addi held her chin high. She wouldn't cry a single tear over him. She would mourn the loss of their relationship but not the loss of *him*. She watched as Sweeney pulled out his phone from one of the pockets of his cargo pants.

"Hey, Sweeney, are the girls safe?" Einstein inquired as he answered the phone.

"They split up the girls. Addi is safe. Haven't heard from Hunter about Serenity."

Einstein sighed. "Glad at least she's ok."

"I need a reservation for two. I'll drop a pin on the location for you." He spoke casually, causing Addi to cock her head in confusion at his odd statement.

"You got it!" Einstein laughed and hung up.

"Reservations for two?" she questioned as he pinned their location and sent it to Einstein.

"Yeah, it's a code we use when we need a cleanup crew so local authorities don't get involved. There's no way I can claim this as self-defense." He laughed. "The reservation amount is the body count," he informed her as he tucked his phone back into his pants pocket and took her hand in his.

"Oh, makes sense. Where do you get the cleanup crew?" she asked, but then thought better of it. "You know what, forget I asked. I don't need to know."

Ignorance is bliss, right? Sweeney laughed and shook his head as he retraced their steps, escorting her back through the woods to the car.

CHAPTER 39

As the front door closed, an eerie silence fell between Jack and Serenity as they stood alone in the living room. "You have to get her back! Jack, please, don't do this."

"What must be done isn't always easy." His words were gentle compared to the vicious act he just committed against Addi. "I know you'll need some time to grieve and it will be painful, but I'll be here, by your side, always."

"Jack, you're not a bad person. You may not have loved Addi, but you can't sit around while she gets murdered."

He repeated the words he said to her outside the bar last night. "You can feel like you truly know someone and never see the real them."

They locked gazes. "So, this is the real you? Someone who would hire men to murder an innocent woman for no reason?" She tried to remain calm, but anger was boiling inside of her, threatening to overflow.

"There was always a reason. Us, Renny," he corrected as he took a slow step toward her. "Everything I did was for us."

Serenity threw her hands up in frustration. "There is no *us*, Jack!"

"Don't say that. I know you have feelings for me. Our time here will prove that." He shortened the distance with another step, then another.

"As a friend, yeah. As anything more than that, no. I've never thought of you like that." With each step he took forward, she took one back. "That was something you created, some fantasy you cooked up in that psychotic brain of yours."

"It's a beautiful fantasy that we'll turn into an even more beautiful reality." He grinned as her back hit the wall of the kitchen. She shifted her eyes around for somewhere to go but she was trapped as he kept stalking toward her.

"How were you getting into the house?" Her voice cracked at the end.

He was so close, his rich cologne filling her senses and his smile sickeningly sweet. "It's my parents' house, Renny. I know where the spare key is hidden."

She cursed inwardly for not even considering the possibility of a hidden key. "Why go through the trouble of setting up the cameras?"

Keep him distracted, keep him talking, she coached herself as she sidestepped the counter and started backing further into the kitchen to the knife set that rested on the counter.

He continued toward her, one slow step at a time, loving the game. "I had to keep up my cover. How would it look if Addi told me what was going on and I refused to set them up?"

Serenity continued her retreat. "You aren't tech savvy. How did you erase your presence from them?"

"In my line of work, you represent an array of people with… colorful backgrounds." Jack grinned as he took another step forward. "You get them cleared of whatever charges they faced, and they owe you a favor."

Her heart sank to the pit of her stomach upon hearing those words. "Did… Did you burn down my house?" she asked hesitantly with eyes widened in fear.

"Well, technically an arsonist did, but yes, I hired him."

"Why would you do that? I could've been hurt or killed!" she shouted in frustration.

"I *would* never and *will* never hurt you, Renny." A small part of her believed him.

Maybe not physically, but you've hurt me emotionally. She kept that thought to herself.

"I needed a way to get you closer to me. What's closer than living in my old childhood home where I could see you any time I desired?" He gave her a dark emerald wink.

Serenity was halfway through the kitchen, just a little further and she could grab one of the knives. "I'm guessing our kidnappers were favors you called in as well?"

"You always were very smart. It's one of the things I love so much about you." His eyes darkened as his grin widened across his face. "So, don't insult my own intelligence by trying to lure me in here so you can grab a knife." He laughed at the shocked look she tried to hide. "I have a gun, remember?" He gently waved it in front of her.

"Motion detected on the east lawn," a feminine automated voice sounded from somewhere close by.

Serenity halted, her vision narrowing as she watched him remove a cell phone from the pocket of his slacks. His fingers worked over the screen before he paused and cursed.

"Looks like that *boyfriend* of yours works faster than I thought." Complete disgust dripped from his tone at uttering that word.

Hunter? Hope blossomed in her chest as she fought hard to hide the smile and sigh of relief that tried to surface. *He came for me.*

"Come here," Jack demanded as he held the gun toward her.

That motivated her enough to get her feet moving toward him. He gripped her bicep, careful not to hurt her, and walked her through the living room and up the wooden stairs to the second floor. If the house wasn't as quiet as a graveyard, they would have never heard the gentle creak of the stairs as Hunter stealthily made his way up a few minutes later.

"Welcome to our home, Hunter," Jack greeted loudly so his voice would carry to their unwelcome guest. "Come out with your hands up. I would hate to have to harm Serenity just to motivate you."

There were no footsteps to be heard, no other noise that would indicate another person was in the home with them, just a few more small creaks as Hunter rounded the top stair and walked into the open sitting room with multiple doors lining the wall, most likely leading to the bedrooms. He stopped a few feet away with his hands held open about chest high. The sight of him sent Serenity's heart racing.

"Toss me your gun," Jack demanded.

Hunter slowly crouched, making it a point to keep his free hand held open in plain sight for Jack to see. He gently placed his gun atop the hardwood floor and slid it across the space. Jack picked it up and tucked it in the waistline of his pants.

"Nice place you got here," Hunter noted calmly as he stood to his full height again.

"Thank you. Cost me a pretty penny, but it's worth it to make my girl happy." Jack leaned in and placed a quick kiss on her cheek.

Serenity visibly shuttered and pulled away from him.

A tick of Hunter's jaw was the only indication that what he saw bothered him, otherwise he kept a bored exterior. "Doesn't look to me like *your girl* likes you touching her."

"Oh, she does," he boasted confidently. "Didn't you see the videos I took of her? Her body reacted so well to my touch. She even moaned for me."

"You mean the video of you violating her while she slept? I remember," Hunter threw back with a half-laugh. "Who's to say she wasn't dreaming of *me* touching her?"

Jack's face contorted in rage, but he quickly relaxed it. "You're not worth my time. Get on your knees, now," he ordered as he aimed his gun toward Hunter. Hunter didn't flinch, merely perched an eyebrow high on his head in amusement. When he made no move to comply, Jack ordered again. "Get on the fucking ground or I will hurt her!" he threatened as he turned the gun on Serenity.

A soft whimper escaped her throat as she stared down the barrel of the gun. "You love her. You won't physically hurt her." Hunter spoke confidently. "Turn the gun back on me."

Jack's gaze traveled down Hunter's large frame and back up before he turned the gun back toward him. Hunter slowly dropped to his knees as he kept his hands up.

"You've got one shot," he threatened in a low tone. "You better make it count."

"What's that supposed to mean?" Jack cocked his head to the side.

"By the time you fire off that first shot, I'll be on you before you get off a second. So, I suggest you don't miss."

"Hunter," Serenity whispered in disbelief.

Why would he say that? What if Jack doesn't miss and kills him?

Panic and fear started to constrict her lungs as if it were impossible for her to take a full breath. Her chest rose and fell at a quicker rate as she was forced to take multiple shallow breaths instead.

"Don't worry, Angel. Everything is going to be ok," Hunter reassured her, most likely noticing the shift in her breathing.

"How touching. Everything *will* be ok, but not for you. Gentleman!" Jack called out loudly and one of the bedroom doors opened to their left as two strong and sturdy-looking men walked out.

Hunter arched a brow. "Bodyguards?"

"No, just some men who owe me a favor. I had a guy do some digging on you when I first saw you at Renny's house. I know all about you and your background. Your time in the Navy SEALs, your private security company, everything. So, when I took the girls, I planned accordingly." The two men strode over and stopped behind Jack and Serenity. "Make it quick and keep it clean. I don't want to come home to a mess. Come on, baby. Let's go for a drive."

Jack pulled Serenity toward the stairs. "No! Hunter! Get your fucking hands off of me!" she screamed as Jack hauled her down the stairs and out of the home. Hunter and his two new friends remained quiet until they heard Jack's car pull down the driveway.

CHAPTER 40

"So, how do you want to do this, boys? Shall we go outside or is right here fine with you?" An amused expression crossed Hunter's face as he pointed to the ground in front of him.

"You heard the man. He wants it kept clean. Get the fuck up," one of the men, slim but tall, with black-painted nails said with a wicked grin as he pulled out a pistol from the waistband of his pants.

He motioned with his gun for Hunter to stand as the second guy, who was shorter but just as broad as Hunter pulled out his own pistol, turned around, and jammed it into Hunter's back as he pushed him in the direction of the stairs.

Hunter kept his hands visible as he walked a few steps before taking them by surprise. He spun his body around in the blink of an eye and secured the gun that was in his back with both hands. He twisted the broad man's wrists to an unnatural angle, causing him to drop his weapon. Hunter kicked out his foot, sending the gun sliding across the room so neither of them could get to it.

The taller man aimed his own weapon toward Hunter, but he didn't have a clear shot, not without shooting through his partner. Hunter, still with a hold of the broad man's wrists, pushed the weight of his body into him, forcing the criminal to stumble backward. He charged forward, sending the criminal into his taller partner and knocking him off balance. He didn't stop there as he continued rushing toward the large window that overlooked the backyard.

Glass shattered as both men tumbled out, rolled over the shingled roof of the back lanai, and fell to the lush grass below. Both men landed with a heavy thud, causing the shorter criminal to become dazed as Hunter recovered quickly. He jumped to his feet and ran back inside the home, ducking behind the island in the kitchen as he heard footsteps stomping down the stairs. The taller man came racing through the kitchen and out the back door to his partner. He waited for the man to pass before he kept low and moved to a hidden spot in the home.

"Where the fuck is he?" the taller man asked as he reached his partner.

The broad man grunted as he stood up and shook off the pain from the unexpected fall. "He took off back inside the house."

"Alright, you take downstairs, I'll search upstairs," the taller man said as they both entered the home again.

They parted ways as the broad man grabbed a large knife from the set in the kitchen since his gun was still discarded upstairs.

He slowly made his way through the living room, making sure to clear every corner and closet along the way. As he kept his steps light down the tiled hallway, he stopped in front of a closet, brought his knife up, and opened it. It was empty, so he moved on toward the laundry room.

As he opened the door and stepped in, Hunter sent his foot flying into the man's chest. He grunted as he stumbled back but recovered quickly. The broad man swung the knife, but Hunter dodged it as he sent a right fist into the criminal's face. The broad man threw a quick combo that consisted of a left hook that struck true and swung the knife clutched in his right hand, slicing Hunter's left bicep.

Each man traded kicks and punches, some blocked while others landed. Hunter quickly realized that these men were not average criminals. Their fighting skills suggested they were trained mercenaries. Hunter threw another right hook, but the broad man blocked it as he swung the knife around.

Hunter saw an opening, but he knew he would have to take that hit if he wanted to win. Hunter pivoted, turning his torso slightly, so the knife entered his left side, slicing through the flesh just below his ribs. Before the broad man could withdraw the knife, Hunter trapped the man's arm and knife in place with his left arm as he threw all his weight into his next swing. His right hand clenched tightly around the broad man's throat and yanked, ripping the meaty flesh from his body, killing him instantly.

The broad man's lifeless corpse dropped to the floor as Hunter gripped the hilt of the knife still protruding from his side. He clenched his jaw tightly as he withdrew the blade and used his left hand to put pressure on the bleeding. He wiped the blade clean on his jeans and grasped it tightly in his free hand as he exited the laundry room in search of a new place to hide and wait.

Footsteps sounded on the stairs as the taller man called out. "Did you find him?" When his partner didn't answer, he called out again. "Presley?" Still no answer. The tall man strode into the living room in search of his partner as Hunter snuck around and quietly climbed the stairs.

"Motherfucker!" the second mercenary cursed, and a wicked grin slid across Hunter's features at knowing he had just found his partner's body.

Hunter deliberately made some noise, indicating to the man that he was now upstairs. The tall man aimed his gun as he climbed the stairs with lethal quiet, not even making the wood squeak. He slowed his movements when the top floor became visible to him. He quickly cleared what he could see of the room and made his way toward one of the bedrooms.

He climbed the last step cautiously, but Hunter jumped out from behind the half wall at the top of the stairs and slammed all his weight into the man, sending him smashing into the wall and causing him to drop his gun. The tall man lost his footing and took Hunter with him as they both tumbled down the wooden stairs.

The tall man landed on his back as Hunter landed on top of him and jabbed the knife into the side of the tall man's neck faster than a flash. The criminal's eyes widened in shock as he began to choke on his own blood. He withdrew the knife, and the mercenary died moments later.

"Fuck me," Hunter groaned as he rolled off the man and lay on the ground for a moment, trying to recover. The wound on his side still bled but it had slowed. He had lost a good amount of blood, but the amount wasn't life-threatening yet.

With a deep breath, he set the knife down as he got up and padded down the bodies of the mercenaries, in search of a cell phone. The burner phone didn't have a passcode to it, so he was able to access it easily. He pulled up the text messages and found one to a number he recognized as Jack's.

Mercenary's phone: It's done.
Jack: Good. Did you make a mess?
Mercenary's phone: No.

Jack: The other half of your money is in the drawer of the end table in the living room. Be gone by the time I get back.

No word from Sweeney, he thought as he checked his own phone. *No news is better than bad news.* He walked to the kitchen, grabbed a dish towel, and pressed it against his bleeding side as he took a seat on the couch and waited patiently in the deafening silence. About ten minutes later, he heard a vehicle pull down the gravel driveway. Two car doors opened and closed as he stood, crossed the room, and waited behind the front door.

He pushed himself flat against the wall, so the door wouldn't hit him as Jack opened it. Serenity walked through first as Jack entered and shut the door without turning around. *Complacency kills,* Hunter thought.

She gasped in horror, using a hand to cover her mouth as she froze in the middle of the living room. Jack approached her quickly and stopped next to her. His body went rigid as he took in the sight of the dead mercenary at the foot of the stairs. He turned around quickly only to find Hunter standing right behind him.

Before Jack could react, Hunter sent a fist flying straight into his nose, sending the man staggering back a few steps. Serenity turned at the sound and gasped for a second time.

"Hunter!" she shouted in relief.

He didn't spare her a glance. His mind was solely focused on the fight at hand. He didn't miss a beat as he ducked down and went in for a double leg takedown, sending Jack's back smacking into the tiled floor. A breath of air escaped Jack's mouth at the hard impact, stunning him for a second but he quickly recovered.

Hunter got between Jack's legs as he sent another right fist into the man's face. Jack pulled his hands up as he blocked the third shot and then reached for the gun that fell out of his waistband when he hit the ground. He grasped it and brought it up, but Hunter quickly secured that hand and knocked the gun out of it, sending it sliding across the living room tile.

Jack's vision dropped, noticing a large amount of blood on Hunter's left side and threw his fist into the sensitive wound. Hunter grunted in pain as Jack grabbed the leg of a nearby side table and flung it toward Hunter with all his strength. The table shattered as he threw up his arms, blocking it from hitting his head. The force of the hit knocked him off balance and Jack rolled with him until he was on top, and Hunter had his back flat against the ground.

"Is that all you got?" Hunter said, a bit winded from the previous fights and the injuries he obtained.

"Fuck you!" Jack spat as he sent a fist flying into Hunter's face.

He pulled back and sent another punch, but Hunter jerked his head to the side, causing Jack's knuckles to smack into the tile floor. Jack groaned as he heard a cracking sound. Hunter knew it wasn't broken, but Jack's hand was definitely sprained.

Jack turned his head and saw a bloodied knife lying on the ground beside them. He quickly grabbed it and brought it down toward Hunter's throat. Hunter's hands grabbed Jack's wrists and halted the knife mere inches above his skin.

It became a battle of strength as Jack used both hands and his body weight to push the knife down as Hunter pushed against it. With Hunter's strength fading rapidly, the knife inched closer to his flesh.

"Fucking die already!" Jack gritted out through clenched teeth as he strained against the knife.

"You first," he threw back.

A gunshot rang through the home, echoing off the walls. Both men froze in place as their eyes shifted to the growing crimson stain on Jack's chest. Jack loosened his grip on the knife as he turned his head around and peered toward Serenity in confusion. She stood there with a pistol gripped tightly in white-knuckled hands, aimed right toward him.

Hunter swiftly took the slackened knife from Jack's hand, wanting nothing more than to plunge it through his cold, dead heart, but he knew his angel had to be the one to end her stalker. Against all his years of training and every protective instinct in his body, Hunter allowed Jack to rise and turn toward her.

"Renny?" Jack choked out in disbelief, hurt and betrayal clear in his emerald eyes. "Why?"

Hunter quickly got to his feet and stood off to the side as he watched the interaction between the two.

"You brought this on yourself, Jack." Tears flowed heavily down her cheeks. "You hurt the people I care about."

"But I love you, Renny!" he shouted in frustration. "Why can't you see that?"

"But I don't love you, Jack!" Her voice broke.

"You never even gave us a shot! We could've been so fucking great together. If you only gave me time, I would've given you the world!" A single tear fell from his eye. He outstretched an open hand and took a step toward her. "Please," he pleaded with her, his eyes filled with so much pain and emotion.

"I'm sorry," she whispered as another shot rang out and created a second hole in Jack's chest.

More blood leaked out and colored his shirt. He staggered back a few steps but kept his hand outstretched toward her as he tried to take another step, giving her one more chance to choose him. She pulled the trigger a third time, sending the bullet deep into his heart as his lifeless body finally dropped to the ground.

CHAPTER 41

Serenity didn't move. She couldn't. Her body had locked itself in place as the realization of her actions sank in. "Oh, God," she cried out as she finally dropped the gun. It landed hard against the tile floor, the metal echoing off the walls.

Hunter was by her side in a second with his hands cupping her face gently. "Angel, look at me." Her tear-filled eyes lifted to his.

"I… killed him," she said numbly, her words barely audible.

"I wish you didn't have to carry that burden, but after everything he did to you and Addi, I knew you had to be the one to stop him. Taking a life is never easy. But know that he deserved this. He wouldn't have stopped coming for you and wouldn't have ever let you go." The look in his ice-blue and hazel eyes said he meant every word he spoke.

"Addi!" The sudden remembrance of her friend sent her watery eyes widening in fear.

"Sweeney went after her," he reassured her as he pulled her against his front, wrapping both arms around her securely. "Trust me, that man would give his life for her. She'll be ok."

She threw her arms around his middle and wept into his chest. *It's over*, she thought. *It's finally over*. She didn't know how to feel at that moment. She was relieved that her intruder was stopped, that she would not have to fear him anymore, but she was sad that Jack turned out to be the bad guy. She shot and killed him, her friend, the man Addi loved.

Would Addi hate her for killing him? Would she have lost two friends by the time this was all over? The thought made her want to retch, but she clamped her mouth shut and willed it to stay down. Hunter gently stroked her raven hair as she cried into him for what felt like hours. Her head was pounding by the time she ran out of tears. She pulled away from him and ran her hands across her cheeks, drying them.

"Angel, I need you to know that I would never cheat on you. Jack paid—"

"I know," she said gently. He looked at her with his brows furrowed tightly. "Addi told me Jack set the whole thing up."

"Do you forgive me?" He held his breath as he waited for her answer.

Serenity let out a small laugh. "There's nothing to forgive."

"I should've seen it coming, should've stopped it or pulled away sooner." He cursed inwardly at himself. "And I shouldn't have let you walk away."

"Shhh." She placed her index finger gently on his full lips, quieting him. "We are not going to play the shoulda, woulda, coulda game. It was just a big misunderstanding."

"One that led to you getting kidnapped," he grumbled.

"After which you found and saved me," she said gently, looking into his beautiful eyes. "Thank you."

"I'll always come for you, Angel." Hunter rested his forehead gently against hers. "You're my whole world."

"I don't plan on getting kidnapped often," she joked, and he laughed, the sound healing her broken heart just a little.

He pulled away and cupped her cheeks again, looking deep into her eyes. "I love you, Serenity."

The declaration caught her off guard. That was the first time either of them had ever voiced those words. Hearing him confess the truth of his feelings made her feel as if she could fly. It was confirmation that everything she'd been feeling wasn't one-sided. She didn't have to think if she loved him back, she knew she did.

"I love you too," she said with a smile.

Hunter's lips were on hers before she knew it as their mouths parted and their tongues tangled in a familiar dance.

"Big Daddy?" Serenity heard a muffled voice call from somewhere close by. "Are you fucking making out right now?" She pulled back, breaking their kiss as she peered around the room for the source of the voice.

"Fuck off, Sweeney," he grumbled as he pointed to the earpiece he had secured deep in his left ear. She nodded her head in understanding as she stood there quietly. "All good?"

"Addi's safe." Sweeney exhaled heavily. "Things all good there?"

Hunter took in the wreckage around them as he said, "Yeah, all good. Serenity's safe too. Where are you?"

"We're down the road from the house. Is it clear to come up?"

He may have asked that out loud, but Hunter knew what he was truly asking. Was it ok for Addi to see the state of things at the house?

"Yeah, we'll meet you out front." He took Serenity's hand and left the home, shutting the door behind him. A minute later, their rental car pulled down the gravel driveway.

Addi didn't let the car come to a complete stop before she

jumped out and threw her arms around her friend. "Renny! Thank God, you're ok. I was so worried about you."

Serenity hugged her friend back. "I was worried about you too."

A part of Serenity wondered if this was the last time her friend would hug her once Addi learned the truth of Jack's fate. She pulled back and finally noticed the state of her friend. She took in the busted lip, light bruising beginning to form on her cheek, and a T-shirt that looked like it would fit Sweeney.

"Are you ok? What happened?"

"I'm ok. It's nothing really. It would've been a whole lot worse if Sweeney didn't show up when he did." Addi turned her head and gave her rescuer a kind smile. He gave her a curt nod and walked toward Hunter.

"You look like shit." Sweeney laughed and slapped his friend on the back.

Hunter groaned from the soreness that was starting to settle in. "Thanks."

"You're starting to lose your touch if one guy did all that to you," Sweeney joked.

"Technically, it was three." Hunter rolled his eyes at his friend. "He hired two mercenaries to take me out."

"Is he… Is Jack…" Addi tried to ask but couldn't get herself to say the words.

"He's gone, Addi." Sorrow filled Serenity's voice.

She didn't want to kill Jack, but he left her no other choice. She knew he would've kept coming for her if she hadn't stopped him.

A sob escaped Addi's throat, but she quickly composed herself. She did enough crying back in the woods. She took a few steps toward the house, only to be stopped by Hunter as he held up a hand to her.

"I wouldn't suggest going in there," he warned. "It would be hard for you to see him like that."

Addi angled her chin in the air slightly and took a deep breath. "I have to say goodbye."

Hunter dropped his hand and gave her an understanding nod.

"I'll go with you," Serenity laced her fingers through her friends, and they walked up the steps together.

Addi gasped as she entered the home. It looked like a war zone with a busted side table scattered around and two bodies littering the floor.

"Oh, shit…" She trailed off as she took in the state of Jack's body in the middle of the living room floor. Three large bloodstains soaked the front of his shirt, and a pool of crimson had puddled beneath his body, stating clearly how he met his demise.

"I had to stop him. I'm so sorry, Addi," Serenity confessed as fresh tears fell down her already tear-stained face.

"You have nothing to be sorry for, Renny. He's the one who did all this, not you." Addi took a few steps further inside and knelt beside her husband. "You were a victim of his sick games just as much as I was." She couldn't contain the sobs that escaped now. "Damnit! I thought I cried everything out back in those woods."

"I'm so sorry, Addi."

She wasn't apologizing for killing him, she was sorry for all the pain and heartache he caused her. Addi swiped her cheeks clean again as she gazed down at Jack, his eyes staring blankly at the ceiling. She reached two shaky fingers out and closed them, putting him to rest. Then, she composed herself again as she stood up and turned to face her friend.

"We will not shed another tear for that fucker." She pointed to Jack's body. "He doesn't deserve it. I'll mourn the loss of what I thought my relationship with him was and you'll mourn the loss of a friend, but nothing more."

"Agreed." A few stray tears fell from Serenity's eyes as she breathed a sigh of relief. She wasn't going to lose Addi after all.

The girls turned to find the men standing in the doorway, watching them closely with worry filling both of their eyes.

"What do we do now?" Addi asked as she walked out the door with Serenity as the guys followed.

"We call the cops and tell them exactly what happened. Well, not everything, but as close to the truth as possible. Einstein has all the evidence we have obtained so far to back up our story about Jack and his motives. We'll give everything to the authorities and let them handle it." Hunter addressed the group. "We will, however, leave out the fact that Sweeney killed the two kidnappers. We'll just say they ran off into the woods at the sight of him coming to your aid."

Everyone agreed as Hunter dialed 9-1-1. The cops arrived, gathered evidence, took photos and statements from everyone, and hauled away the bodies before leaving.

Hunter, Serenity, Addi, and Sweeney had to stay in town a few more days while the investigation was underway. Einstein had sent over all the evidence they gathered to the authorities and after a few nerve-wracking days, they ended up ruling everything as self-defense and closed the case. They were cleared to go home, and everyone met in the lobby of the resort with their luggage as they waited for the shuttle that would take them back to the airport.

The shuttle ride was quiet as everyone stared out their windows. It dropped them off in front of the private airstrip where Hunter's company jet waited for them. They climbed aboard and took their seats around the cozy sitting area that had two chairs facing each other with a white table separating them.

They chatted here and there over the course of the plane ride. Hunter kept his hand on Serenity's thigh the whole time as if he were worried that she would disappear again if he wasn't touching her. She found it comforting so she didn't protest. Sweeney checked in with Addi every now and then, but she mostly kept to herself, and he didn't push her boundaries, no matter how badly he wanted to pull her into his lap and make everything better.

Sweeney knew Addi would need time and space and he was giving it to her. Serenity's phone rang as they exited the plane and got into a vehicle that would take them to Hunter's Jeep still parked in the long-term parking lot.

She answered, despite not recognizing the number. "Hello?"

"Is this Ms. Serenity Jinx?" a gentleman asked in an aged voice.

"It is." She hesitated and furrowed her brows. "May I ask who this is?"

"My name is Mr. Stanley. I am—" He cleared his throat before continuing, "I *was* Jack Maddlen's lawyer. I have his last will and testament, and I need to speak with you as soon as possible."

"Oh, ok. I'm free anytime." She exhaled in relief. *Why was he calling me though, and not Addi?*

"Would you be willing to come to my office in half an hour?" he asked and she checked the time on her phone before answering.

"Yeah. If you text me the address, I'll head right over."

They said goodbye and hung up before her phone dinged a minute later with the address.

"Who was that?" Hunter questioned as they all reached his

Jeep.

"That was Jack's lawyer. He needs me to come in so he can read his last will and testament."

Hunter spoke as he and Sweeney loaded up all the luggage into the back. "That's no problem. We can swing by real quick."

CHAPTER 42

The drive to the lawyer's office was rather quick. They parked, walked inside, and took the elevator to the fifth floor. The red-carpeted hallway quieted everyone's footsteps as they passed wooden doors with frosted glass windows that led to other offices. The group of four came to a stop outside the one with *Mr. Stanley* stenciled on the door in big black letters.

They filed into the small waiting room as a middle-aged woman greeted them from behind a mahogany desk. "Good afternoon. How can I help you?"

"My name is Serenity Jinx. I'm supposed to meet Mr. Stanley about the last will and testament for Jack Maddlen."

She smiled sweetly at everyone. "Please, have a seat. I'll let him know you've arrived."

They turned around and each took a seat in the black padded armchairs. About five minutes later, an older man, about mid-sixties, with white thinning hair and a chubby face walked through the door across the waiting room.

"Ah, Ms. Jinx, please come on back."

The poor guy's face looked shocked and confused when all four of them stood and followed one behind the other through the door and into his office.

"I'm sorry, I don't have enough chairs for everyone, but please make yourselves comfortable," he said kindly as he pointed to a black leather couch off to the side.

Sweeney and Addi took a seat on the couch as Serenity and Hunter took a seat in the two chairs that sat opposite his large desk.

"Were you all friends of Jack's?" he asked politely as he rounded his desk and took a seat in the large black swiveling chair.

"Something like that," Hunter responded cryptically.

"I'm so sorry for your loss," Mr. Stanley began as he withdrew a few papers from a manila envelope and cleared his throat. "This should go relatively quickly. It appears, Ms. Jinx, that Jack left everything to you."

Serenity opened her mouth but closed it again, not sure what to say. *There's no way I heard that correctly.* "I'm sorry, could you repeat that?"

"Jack left everything in his will to you, Ms. Jinx," he repeated with a kind smile on his face.

"Everything?" She sat up straight and pulled her brows together.

"Yes, ma'am. It states his parents' house and all its possessions, his current house and all its possessions, the property he just purchased in Hawaii and all its possessions, his car, his life insurance money, and the entirety of his bank accounts." Mr. Stanley pulled his head back up to look at her and removed his reading glasses, setting them down atop the papers on his desk.

"But why me? Addi was his wife." She pointed back to her friend who was completely white in the face with eyes as round as saucers while Sweeney rubbed soothing circles across her back.

"I was informed that he had gotten married last week, but he made no change to his will after that. In fact, this will has been the same since his parents passed a few years ago, except for adding new assets," Mr. Stanley informed her as gently as possible.

Oh... my... God... He truly was obsessed with me from the very start. How could Jack do this to Addi?

She put her foot down as she shook her head from side to side in disgust. "I don't want it, any of it. If anyone deserves that stuff, it's Addi."

"You have a few options if that's how you truly feel. Option one, you can sign everything over to Addison. That would involve a lot of paperwork to sign ownership over to someone else and we would have to do it for everything he owned. So that would take a while. Option two, you can sell what you don't want and give her the money. Or option three, you can keep it all. This is completely up to you."

Serenity turned toward her friend, who finally started getting some color back into her face. "Addi, what do you want to do?"

A piece of her heart broke. Not only did Jack screw Addi over in so many ways while he was alive, but he also had to go and fuck her over again from the grave.

"I don't want any of it either. I want nothing that reminds me of that piece of shit," Addi said quietly as she turned her eyes toward the lawyer. "Sorry about the language."

Mr. Stanley did nothing wrong. He was just an innocent messenger who unknowingly delivered another sick piece of Jack's game to them.

Addi couldn't wait for it all to be done with and for everything to blow over. She just wanted to try and get back to some resemblance of normalcy in a life without Jack. That thought terrified Addi. She had been with him for years and was even living with him. She didn't know what normal looked like anymore. She also didn't want to go home to a place she shared with Jack, a home where every room, every piece of furniture had some story that reminded her of him.

She felt her lungs constrict and she couldn't take a full breath. She wouldn't let these panic attacks rule her. She wouldn't let Jack have any more effect on her. Her chest rose and fell quicker as her breath became shorter.

"Eyes on me, sweetheart," Sweeney whispered to Addi in a tone so low that she almost didn't hear it. Her brown eyes snapped to his as one of his hands came up to gently cup her face. "He doesn't get to decide how you feel anymore. Don't give him back that power."

"I'm trying," she whispered as tears threatened to fall. "After everything he did, he had to get one last "fuck you" to me. I... I don't even want to go home because of him."

He paused, as if pondering something. "Then you'll come home with me until you find a place that's all your own."

"No, no I can't. I don't want to impose—"

"It's not imposing if I offered first, and if we're being honest, it wasn't an offer. You *will* come home with me. You *will* stay there until you get a place of your own. You *will* let me help you heal in any way I can." His words were demanding but his eyes pleaded with her, begging her to let him help.

Addi knew Sweeney would never hurt her as Jack did. She knew he would keep his promise and help her in any way he could. She knew she could trust him completely, a man who literally killed two men to protect and save her. And she knew he wouldn't expect anything in return.

He wouldn't touch her or try to pressure her into something she wasn't ready for. Her husband had just betrayed her the day after their wedding for Christ's sake. A relationship, even one that was purely physical, was the furthest fucking thing from her mind at the moment. But a friend to help her heal was exactly what she needed.

"Ok," she whispered, and the spark of joy that ignited within his golden eyes confirmed her thoughts.

He flashed her a bright smile before he dropped his hand from her face and turned forward, still rubbing small circles across her back with his other hand.

"Then your best bet would be to sell everything and put the money into an account until y'all decide what you want to do with it," Mr. Stanley offered.

"Let's do that then," Serenity agreed. Mr. Stanley had her sign a few papers before they were free to go.

Over the next few weeks, Serenity took leave from work so she could handle all of Jack's burdens he left behind for her. She sold his car, the house in Hawaii, his current house, and his parents' house. She had donated all the possessions within the homes to charity and closed out every account he had in the bank.

She had multiple savings accounts that were maxed out from all the money she collected. Her heart skipped a beat every time she looked at the total amount. After selling everything, getting the check from his life insurance, and taking over his bank accounts, she had just over six million to figure out what to do with.

Hunter had invited her to live with him until she found a place of her own, but she knew that if she said yes, she would never leave. A part of her was ok with that. Living with him had been wonderful. She got to wake up to his handsome face every morning, cook and eat breakfast with him, have sex with him multiple times a day, and fall asleep in his arms just to wake up and repeat it all the next day.

Serenity walked into a local bar and grill where she was meeting Addi for dinner. She spotted her friend already sitting at a table and walked up, taking the seat opposite her.

"Hey, Renny!" Addi greeted cheerfully.

"Hey, girl!" Serenity laughed. It was good to see her friend smile again. After everything, she feared she'd never see it again. "You seem like you're doing better."

"Way better! I mean, I still have bad moments, but those are growing fewer with each passing day. I feel like I'm starting to feel like the old me again." Addi took a sip from her wine glass.

"I'm so glad to hear that." Serenity smiled brightly as she sipped from her own glass of wine that was waiting for her.

"So, how have you been?" Addi inquired.

"Besides dealing with legal crap, I've been great. Hunter is amazing and living with him is like a dream that I never want to wake up from. A part of me doesn't want to find my own place anymore."

"Then don't." Addi wiggled her eyebrows suggestively.

"Don't let Hunter hear you say that. He would have you trying to convince me to stay at his place." Serenity laughed. "How's living with Sweeney?"

"Honestly, it's been great." A small blush tinted her cheeks.

"If he has been anything less than a gentleman, tell me and I'll kick his ass for you."

"No, he's been wonderful." She filled Serenity in on the progress she had been making with the help of a new friend. "I have my own room and bathroom at his place. He gives me space when I need it. He helps me through my panic attacks, which are getting better by the way. He makes me laugh when I feel like crying, and he cooks for me. He also got me in touch with the lawyer who works for Red Sky Security and helped me get my marriage annulled. It's as if it never happened."

Serenity didn't miss the way her friend's eyes lit up when she talked about Sweeney. "How's the house search going?"

"Not so great." Addi's shoulders slouched, and she groaned. "Every time I find a place that might work, Sweeney finds something wrong with it. Sometimes they're legit reasons but other times it seems like he tries to find something wrong, so I have to stay there with him."

Their server delivered their food, and they wasted no time digging in.

"So, then stay there with him for a while," Serenity suggested. "From what you tell me, he's been helping tremendously with your healing process. Why not stay a while longer, until you're fully healed and ready to be on your own?"

Serenity had to hide the smile that tried to work its way across her lips. She knew the reason why Sweeney was being so picky with Addi's house search. That man had fallen for her the moment he saw her and had stuck by her side through the roughest patch of her life because he truly cared for her and wanted her to get better.

When Addi was fully healed, Sweeney would claim her as his, and Serenity couldn't wait for that. Addi deserved to be truly loved in this world, and she knew Sweeney would be the one to give that to her when their time was right.

"I don't know." Addi exhaled heavily. "Maybe you're right."

"Haven't you learned by now? I'm always right." Serenity laughed and Addi joined her. The sound warmed her heart. "On to a more serious topic. I want you to have the money. Everything's been handled and dealt with, so you won't have to worry about anything except what you want to spend it on."

She knew Addi deserved the money. She'd dealt with all the legal headaches so her friend wouldn't have to. Now she could just take the money and live comfortably for the rest of her life.

"I can't do that, Renny. After what he did, you should take it."

"Then let's split it, please. It's too much for one to have alone," she countered. "You can leave it sitting in accounts to grow off interest for the rest of your life or you can buy your dream house with it. It's totally up to you."

"Fine, half," Addi finally agreed with a small smile. "How much was there anyway?" she casually asked. The amount had never once crossed her mind.

"Just over six million."

Addi nearly choked on her wine as her brown eyes widened in surprise.

"Holy shit!" she shouted. "And he gave me a hard time for buying new towels for the bathroom when I first moved in. Cheapskate." She shook her head and looked toward Serenity. They both paused then burst out laughing.

THE END... FOR NOW

DON'T MISS OUT!

Sweeney, Doc, Fuse, and Einstein deserve their own happily ever after, don't you agree? Here's a sneak peek at Sweeney and Addi's story!

A Healing Love
Brothers of the Red Sky – Book 1

Prologue

Addison

My name is Addison Thatcher, and this is the story of how my life went from a magical fairytale to an utter nightmare in the span of a single day. Literally, one fucking day. I wish I were joking, but my ugly reality is a constant unfortunate reminder of the shitty hand Fate dealt me. Whatever I did to deserve this eludes me.

What should've been the best day of my life, of any girl's life, turned into something straight from a Blumhouse horror film. It's the day every girl spends years of their childhood planning, from clipping out various pages from bridal magazines to creating their dream wedding board. I should know. I was one of them.

Then Jack Maddlen waltzed into my life. A man for whom I quickly fell head over heels. A man I found myself wanting to build a future and share my life with as much as the body needs a heart and the earth needs the sun. He was smart, funny, and not to mention, the most attractive man I've ever had the pleasure of touching.

Six feet packed with mouthwatering lean muscles, wavy brown hair that made you want to sink your fingers into it, and deep emerald eyes that could turn any woman on with just one look. Not to mention he was a defense attorney with a plush bank account.

He was the entire package… Or so I thought.

My rose-colored glasses must've been sewn onto my face or else I would have seen the true demon that lay beneath his gorgeous exterior. The truth is, Jack never loved me. He only used me to get close to my best friend, Serenity Jinx. He said as much not even twenty-four hours after we were married. What a fucking dick.

He'd bought a property there in Hawaii, had both Serenity and I kidnapped from the resort where we got married, and hired two hit men to kill me so he could collect the multi-million dollar life insurance policy he took out on me without my knowledge. He'd planned on living in that home with Serenity, the woman he truly loved.

I don't blame Serenity or hold a grudge against her for what happened. She loved Jack, but only as one loves a close friend or a member of one's family. She was the one to stop him, sending three bullets deep into his chest cavity where his heart should've been. And rightfully so. I don't hold it against her for killing him either. He deserved it and much more.

My only regret is that I didn't do it myself for what he did to me. To us. He had stalked and tormented Serenity in the weeks leading up to our wedding so much that she was a paranoid and nervous wreck.

Boy, I sure do know how to pick 'em, huh? So where does this leave me? At twenty-four, I've been reduced to an emotionally shattered shell of my former self with my trust in men *completely* broken with no light at the end of the tunnel. A tunnel so dark that you couldn't see your hand in front of your face. A tunnel that claims thousands of victims each year without remorse by showing no mercy and sucking you in to drown you with depression, grief, and heartache

Chapter 1

Addison

The drive to the lawyer's office from the airport was rather quick. I don't remember much though. I don't even remember much about the flight back from Hawaii. I couldn't even tell you what the inside of Hunter's company jet looked like or any conversations that were had.

I kept to myself, with my knees pulled to my chest, my arms wrapped securely around my legs, and my vision trained on the clouds beyond my window. I wished more than once that I could turn into one so I could simply float away, without a care in the world, forgetting all about my troubles and my obliterated heart.

I do recall Sweeney checking in on me every now and then. However, I didn't speak. I simply didn't want to. All I wanted was to crawl into bed in a pitch-black room and never leave. I merely nodded weakly in answer to his questions. Thankfully everyone left me alone so I could further process the horrors of what happened just a few days ago.

Had it only been a matter of days? It feels like a lifetime ago. Jack and I would've been wrapping up our honeymoon right about now. I should've been exhausted from exploring the islands, sightseeing, having so much mind-blowing sex with my new husband, and glowing with a golden tan from all the time spent relaxing on the beach.

Instead, I'm broken and bruised, metaphorically and physically, both inside and out. My husband was a monster that crawled out of the deepest darkest pit of hell. My husband… God, how could I have been so stupid? How did I not see the signs?

After having a few days to reflect, the signs were there. How overly friendly Jack was with Serenity. The look in his eyes anytime she was around, as if she hung the moon. How he clung to every word she said, as if she was the center of his universe. Fuck, I'm such a fool!

Again, I don't blame Serenity. Not one bit. She never crossed that line with Jack. She's my best friend, my sister from another mister, and I trust her with my life. She loved Jack, but not in the way he wished. Not in the way he so desperately wanted.

A blinding light stings my vision as the car door opens. I hadn't realized we'd reached our destination. Hell, I didn't even realize that we were no longer on the jet. Not until I focus my gaze on Sweeney, who now stands outside my door with an outstretched hand and a kind smile on his ruggedly handsome face.

"Do we have to do this right now?" I grimace.

My voice is hoarse from crying and screaming into my pillow the last few days. On second thought, screw the bed in a pitch-black room. I'll settle for nothing less than a cold, dark hole to crawl into and never leave.

"Unfortunately." He holds my gaze, his honey eyes shining bright in the sun, showing off breathtaking hues of yellow and brown. "But it will be over soon, and you can put this behind you too."

I let out an exhausted sigh because he's right. I unbuckle my seatbelt and reach for his hand. I don't remember buckling myself in. Sweeney must've done it when he sat in the back with me as we left the airport. He helps me out of the car and closes the door behind me.

Hunter holds the door open for us as Serenity, Sweeney, and I enter the lawyer's office building. Why Mr. Stanley called Serenity and asked to speak with her about Jack's last will and testament instead of me has a bad feeling settling deep in the pit of my stomach.

We pack into the confined elevator and Hunter presses the button for the fifth floor. My broken heart aches as I take in my best friend clutching her boyfriend's muscular arm like it's her life support. I'm so thankful that she was at least blessed with one of the good ones.

She'd met Hunter a few weeks ago on a dating site called Desire when she was searching for a new date for my wedding. She'd broken up with her long-term boyfriend after he'd cheated on her and she didn't want to spend the weekend at the resort alone. I suggested she use the dating site to try and find a replacement date.

And in walked Hunter Gatlin. A six-foot-three former Navy SEAL packed with bulky muscles, shoulder-length brown hair he keeps mostly tied in a knot on the back of his head, a full brown beard he keeps neatly groomed close to his face, and unique ice-blue eyes with a warm hazel center. Dark ink that's disturbed by occasional scars covers both arms before disappearing beneath a T-shirt that forms tightly around his broad shoulders.

After separating from the military, he started his own security company, Red Sky Security, which provides temporary security details to affluent clients.

Hunter leans down and places a gentle kiss atop Serenity's

raven hair as he rubs soothing circles across her back, causing emotions to constrict my throat like a boa with its prey. But in a good way. I wrap my arms around my middle, wishing I could crawl into myself and disappear as the metal doors part and we step off the elevator.

The red-carpeted hallway quiets our footsteps as we pass wooden doors with frosted glass windows that lead to other offices. We come to a stop outside one with *Mr. Stanley* stenciled on the door in big black letters.

We file into the small waiting room where a middle-aged woman greets us from behind a mahogany desk. "Good afternoon. How can I help you?"

"My name is Serenity Jinx. I'm supposed to meet Mr. Stanley about the last will and testament for Jack Maddlen."

The receptionist smiles sweetly at us all. "Please, have a seat. I'll let him know you have arrived."

We turn and take a seat in black padded armchairs. About five minutes later, a man in his sixties with thinning white hair and a chubby face walks through a thick wooden door across the waiting room.

"Ah, Ms. Jinx, please come on back."

Shock and confusion mar the old man's rounded features when all four of us stand and follow one behind the other through the door and into his office.

"I'm sorry, I don't have enough chairs for everyone, but please, make yourselves comfortable," he says kindly and points to a black leather couch off to the side.

Sweeney and I take a seat on the couch as Serenity and Hunter take a seat in the two chairs that sit opposite the large desk.

"Were you all friends of Jack's?" he asks politely as he rounds his desk and takes a seat in the large, black swiveling chair.

"Something like that." Hunter's deep voice is cryptic.

"I'm so sorry for your loss," Mr. Stanley begins as he withdraws a few papers from a manila envelope and clears his throat. "This should go relatively quickly. It appears, Ms. Jinx, that Jack left everything to you."

Blood roars in my ears and my stomach churns as the lawyer's words sink in, unknowingly delivering news that only serves to twist the metaphoric knife Jack stabbed into my heart even deeper. I didn't think it was possible, but the fresh wave of pain is undeniable.

Serenity opens her mouth but closes it again, unsure what to say.

"I'm sorry, could you repeat that?" Her words come out shaky.

"Jack left everything in his will to you, Ms. Jinx," he repeats with a kind smile on his face.

This can't be happening...

Serenity sits up straight in her chair. "Everything?"

"Yes, ma'am. It states his parents' house and all its possessions, his current house and all its possessions, the property he just purchased in Hawaii and all its possessions, his car, his life insurance money, and the entirety of his bank accounts."

Mr. Stanley pulls his head back up to peer at her and removes his reading glasses, setting them down atop the papers on his desk.

Serenity points toward me. "But why me? Addi was his wife."

I know by the look on my friend's face that my features must be as white as the papers the lawyer clutches in his wrinkled hands. It feels as if someone sucked all the oxygen from the room. I try to take deep breaths, but my lungs won't fill, forcing me to take multiple shallow breaths instead. I'm vaguely aware of Sweeney next to me, his strong hand rubbing soothing circles across my back, but my mind is elsewhere.

"I was informed that he had gotten married last week, but he made no change to his will after that. In fact, this will has been the same since his parents passed a few years ago, except for the addition of new assets," Mr. Stanley informs us while keeping his tone as gentle as possible.

Holy... hell...

He truly was obsessed with Renny... from the very fucking start...

Serenity puts her foot down and shakes her head in disgust. "I don't want it. Any of it. If anyone deserves that stuff, it's Addi."

"You have a few options if that's how you truly feel. Option one, you can sign everything over to Addison. That would involve a lot of paperwork to sign ownership over to someone else and we would have to do it for everything he owned. So, that would take a while. Option two, you can sell what you don't want and give her the money. Or option three, you can keep it all. This is completely up to you."

Serenity turns toward me. Her mossy eyes soften with sympathy. Or is it pity? I can't tell the difference anymore, and frankly, I don't care.

"Addi, what do you want to do?"

I open my mouth, but no sound comes out, forcing me to close it. My clammy grip on the couch tightens, and I know that without looking my knuckles are bleached. My breaths begin to come faster, and I feel as if a panic attack is on the horizon.

I can't do this... I can't do this...

Finally, I manage to pull myself together enough to speak a few sentences.

"I don't want any of it either. I want nothing that reminds me of that piece of shit." I drop my gaze to the carpet and apologize no louder than a shaky whisper. "Sorry about the language."

Mr. Stanley has done nothing wrong. He's just an innocent messenger who unknowingly delivered another sick piece of Jack's game to us, putting the icing on the "fuck you" cake he spent the entirety of our relationship baking. Years of my life up in smoke, with nothing to show for it but devastation and pain. So much fucking pain...

I can't wait for all this to be done with and for everything to blow over. I just want to try and get back to some semblance of normalcy in a life without Jack. However, the thought is utterly terrifying and makes me physically ill to my stomach. I've been with Jack for years. I was even living with him. What does *normal* even look like now?

Home... How can I go home to a place I shared with a monster? A home where every room and every piece of furniture has some story that reminds me of him. I can't. It would be too much.

I can't... I can't breathe...

My lungs constrict further, causing my chest to rise and fall at an alarming rate. I feel as if the walls of this small office are closing in on me and escape seems impossible.

Get a hold of yourself! I won't let these panic attacks rule me. I refuse to let Jack have any more effect on me.

"Eyes on me, sweetheart," Sweeney whispers in a tone so low that I almost miss it.

My brown eyes snap to him as one of his hands comes up to gently cup my face.

If my panic attack hadn't stolen my breath, the sight before my eyes would have. Sweeney is just as tall and broad as Hunter, with sun-kissed skin and eyes like ambered whiskey. His brown hair is cut short on the sides and just long enough on top to run your fingers through. His square jawline is free from hair, showing off his rugged, manly features. Colorful ink covers his right arm, disappearing beneath his T-shirt.

His face is an unreadable mask but worry swirls in his gaze as he peers at me. His thick dark brows are pulled together as if trying to read the solution to helping me lies somewhere within my irises.

"He doesn't get to decide how you feel anymore. Don't give him back that power."

"I'm trying," I choke out as tears threaten to fall. "After everything he did, he had to get one last fuck you to me. I... I don't even want to go home because of him."

He's quiet for a moment, as if pondering something. His vision shifts between mine, unsure of which to focus on.

"Then you'll come home with me until you find a place that's all your own."

I open my mouth, but the words get clogged in my throat. I close it and my eyes as I try to collect myself. After a few deep breaths, I manage, "No, no. I can't. I don't want to impose—"

"It's not imposing if I offered first, and if we're being honest, it wasn't even an offer. You *will* come home with me. You *will* stay there until you get a place of your own. You *will* let me help you heal in any way I can."

His words are demanding but his eyes plead with me, desperately begging me to let him help.

Should I? Jack has completely shattered my trust, but I know from Sweeney's actions alone that he's nothing like Jack. They aren't even in the same universe by comparison. I know he'll keep his promise to help me in any way he can. And though Sweeney flew to Hawaii to help aid Hunter in rescuing us, killing two men to protect and save me, so effortlessly like a human squashing an ant, I know that he'd never hurt me as Jack did. Physically or mentally.

But *living* with another man? So soon after everything that had happened? I know he wouldn't touch me or try to pressure me into anything I wasn't ready for. My husband just betrayed me the day after our wedding, for Christ's sake. A relationship, even one that's purely physical, is the furthest fucking thing from my mind. I know I can't handle that right now, no matter how handsome the man is. But can I be roommates with another man so soon?

On the other hand, I truly don't want to live alone. I feel that's the quickest way to slip into a dangerous depression. Maybe I can room with Serenity for a little while? However, she is technically homeless.

Her house had burnt down over two weeks ago. Jack, no surprise there, offered up his childhood home to her until she found a new place to live. That sick fuck just wanted her as close to him as possible. Another huge flashing neon sign that I so blindly missed. He stalked her inside that house in the days leading up to our wedding.

With how close Serenity and Hunter have grown, she'll probably want to stay with him. And if those two are living together, the last thing I want is to intrude and have to listen to them having sex all the time.

So... stay with Sweeney or live alone? A friend to help me heal *does* sound pretty nice right now.

"Ok," I whisper and the spark of joy that flashes through his golden eyes tells me I made the right decision.

I hope...

He smiles brightly before dropping his hand from my face and turning forward, still rubbing small circles across my back with his other. His simple touch grounds me long enough to make it through the rest of this uncomfortable meeting.

"Then your best bet would be to sell everything and put the money into an account until y'all decide what you want to do with it," Mr. Stanley offers.

"Let's do that then," Serenity agrees with a curt nod.

Mr. Stanley has her sign a few papers before we're finally free to go.

Chapter 2

Addison

The silence amongst us was heavy when we finally left the lawyer's office. No one spoke until we piled into Hunter's gunmetal grey Jeep Wrangler. With a twist of his wrist, the engine roared to life, and rock music turned low filled the cabin as we buckled up.

With a heavy sigh, Serenity is the first to break the silence. She twists in the front passenger seat to peer back at me, concern marring her pointed features. "How are you doing, Addi?"

"Oh, just peachy." Sarcasm drips from my words as I try to plaster a fake smile across my tired face.

"Honey," Serenity says with a sigh, seeing through the mask to the truth that lies beneath like she always has with me.

I cut her off, not wanting to talk anymore. "I just want a hot bath and some sleep."

I don't think I can take any more pity. From anyone.

"Can do." Hunter peers over his shoulder at me with a genuine smile. "What's your address? I'll drop you off first."

Before I can answer, Sweeney speaks up from beside me. "She's staying with me."

Hunter arches a brow at his friend, silently communicating his question. His eyes shift to me before flicking back to Sweeney.

"Don't worry, Big Daddy." Sweeney gives him a wide smile. "It's just until she gets back on her feet."

Hunter shifts his ice-blue and hazel gaze back to me. "Are you ok with this?"

"Yes." I give him a weak nod. "I..." My voice cracks so I quietly clear my throat and try again. "I can't go back to that house. There are too many memories..."

"You don't have to explain. I understand. You could stay with Angel and me if you want," Hunter offers.

I knew Serenity would want to stay with him after all this. A small smile tugs at the corner of my mouth. "And listen to you two have crazy hot sex every night? No thanks."

Serenity blushes hard and tries to bury her face in her hand while Hunter chuckles softly to himself.

"How do you know what their sex is like?" Sweeney squints his gaze and wiggles his brows at me with a mischievous grin lightening up his face.

"Girls talk." I shrug a shoulder before continuing. "Plus, just look at him, all hot, muscular, and manly. He doesn't strike me as the soft and gentle type."

"Alright!" Serenity is now as red as an apple as she cuts the conversation from going any further. Hunter and Sweeney both roar with laughter. "If you're truly ok with this, we can drop y'all off and go pack up your things and bring them to you."

My aching heart swells with love for my sister. "You don't have to do that, Renny."

"It's no bother at all, I promise. I wouldn't want to go back there either if I were you. I got you, sis."

She shoots me a wink before turning back around and signaling for Hunter to start driving.

He must know where to go because he drives without turning on the GPS. It would make sense though. Sweeney has worked with him for years now. I'm sure they've been over to each other's houses numerous times over the years.

Twenty minutes later, we pull into a small neighborhood with beautiful two-story duplexes. The houses couldn't be more than ten years old, each covered with brick, wood, or a combination of both. Each home is equipped with a two-car garage with beautiful flower beds lining the front walkways.

I can't help but gape in awe. I didn't know what to expect when it came to the type of home Sweeney would live in, but this caught me by surprise. We pass a handful of duplexes before Hunter pulls into the left driveway of a stunning house. It's built of beautiful grey brick halfway up, then dark blue painted wood the rest of the way, topped with a black shingled roof.

Sweeney jumps out and rounds the back of the Jeep as he begins to unload our luggage. I climb out and try to school my features from a mixture of shock and admiration.

Serenity rolls her window down and peers over at me. "We'll be back in about an hour or two with your things, ok?"

I turn to her. "Thank you." I shift my gaze toward Hunter. "Both of you."

He nods in return.

I round the front of the Jeep where Sweeney is waiting for me with my luggage in one hand and his black duffle bag slung over a broad shoulder. I don't miss the way his muscles bulge and flex with each movement.

"You look surprised." He's sporting a cocky grin as Hunter backs out of the driveway and drives off down the road.

I follow him up the three steps onto his covered front porch and wait as he sets my suitcase down and digs his keys out of his jeans pocket.

"I just didn't peg you for the suburban, HOA type."

"You can peg me anytime you like." He gives me a playful wink before unlocking his front door and stepping aside, motioning for me to enter first.

"Don't tempt me. I might be into that," I shoot back and don't miss the shock that enters his eyes as I step over the threshold.

He throws his head back with laughter behind me as he shuts the door and locks it, setting our bags down in the small foyer. The space is cozy with a small closet nestled in the left corner and a door to the right that I'm guessing leads to the garage. The walls are painted a soft cream with white baseboards and elegant crown molding. Light hardwood floors run vertically from the front of the house to the back, making the space appear more open.

His keys clink against a small glass bowl that sits on a wooden entry table positioned to the left that contains... photographs?

"A suburban home *and* you set out pictures. Who are you?" I tease as I skim over the five-by-sevens resting in thick dark wood frames.

One is of Sweeney and a young woman dressed in a black graduation robe with a gold sash draped around her neck. *Valedictorian* is stamped into the sash in black font. He has his arm wrapped around the woman's neck as he pulls her to his side and is about to give her a knuckle sandwich.

I take a guess. "Is this your sister?"

They have the same shade of brown hair, though hers falls in luscious waterfall curls that cascade down her shoulders, and they share the same golden eyes. Their smiles are almost identical too. The sight brings the ghost of a smile to my face. A rare occasion this week.

"Yeah. That's Sophie." Love fills his voice. "That was taken last year when she graduated college."

"I see she got all the beauty in the family."

He snorts and I shift my gaze to the next one. A group photo of the men he works with. Sweeney, Hunter, Fuse, Doc, and Einstein are gathered around a bonfire, all with a beer raised in salute and smiles brightening their faces.

I think back to the day I met them all. Serenity had asked if I wanted to join them for a few beers. I was more than happy to get out of the house for a while. Jack had been working late all week, making sure he was caught up on all his case files so he could pass them off to a coworker while he was on leave for our wedding and honeymoon.

My mouth sours as if I swallowed acid and I clench my jaw to keep the nausea down. He wasn't working late… Not every day, at least. It was his excuse so he could freely stalk Serenity.

I close my eyes, take a slow deep breath, and release it even more slowly, clearing my mind of all things Jack-related. I open them and land back on the picture of Sweeney and his friends. I'm not afraid to admit, I was a bit scared when I first met them. They looked rather intimidating. All were either ex-military or worked with government private contractors. You know the type. I try to remember the story they told me behind each of their call signs, but I can't remember the exact details.

I turn back and start down the hallway that leads to the rest of the home. I don't have to turn around to know Sweeney is following close behind. Though his steps are silent, I can feel his dominating presence. We pass a small half-bathroom to the left and a carpeted staircase on the right that leads to the second floor.

The back half opens before me. A large living room, dining room, and kitchen are all open and connected. An entertainer's dream. More photos and artwork adorn the walls and the light from the numerous large windows brightens the space fully without the need for artificial light.

I turn and make my way up the stairs, fully aware of my new roommates' gaze on me the entire way. I observe more photos hanging along the walls of the stairwell. A small loft at the top of the stairs is filled with bookshelves and a cozy lounge chair.

I point to the door on my left. "Bedroom?"

"My room, yes." I turn right to head down another hallway. "Your bathroom." He points to the left.

I let out a small teasing sigh. "I guess it will do."

He snorts and points to the right. "Laundry room, and two bedrooms." He motions to the doors in front of me. "Take your pick."

I point to the one on the right. "Does this one share a wall with your bathroom?"

"Yes."

I step toward the room on the left. "I'll take this one then."

"Too tempting to not picture me when you hear me shower?" he teases.

"Not at all. I just don't care to hear you jerking off in there," I throw back as I enter my new bedroom.

The farthest one away from him as possible. The room is simple. A queen-sized bed with a large, slatted, wooden headboard, a nightstand, and a dresser all in a matching dark walnut color. A simple powder blue bedspread covers the bed with matching throw pillows and drapes.

I can't help but turn around and cross my arms over my chest.

My breath hitches when I see him leaning against the doorframe, hands tucked into the pockets of his black cargo pants. His gaze is locked on me as I take in the space, and my aching heart nearly skips a beat.

I clear my throat of any emotions before I speak. "Does a woman live here with you?"

He hikes a brow in amusement. "Why do you ask?"

"You didn't answer my question," I push back, raising a brow of my own.

He shrugs his shoulders. "If one did, would it matter?"

"Um... Yeah, it would. One, it would be awkward. Very awkward. And two, that's the reason I didn't stay with Hunter and Renny. The last thing I want is to hear two people having sex often."

I push away the ping of jealousy that tries to surface. I barely know the man and I just got out of a horrible relationship. Dating or sleeping with someone is literally the furthest thing from my mind. Even though my heart has been shattered, my body still reacts on its own when in the presence of beauty. Or in Sweeney's case, a goddamn masterpiece. Good to know my hormones still work, for way in the future when I'm ready to date again. Though that thought is enough to churn my empty stomach.

"Is someone jealous?" he teases with a smile.

"I barely know you. Why would I be jealous?"

I ignore the rational part of my brain that tries to scold myself for agreeing to stay in a house with a complete stranger. *Smart move, Addi.*

He removes his hands from his pockets and crosses them over his chest. "Why all the sudden questions?"

I place my fists on my hips and pin him with a glare. "Why are you avoiding answering them?"

"I can see living with you is going to be fun." His grin is full of mischief.

"I won't be living here if someone else lives here with you," I correct.

"Sorry, no take-backsies. And to put your cute little mind at ease, I live alone. Minus Sharleen." My brows pull together, and he explains. "She's a harmless old lady whose spirit lingers here. That's why I have that reading nook. I've found her lounging there too many times to count."

My jaw drops in shock, and I try not to be obvious as I peer around his large frame and down the hallway. "Please tell me you're joking."

A wicked grin and a shrug of his broad shoulders is his only response.

I take a deep breath and try again. "Have you ever lived with a woman?"

"No, sweetheart." He pushes off the doorframe and takes a step toward me. "Why?"

I ignore the way my body tries to wake up when it senses his closeness. "Because this home was definitely furnished and designed by a woman."

"How do you know it wasn't me?"

I motion behind me with my hand. "Because no straight man would ever bother matching the color of the bedspread to the drapes."

He takes another step. "Very observant of you. Do you like it?"

"Your home is beautiful," I answer honestly.

"I'll be sure to relay your compliments to Sophie." He gives me a wink and stops a few feet away.

His sister. I nod in realization and try not to sigh in relief that no other woman lives here.

I take a breath and square my shoulders. "Any rules I should know about, going forward?"

"Like what?" He cocks his head to the side, and I groan inwardly.

"Like Thursday nights are poker with the boys, so I'll need to make myself scarce. The second shelf in the fridge is yours. Sunday nights are for orgies."

Sweeney's laughter echoes off the bedroom walls, the sound scooping the pieces of my broken heart into a neat little pile as if they could be reconstructed. "First, orgy nights are on Fridays. You can't do something like that on the Lord's Day. That's just wrong. Second, I keep my snacks in a private stash, hidden away, so feel free to eat anything in the kitchen. And third, even if I have the boys over, this is your home now just as much as it's mine. I will never make you leave for any reason."

I snort at his first two conditions, finding myself thankful for his wonderful sense of humor. But his third condition settles over me like a security blanket I don't realize I need at this moment.

"Thank you." I let my arms fall to my sides as I begin to pick at the hem of my shirt. "For letting me stay here. I promise I won't be a pain in your ass. And I'm more than happy to split the bills with you until I find my own place."

"As long as it's an enjoyable pain, then we're good." He smiles before his features turn more serious. "You won't pay me a penny. And if you do, I'll put it aside in an envelope for you to use for a new place if you move out."

"We'll see." I purposefully don't let myself linger on the fact that he said *if* I move out, not *when* I move out.

"We will." He chuckles. "Now, get cleaned up and get some rest."

"I don't have anything to change into. Nothing clean, at least. I need to do laundry from... the trip." My voice weakens as the memory of this week settles back over me.

Without a word, Sweeney turns on his heels and disappears down the hallway. I stand there confused and can't stop my gaze from sliding to the reading nook at the end of the hallway. He better've been joking when he mentioned he had a ghost living here. I swallow audibly and pray that if Sharleen is in fact real, she's a gentle old soul who'll leave me alone.

My eyes dart around my room as quick fear causes goosebumps to sprout up my arms. I hope she's not in the room with me now, watching me. A chill rolls down my spine and I quickly force her out of my mind as Sweeney returns a minute later with a black T-shirt and a pair of boxers clutched in his large hand.

He hands the clothes to me. "You can wear these."

"So, you're a boxers guy?" I snort as I accept the clothes from him and drop my gaze to the carpeted floor. "Thank you."

"Anytime, sweetheart." He turns, heads back downstairs, and leaves me all alone.

FOR MY READERS

Thank you for reading Desire's Blessing. I hope you enjoyed Hunter and Serenity's love story as much as I did. I would love to hear your thoughts about it so please leave a review and follow me on social media to stay up to date on my latest writings.

Facebook: Maricca Wood – Author
Instagram: mariccawoodauthor
TikTok: mariccawoodauthor
Website: www.mariccawood.com
Newsletter: www.mariccawood.com/newsletter

ACKNOWLEDGMENTS

First and foremost, to my amazing husband. Thank you for letting me pick your brain with random questions and never once looking at me weirdly for giving you zero context beforehand. You're my biggest cheerleader and if it weren't for you, these stories wouldn't have been published for everyone to read.

To my beta readers, Tara, Shelby, and Jennifer. I love and appreciate the honest feedback you all have given me. It helped me see the story through others' eyes so I could tweak it to be its best. Or at least close to it!

To my editor, The Havoc Archives. You're amazing and if it weren't for your expert eyes, my story wouldn't be as polished and beautiful as it could be.

Last but certainly not least, thank you to all my readers. I hope you enjoyed Hunter and Serenity's love story as much as I did. Thank you for giving my book a chance. I can't wait to write more stories and share them all with you!

ABOUT THE AUTHOR

Maricca Wood is a hopeless romantic who, believe it or not, used to loath reading growing up. Now, she finds it hard to put books down. She writes contemporary romance, some darker than others, and fantasy, all with plenty of angst, relatable characters, and of course, spice!

She lives in Oklahoma with her family and possesses an associate degree in Entrepreneurship. She enjoys reading a wide range of genres, playing video games, watching anime, doing puzzles, and building Lego sets. She can count on one hand all the people who have ever pronounced her name correctly the first time. Good luck!